Land of My Neighbours

The Valley

The Town With No Twin

Land of My Neighbours

Barry Pilton

BLOOMSBURY

LONDON · BERLIN · NEW YORK

First published in Great Britain 2009

Copyright © 2009 by Barry Pilton

The moral right of the author has been asserted

Bloomsbury Publishing, London, Berlin and New York
36 Soho Square, London W1D 3QY

A CIP catalogue record for this book is available from the British Library

ISBN 978 1 4088 0272 4
10 9 8 7 6 5 4 3 2 1

Typeset by Hewer Text UK Ltd, Edinburgh
Printed in Great Britain by Clays Ltd, St Ives plc

Mixed Sources
Product group from well-managed
forests and other controlled sources
www.fsc.org Cert no. SGS-COC-2061
© 1996 Forest Stewardship Council
FSC

www.bloomsbury.com/barrypilton

For Jan

1

A Wednesday in Spring

The Mid-Walian

Wednesday, 11th May, 1988   20p

Vol. XC   5003

TOWN CENTRE ASSAULT

Gareth Richards, 43, of Ty Mawr Farm, near Abernant, will appear at Abernant Magistrates Court on 13th May. He will be charged on nine counts, including criminal damage, theft of council property, affray, and lewd behaviour in a public place.

Mr Richards, a hill-sheep farmer, is expected to enter a plea of guilty, but with extenuating circumstances.

Police sources say that psychiatric enquiries continue to be made into the background of the accused, who is recently separated from his wife. Moira Richards, 25, is believed to have returned to Donegal.

The Welsh Arts Council today issued a statement saying that they had not yet decided whether to pursue a claim for damages against Mr Richards.

It is thought that the high-profile nature of the case, with its unusual sexual overtones, is likely to attract widespread publicity to the town.

(Further articles on pages 8, 9, and 10)

Chapter 1

Arabella slipped unseen across the sunlit lawn, her hips swaying with a lazy, provocative confidence. Then she stepped on to the crazy-paving path, tripped lightly along the line of laburnum arches, navigated the parterre, slipped past the seed trays, and advanced steadily, purposefully, up toward the patio, not once distracted by the wild and scented roses, not even glancing at the water feature, but aiming always at the cracked teak bench on which old Mrs Harpur was dreamily sat, bare-armed in a blue cotton dress, and gazing with a lifetime's contentment upon the floral kaleidoscope that was her cottage garden. Arabella padded gently to a halt beside the rustic seat and, in a display of pride and shy affection, she leaned her head low, parted her lips wide, and deposited a gashed blackbird at the elderly widow's feet.

It was a quiet day at Abernant Police Station, and several key personnel had gone out for doughnuts. There had been an emergency earlier, when a hay lorry had been wrong-footed by a roundabout, and the Panda's radio had crackled with the need for pitchforks, but the guilty driver was found to be the superintendent's sister's stepson and the incident had to be put down to an errant – and anonymous – sheep. The chances of a second arrestable offence on the same weekday were deemed low, and the front line against rural crime was reduced to Griff Griffiths, a safe, if unappealing, pair of hands.

A spherical, slow-moving man, he had peaked at sergeant after twenty-two years of trying to arrest drunks, and now regarded desk duty as his niche, his patch. Over time, he had stamped his interesting personality upon the reception area, and no wall space was without a frayed government poster conveying the legal, moral, sexual, animal, medical, agricultural, and mechanical rules essential to the life of a model citizen. When he had begun in the police force the main threat to the Welsh nation had been the Colorado beetle, a potato-loving immigrant whose gaudy stripes presaged dietary mayhem. But times change, and by the late 1980s, *la crise de nos jours* was pervasive vomit. And prominent amongst Griff's custodial duties was the use of Dettol, alcohol's ultimate chaser.

The two holding cells were a door away, and the bodily contents of criminals were seldom wholesome. Visitors to the station, whether wanting advice on the road signs, reporting a dog gone to the bad, or confessing to wrongful parking, felt entitled to reasonable fragrance, as was befitting for ratepayers. But, following the fashion for old market towns to commit architectural hara-kiri, Abernant's planners had demolished the original building, which bristled with the Victorian stucco and stonework that once stood for rectitude, and opted for a chipboard structure because it was modern. Outside, it had the look of a prefab with pretensions, inside, it was a paean to partitions, and Sgt. Griffiths had dominion over a flimsy, box-like room, at the mercy of unseemly sounds and smells.

The most distinctive smell of crime was fried eggs, urine, and disinfectant. At times, this would waft through walls with the power of a Superman fart, like air on a mission. It was not from liberal instincts that Sgt. Griffiths liked to keep arrests to a minimum. Fortunately, the serious criminals in mid-Wales had mostly moved to Cardiff, tempted by the bright lights and car chases, and today the sergeant's custody suite was empty, leaving him free to bestride the public reception area, in which only a trace element now tingled the nostrils.

Sgt. Griff Griffiths had large nostrils, but they took second place to his mutton-chop whiskers, which in turn were outgunned by his girth. He was a character. Had police regulations allowed it, he would have worn a multicoloured waistcoat. He rarely left home without a viewpoint to purvey, and liked to specialise in reassuring nostrums, the better to put the populace at its ease. If pressed – indeed, if not pressed – the sergeant would describe himself as a sort of father figure to the community. He would also describe himself, breath allowing, as a trouper of the old school, as a Mr Dependable, a man with a storehouse of cautionary tales, a repository of first-aid tips, and a repertoire of humorous stories, each honed to the funny bone by repeated retelling.

But it was a slow May afternoon, with little call for any of these skills, and so Sgt. Griffiths stood with officious idleness behind his counter, and authorised his mind to wander. A vigorous thinker, often reprimanded for overuse of the Suggestion Box, his current big idea was a police station Open Day. The details were still vague, but he envisioned a visiting public of Dickensian diversity, all of them agog at the miracles of police craft. Few treats would be spared: a browse through dead-eyed mug shots, a trial run with handcuffs, a lie-down in the whiffy cells, a feel of the weight of a baton, a seat at the wheel of a Panda, a couple of playful presses on the siren. Not just masterful PR, but crime prevention – the sight of smiling men in blue, bearing tea and sugared buns, would, Sgt. Griffiths liked to imagine, cause many a criminal gene to mutate and reassess its plans. And all these dreams came with the rightful bonus of himself as Master of Ceremonies.

'*Le Figaro*, for goodness sake! They tell me I'm going to be in *Le Figaro*.' A bearded man, early sixties, ramshackle hair, ruddy skin, tweed jacket, dirty white mac, had come in from the high street unnoticed. 'French pin-up of the week, no doubt,' he added in a modest mutter.

'Good afternoon, sir.' Sgt. Griffiths quickly removed his gut from the counter top and aborted his reverie. He glanced with apprehension at the old cardboard box that stood near by.

'Afternoon, Sergeant.'

The man had an easy air of authority that was at odds with the mac. Upon most people of his age, it would have been a dirty old man's mac, and reliable proof of pervertedness, but upon him it was just a rather shabby mac, an ancient mac, and evidence that he cared little for material things; even the tweed showed signs of wear, a rare failure for the women of Harris. Only the eyes had not faded with age, and were still deep brown, still piercing his interlocutors with a twinkle. A trim man of below-average height, he had a brown beard that failed to fully disguise a pointed chin, and first impressions suggested an adult elf of some gravitas.

The sergeant stood silent, and patiently waited.

'Six months.'

The sergeant nodded sagely, but affected mild regret.

'No choice really, Sergeant.'

'No, I guess not, sir.'

'If you chisel off a penis in public, you've got to expect something custodial.'

'Very true, sir.'

'As a deterrent to others, if nothing else.'

The sergeant nodded again, but chose not to pursue this exchange of views on penal policy. It is possible that the recent outbreak of genital vandalism in the town had not left any conversational cranny unexplored, but he also knew that his visitor had not come in for chit-chat. The magistracy did not do chit-chat with coppers, for constitutional reasons, a separation of powers that the sergeant respected. What he respected somewhat less was the attitude that Gwyn Hopkins, JP, displayed towards the world of police work.

Sgt. Griffiths knew himself to be a structural interface – he had seen the strategy document – and was personally developing a policy vis-à-vis the public which he called the 3 'D's: dignity, dedication and duty. And that meant not just a Dettol-dosed reception area, but a place where troubled citizenry could feel the rhythms of a well-ordered universe, where the forms would lie in neat files, the reports in tidy trays, and you could see your face in the Formica.

Yet the magistrate paid little heed to these innovative amenities, and focused instead on the old cardboard box at the end of the counter.

Concern crossed his face as he came closer, and his brief glance at the sergeant held a hint of distrust. Using police training to suppress any surge of resentment, Sgt. Griffiths, who came from the lower socio-economic groupings, made no comment, but moved along the counter and cautiously lifted the lid.

'Got a pigeon for you, sir.'

'Collared dove, Sergeant.'

Sgt. Griffiths wondered briefly if this were some form of word play, pertaining presumably to a bird arrest, but then saw that the magistrate's finger was pointed at the distinctive neck marking.

'Hit by a bike, sir,' the sergeant added, moving to the safer ground of criminal cause, 'but still cooing. Quite a lot of cooing.'

'Good sign,' said the magistrate. 'Good sign.' And he gently ran an ornithologically expert hand over the ruffled grey plumage. 'Pen?'

Sgt. Griffiths handed him the station Biro – attached by a disconcerting chain to the counter – and the magistrate made several air-holes. Then he patted the lid back into place.

'We're doing well, Sergeant. Five last month alone.'

'I'd say six.' It was not a shared enthusiasm.

The policeman blamed the masons, though wrongly. Gwyn Hopkins was a very persuasive person when it came to nature. The last time anyone counted, he was on sixty-two committees, and a Roneo in his bedroom cranked out his causes. Builders of bypasses and dreamers of dams knew it was best to beware. Edwardian in his enthusiasms, and founder of the Abernant Naturalists' Trust, Gwyn was an all-weather friend to fish, flesh and fowl. Only in court were his binoculars not to hand.

The bench was not his natural habitat, nor JPs his favourite species, but he understood the pecking orders of power. As an arbiter of justice, albeit unable to transport egg-stealers to Australia, he was guaranteed his tithe of respect, with or without mud on his mac. (In a town of just eight thousand, nearly all related, the backs to scratch were no secret.) It only took a nod and a wink – and not a funny handshake – to get the men with braid onside, and now he had a clearing house for birds that were poorly, or suffering from traffic. With a multitasking sergeant to pay heed to their cries.

So every Wednesday, after his weekly court, Gwyn Hopkins, JP, came by, and would take away the wounded. And every Wednesday, Sgt. Griff Griffiths gritted his teeth, and would refer once more to his feathered friends. The sergeant was a man who did not wish to share his personal space with any of God's creatures, whatever their state of health. Cardboard boxes were, he felt, a threat to his professionalism. And if it flapped, he could not file it.

'It's the wood pigeon that normally cops it. Take-off velocity of a hippo.'

The sergeant nodded, as if he gave a damn.

'You'd think they'd die out, but they're still spreading. As is the collared dove.'

'Looked foreign,' said Griff dubiously. 'A Continental sort of bird.'

'And you would be right. Circa 1955 they first arrived, possibly unhappy with the Fourth Republic.'

The joke was lost, though it gave Gwyn a private pleasure.

Years of studying prisoners in the dock, like a naturalist whose speciality was man, had brought him up to spy-speed in the decoding of body language. So he was under no illusion that Sgt. Griffiths was besotted with birds, or even had a mild liking for them. Given the chance, the man would have nursed them to death with disinfectant. But it gave Gwyn satisfaction to toy with his deceit, and hope that the nuggets of bird knowledge he scattered might one day prove useful, even if only in a pub quiz.

The magistrate took hold of the cardboard box and eased it from the counter.

'I'll get the door for you, sir.' Trying not to be overly eager, Sgt. Griffiths led the way across his partitioned domain. 'Oh, and you have a message.'

'A message?'

'Yes. *Would you drop into Mill Cottage on your way home?*'

'Oh dear,' sighed the JP. He paused in the doorway. 'Oh dear, I think Arabella's struck again.'

Chapter 2

Nico edged slowly down the stone steps of the old courthouse, his pace dictated by the departing crowd, and then a hundred yards on, eager for a restorative roll-up, he paused to gather his thoughts in the sleepy town square, where the paparazzi had been so busy earlier.

Had Nico been an introspective man, or appreciative of irony, he would have judged it a minor miracle that his first time in a law court had not been from the perspective of the dock – a fact which many in the antiques trade found to be cause for regret. A wheeler-dealer who had begun in bric-à-brac, Nico hid the morals of a shark beneath the stubble of a yokel, and his ducking and diving had now so diversified that nothing saleable was safe from his clutch. Although his hallmark was a hooded zip-up jumper of the yob brand, he also had the arm-twisting charm of a man whose hobby was to commit *Miller's Guide* to memory. Few were the townie tourists who escaped his back-street shop without some essential like a hay-rake.

Normally aloof from the pack, disdainful of mainstream mores, he had – like so many in the town – found the trial of Gareth Richards too tempting a tragedy to ignore. This was not from a wellspring of personal warmth. He could not himself claim a friendship with the hill-sheep farmer, though a candlestick had once changed hands. (At a profit, Nico recalled, of £17.50, with a mark-up, he also recalled, of 800 per cent.) But then, few could claim a friendship, except possibly Dafydd the ex-postman, with whom mail had formed a tenuous bond. Today's packed house was because Abernant seldom had operatic tales of passion and revenge, cold and wet being the wrong kind of climate.

But as Nico had sat upon the ancient oak benches – worth, he reckoned, three noughts in salvage – and concentrated on the drink-fuelled saga, his business brain had ticked over on standby. Whilst the good burghers, eager to be shocked, listened to a stumbling account of lust and loneliness, Nico could not help computing. The charges were many, stretching even to legal spite about a bald tyre, but it was not compassion that had first call upon his undersized soul. Over one hundred acres were at stake. And when the sentence came, the consequence was sheep without their shepherd, a farm without its farmer.

Nico scuffed pensively at the gravel, and leaned against the war memorial. Abernant was a town of some history, kick-started by drovers, still bearing a faint imprint of moneyed monks, and at its heart lay the ancient town square, now municipalised into neatness. Yet it had a new notoriety. This was a notoriety that brought despair to the museum curator, whose exhibitions – always the fruit of long months' lucubration – were opened by wine-and-cheese evenings that made little inroad into eight ounces of Cheddar. Intellectual life, she sometimes felt, was going to hell in a handcart. Despite centuries of Celtic culture, and multicoloured mosaics at a nearby Roman ruin, and royal visits by boar-hunting kings, and a church with a rare rood, Abernant had finally been put on the map by a statue subjected to sexual assault.

Nico stubbed out his faltering fag upon the plinth, and thought some more. Like all his thoughts, they were business thoughts; he was not given to thoughts which did not lead to money. And his money had, of late, come in ever bigger wads. To his areas of expertise he had added art, archives, and combine harvesters. And to his ambitions he had added land.

In land itself, in land qua land, he had no interest. He neither communed with it, nor rambled on it. On the days when the clouds lifted, he felt no urge to look at it. As a man who lived on pizzas, he gave no thought to what people did with it. Land had for him no history, no sense to its shape, no proof of endeavour. Nor did it come with geology or flora or fauna or fossils. Land, like life, was simply there. Waiting for someone to take advantage of it.

And Nico was rural enough and local enough to know of the new agronomics, and the fate that faced the hilltop fields.

The land needed for a living now doubled in size every decade, and farmers were the latest surplus crop. Behind the hedges, the new breed stalking the hills was the rural asset-stripper. The hottest Monopoly game in town was to split the farm from its farmhouse, and rearrange the countryside at big-time profit. And the spare farmers could go hang, which they often did.

Nico wondered about prison visiting hours.

Chapter 3

Stéfan was bored. He was standing on the sunny bank of his buttercup meadow, beside his private stretch of the unruly River Nant, and was blankly staring at some bobbing wagtails while he waited for a bite from his brown trout. He had been waiting for over three minutes. He was easily bored.

Waiting was for wimps, he always declared. And he always declared it loudly, as whispering was also for wimps. Waiting was, he held, an indignity for a wealthy man. Only life's failures ever waited. Even traffic jams he took as a slur on his power; he had, so far, five summonses for using the M4's hard shoulder as his personal lane. A compelling need to reach his new Welsh estate had cut no legal ice.

He had wanted a helicopter, but the weather of mid-Wales specialised in mist, and landing was considered a luxury. This meant not just a transport shortfall, but a social setback. He already had to bear the shame of being nearly thirty and still without a jet.

Two years it had taken to make his new home habitable. Two years of damp and rot and absent artisans. Two years of tantrums and threats and special pleading. Back in his native Georgia, he would have brought in brigands with guns, and done away with the decorators' next of kin. In the timeless world of the upper Nant Valley, all he could do was wait and wave money. And still he had not got the respect that was owed to a squire.

He had raised funds for the hunt, and had put something called tombola on his very large lawn. He had been a judge at the annual valley show, and pinned rosettes on doilies and damsons. He had donated a vast vegetable medley from Harrods to the harvest supper evening. And yet still he was waiting for cap-doffing deference, which apparently only fell due when he had been around as long as his Jacobean mansion. Sometimes he reckoned he would get more status if he got more land – and ideally land with a view of the rest of his land, to add to his visions of grandeur.

But nature was the worst when it came to waiting. Nothing grew to command, nothing blossomed to order. Spring came late or not at all. Welsh seasons were merely guidelines, with no sign of central planning. His new trees rose slowly and at unwanted angles; his bolshie new bushes held back their berries; his flowerbeds mocked him with species in miniature.

And his fish were fickle.

The trout were now four minutes late. Stéfan reached into his blazer for the fisherman's secret friend, obtained for him by Eryl, his surly handyman. Then he clicked his silver cigarette-lighter underneath its fuse, and hurled the dynamite into the river.

To help strategy facilitation and develop commitment potential, wrote Rhys with fastidious slowness. Then added, after further thought, *using the medium of experiential projects.* This he underlined, a little wavily.

It was not easy writing in a hammock, and lunch had made him drowsy. He swung his legs out and down, and on to the grass. He felt his creativity flourished better when he was on the move. All that extra external stimuli. He made his way through the small pasture, close-cropped by a handful of geese, and took the path into the sessile-oak wood on the slopes above.

To enhance strategy development and motivate commitment, rewrote Rhys, as he paused at the stile, notebook resting on his raised knee.

The bracken was making inroads here, he realised, taking advantage already of the death of his grandfather. In the old man's declining years, the fronds had noticed that he thwacked less well, that his flailing arm was weakening. Country lore stated, according to Gwyn the JP, Granddad's lifelong friend and sometime mentor, that it took seven years of thwacking bracken for it to be deterred. But this year it had not even been mildly discouraged, and green tendrils were advancing like a blind and hydra-headed army.

Rhys moved on into the cool bluebell clearings of the wood, where there was a gentle buzz of bees and a faint scent of wild garlic. The undergrowth twitched every now and then with the secret life of small mammals, adding a pleasing touch of naturalist mystery to the scene. From the distance, there came courtship calls of birds who remained coquettishly unseen, and overhead, the canopy of leaves rustled in the light wind, evoking dreamlike memories of childhood summers.

Rhys paused to check the position of the trees in the largest glade, as if engaged upon some abstract calculation. Then he sat down on a fallen trunk, its mossy bark like a damp cushion-cover, and reached again for his pen.

To generate strategic visions and enhance commitment.

Perfect! He crossed out versions one and two. But, his satisfaction still not complete, he flicked back and forth over half a dozen pages of notes, making further alterations and inserting *psychometric profiling* in a margin. He also muttered *facilitated review* and *theory input* out loud several times, road-testing their appeal in the real world. And he did some more thinking.

After ten minutes of this, he straightened up and continued along the circular path, now thin as a hair parting, that followed the perimeter of the wood. He remembered the path from his youth, from the time when he and his parents would come up from Cardiff for a day of rural treats. Little had he known that the land would one day be his, and ripe for rich rewards. It was just a shame that the land on the windy rocky ridge was not also his, as that could, he thought, be of great benefit to his plans.

He soon had to leave the path, to divert around a mound of earth – that traditional sign of badgers indulging in their lovable acts of destruction – but this he scarcely noticed for he was doing a mental cut-and-paste as he walked, and was blotting out the backdrop of nature. This ability to focus so fully was, to date, the most tangible gain from his business studies course, whose diploma was very prominently framed upon the wall of his entrance hall. It was a focus only broken by a puzzling explosion, the second of the day, that came from a little further up the valley. He put this down to the Army, who were known to be practising for World War Three on the moors. And then he returned to the editing suite of his mind.

As Rhys worked his way back down the brackened hill, past the scattered nest-boxes that offered accommodation for the pickier bird, he already had a clear idea of the brochure. As yet, he lacked a clear idea of the photographs that would best illustrate *behavioural monitoring* and *group specific objectives*, but he did now have a collection of first-rate jargon. And he had also found a new name for the estate: *Demeter*. A little-known goddess of the harvest, apparently. Just the sort of high-sounding classical nonsense so beloved by the modern exec, even if such men did struggle with apostrophes. Soon, thought Rhys, he could start to seductively package the wilderness training weekends that would claim to transform the careers of mediocre management. The prices that would transform his own career were yet to be brainstormed.

Chapter 4

To reach Mill Cottage one had first to go past the mill. A rutted track descended from the road, and went by the watermill at roof height, except there was now more ivy than roof. Where nature had not forced its way in with wind and rain, unscrupulous scrap dealers (Nico by name) had repeatedly invaded, and taken away anything loose – or not so loose – of value. Slates and flagstones, even a lintel or two, had gone into his overloaded Volvo at the dead of night, off to a new life at a more caring postcode. Only the giant wooden waterwheel, which had not turned for a hundred years, was still intact, too difficult to detach, too recherché for even the most cutting-edge of homemakers, normally so keen on an *objet trouvé*.

It was one of thirteen ruined mills on the Nant, and was now so ruined it was only ever noticed by those in the know. Every few years some historically minded incomer would propose its salvation, and cast around for a committee. Titles would be thought up for a trust – The Nant Mill Trust was favourite – and charities approached for funds. But the mid-Wales world is full of ruined mills, some only a handful of bricks in total, and the forces of form-filling would soon induce restoration lethargy, so minds would turn instead to saving the likes of the red kite, which at least flew about a bit.

Damp and overgrown and dark in daylight, with saplings growing through the roof and *DANGER!* written on the walls, it was one of Gwyn's favourite places.

He would visit it at dusk, and count out the bats as they left. His most successful twilight had seen him reach four hundred, his finger a blur on the bat-counter, the last bat all but imperceptible. He would watch till the last of the light had gone, straining to see them jerk about the sky as they forayed for low-flying food, their snack bar of choice beneath the little humpback bridge that stood downstream. It added to his pleasure, Gwyn would say with a smile, that these were not just run-of-the-mill bats, they were Daubenton's – a joke that worked best in bat circles.

And today it was cats. He drove slowly on down the dead-end track, treating his beat-up banger estate with a rare reverence, due wholly to the delicate state of the dove, whose cooing had begun to grate. A hundred yards farther on, and Gwyn eased to a halt, choosing the shade of some alders.

In front of him, beside the river and next to a meadow, was a long and narrow cottage with three front doors ... and just the one wisteria, writhing over their token porches in a unifying purple. When this had been planted in the reign of Queen Victoria, no doubt by some house-proud mill-hand, there had been three mill cottages – each with tenants enough for a football team. Today there was but one old lady, owner and gardener, with a surfeit of drawing rooms.

Quite how long Mrs Harpur had been here, no one knew. Best guess was before the war. Photos on a writing desk showed her in Land Army breeches and jersey, hoeing a sea of mud. She had had help, as other photos showed an elegant, angular man, sometimes in the garden, sometimes on elephants, sometimes at masked balls. But all she had left of her husband was half a boat. It stood on struts in the extra-large lean-to, kept dry by an ageing corrugated roof. They had planned to celebrate the Sixties by building a schooner to sail round the world, she had once said, and Mill Cottage had briefly taken on the look of a boatyard. Not a practical man, he had dropped dead on the transom. Something to do with misjudging the weight of the rudder, the coroner had thought. But mostly she and Mr Hopkins talked about the wildlife in her garden.

'The cat meant no harm,' she said, as he came into view on the patio.

He sat down on the bench beside her, and poured a glass of the lemonade she had provided.

'I'd still hang it,' he replied, his views on cats well known. He looked into the wicker basket between them, and at the bloodied bird lying in shock on fresh grass-clippings. 'Or possibly put it in front of a firing squad.'

'They fly too low, blackbirds.'

Mr Hopkins gently inspected a wing and a breast, and nudged the saucer of watery milk closer to its beak.

'How negligent of them.'

He had this conversation with her every year, some years more than once.

'Thank you for coming,' she said. 'Will this one be all right, Mr Hopkins?'

'... too soon to say.' He felt its hurrying heartbeat, with a finger more calloused than was normal for a magistrate. 'Post-traumatic stress is difficult to assess in blackbirds.'

He liked to convey an irritation at such incidents, in the vague hope that this effect change. But Arabella was her sole companion, and unlikely to be sacrificed for the greater avian good. Besides, he sometimes wondered whether she rang to assist the bird or assuage her guilt. He leaned back on the bench, noticing almost for the first time that the early morning rain had given way to warm sun.

'*Turdus merula*,' he said. 'From the *Turdus* family. A very disappointing name, I always think. Though I doubt it bothers the bird.'

'Did you do Latin at school?'

'No. No, my knowledge ends with animal names. Animals and birds. And I can identify a *Homo sapiens*, of course. Cause of all our trouble.'

If Mrs Harpur disagreed, she did not say. There was a brief, but not awkward pause, as they took time to gaze upon her garden.

Like the best of cottage gardens, it initially appeared that nature had had a free hand, yet the colour was rioting to order. And fortunately the orders came from a libertarian botanist, for whom foxgloves were as welcome as Aquilegia, who let honeysuckle climb her trees, and who allowed her lawn to be a sanctuary for speedwell. Nor did the garden's charm end at its low box hedge, for the vista beyond was of a meadow now streaked with late-spring tints. It was her visitor who had last year advised a delay to the cutting regime, in the hope of luring out rare yellow rattle, and already there were various minor-league orchids and an unusual hellebore marked by a milk crate for makeshift protection. But best of all, whenever one was in the garden, and wherever one was in the garden, nature laid on one beguiling constant: the backing track of the river, never silent on its thirteen-mile tumble to town.

'Most of the time it's just mice she brings me.'

'What sort of mice?'

'What sort of mice are there?'

'House mice, field mice, wood mice, also known as long-tailed field mice, yellow-necked mice …' Mr Hopkins gestured in the general area of the countryside. 'If you can find them, that is.'

'Oh. So some of them are rare?'

'And getting rarer. Sadly.'

'Well, I think mice are overrated.'

She spoke with the authority of the gentry, whose stance on mammals was often unsound. But her years of solitude and lumbago had encouraged a dogmatism, and despite being shrivelled by age, she was never easily uncoupled from her views.

'Will it fly again?'

'… possibly. Given time.'

'You mean, given time and proper care?'

'Oh yes, lots of proper care.' He looked down at the sorry bird, its feathers matted and askew. He smiled, knowing what was to come next in the ritual of the visit.

'I see … It would be awful to do something wrong. By mistake.'

'Indeed.'

'Because it's such a fragile creature.'

'No doubt about that.' He embarked upon a pause. Dragged it out. And added a beat for devilment. 'If you wish, I could take the bird back with me.'

'Oh, *would you*, Mr Hopkins? That would be so kind.'

'Not at all, Mrs Harpur.'

'It's probably for the best, you being the expert.'

He inclined his head, accepting the flattery with a modesty born of no effort.

'More lemonade?'

'No. No, thank you. Places to go, people to see, like my wife.'

He pushed himself to his feet, and reached for the basket.

'Do give my regards to her – and apologise for my sending another lodger.'

'Of course.' And with a friendly nod, he set off with his second sick bird of the day.

Outside, on the track, Gwyn did not immediately get into his car, but crossed the few yards to the river. He lived up on the exposed side of the valley, where you could see twenty miles of sky from your bed, and sometimes the only sound was the wind. Down here, the reed-fringed river was a world of mist and early shadows and gurgling secrets. From somewhere came the sound of ducks, while little hoofprints upon a mudflat were the mark of the very private muntjac. And almost hidden from view, the old concrete mill-race still survived, although the current had long ago abated, and in its wake had left a habitat for watercress, a scene so tranquil that even Pooh-sticks would struggle.

Gwyn walked a little way along the bank, the wicker basket in his hand, his eyes on alert for a flash of kingfisher or an incautious otter. He stopped when he reached the mill, set back by the rock face below the track. And then he tenderly raised the gashed blackbird from its bed of grass, held it by both feet, and swung its head swiftly, terminally, mercifully, against the redundant stone wall.

Chapter 5

There was a double bill of dead bodies at Ebenezer Chapel, and not a free seat to be had.

It was the custom of the valley, of the stolid, stoic, flat-capped farmers, to pay their last respects even when they did not know the dear departed. A solemn mien, hewn by wind and rain, made these men naturals for a funeral. Theirs was not the culture for a wild wake, or a knees-up at any time of life, since by character and tradition they always sought an outlet to be sombre. So when death came to anywhere near the Nant, most heads of household were on hand with subfusc suits and ready-made faces of deepest regret, primed to mime mourning for a stranger.

But everyone knew Teg and Ben.

That was why the narrow lane up off the valley road was clogged with 4 × 4s that afternoon, mostly abandoned on the bank at an angle of thirty degrees. Scarcely a farm had not cause to thank these two old men. With them had died sixty years of mole-catching memories and left behind them was a legacy of flatter fields, albeit fleetingly. Their life of dedication to digging holes in pursuit of moles had smoothed the path of untold ploughs. They were almost the last of the professional rustics, in a line that stretched back to Bottom. Which made it all the more appalling that the pair had spent their last night dying in a ditch.

The probable cause of death was a disputed double six. Their lives, off-duty, were dominated by drink and dominoes. Ungainly and muddy, Big Teg and Small Ben were of little appeal to ladies, and as the two men aged they had kept each other company, in a drear and fractious way. In public bars with dirty flagstones they hid from the cold of their cottages and gambled a few pence of their pay … and the gruff no-nonsense of the working day turned rancid with the evening ale. The late-night hedgerows would then echo to grudges and loud petty quarrels as they lurched back to bed along the byways.

It was a deep, steep ditch, with muddy sides, standing water, and a rock – on which two interlocked bodies had landed. Eight pints put paid to escape.

Ebenezer Chapel stood in bright sunlight on a hillside gleaming with yellow gorse, at the end of the line for the lane. Apart from Speckled Face sheep, there was only a cemetery for company. Above and beyond were the moors, purple and moody. To the nonconformist builders of 1841, this lonely lovely dell might well have held the hope that the Promised Land could be found at home in Wales. Substantial and reassuring, Ebenezer Chapel was a fine place to be seen dead in. The only regret to date was calling it Ebenezer, a name done infinite damage by Dickens.

This was the first time that Eryl, Stéfan's surly handyman, had been in the chapel, or indeed in any of the valley's many chapels, whose shuttered shells now littered the roadsides. *His* nonconformity drew strength from a passé ponytail and black bike-leathers, the last surviving symbols of a failed rural roué. He sat near the rear, his acned face troubled less by grief than sourness. Although not yet thirty, Eryl was a man bitter beyond his years, for his life had suffered setbacks across a wide range of fronts, not least a blood group foreign to the rest of his well-bred inbred family.

His hopes of a silver spoon, of razzle-dazzle on a daily basis, had not survived the unfair fate of adoptive parents who died young and intestate in their Lagonda. A distant relative had quickly emerged from the rococo woodwork, and laid a devious claim to the landed luxuries of their many-bedded mansion, with auction as his endgame. Several hundred years of gentry genes had then followed the bloodline, rerouted around the protesting body of Eryl the Illegitimate, and his home had gone under the hammer. So he sat in the chapel not as a man with his own pew but as one of the dispossessed.

The deceased mole-men were not his close friends, not even his friends; they merely got drunk and grunted together, *faute de mieux*. Their common bond was melancholia. They had been four in total, four forlorn regulars in a bleak country alehouse – while the old men were damning their dominoes, the other two drinkers had relentlessly lamented their lot, and their lack of luck with women. Night after night at the Dragon's Head, Eryl would list the downsides to life as a nouveau pauvre who once had plans to be a playboy, and then, in turn, as the pints piled up, he had had to listen to the infidelity fears and midlife crises of a hill-sheep farmer, whose young Irish wife had legs with attitude, and strange desires like salsa.

Eryl had spent much of this day with these facts to the fore of his mind, for in the morning he had gone to town to see that same farmer again, but now facing the public consequences of cuckoldry. Court and chapel, gaol and grave, it had been an unusually busy Wednesday.

And not merely for Eryl. Many a diary in the valley had cancelled a whole day's hoeing and hedging, prurience requiring a presence at the triple tragedies of Gareth, Teg, and Ben. Even old Clydog, mainstay of the weekly *Mid-Walian*, could barely remember when last he had so full a pad, so many were the mourners to list, so lubricious was the account of the court case.

Eryl glowed yellow in his pew, suffused by sunbeams. A great window occupied the wall beyond the lectern as, unlike churchgoers, the chapel faithful are granted full viewing rights of the temporal world outside. Modelled on a meeting-house, this place of worship seated its congregation around three sides of a square, as if in a very modest amphitheatre. But whatever doctrines dictated such design, the distant vision of well-grazed uplands – now glowing almost golden – was a reasonable replication of a hill-farmer's idea of heaven, and so helped take the edge off death.

The massed ranks of men in Sunday tweed sat in dutifully sad silence, doggedly ignoring all the cheerful, chirrupy birdsong that was drifting through the open door. This was a community that still had reverence for decorum, a virtue above all others. And here today, with no known relatives, and no one fighting back tears, they were determined to line up foursquare beside the dead.

As was Revd Joshua Bennett-Jones.

'Two lives of service! *Two lives of duty!* Two lives of toil! *Two men of manners!* Two men of goodness! *Two men of vision!'*

And one style of sentence. Rhetorical.

This was no mousy C of E. This galvanic preacher had a mane of grey hair, which he tossed in time with his punchlines. A visitor to the valley, he stood six foot, with the shoulders of a svelte ox, and arms that kept pointing to heaven.

'These were men in harmony with *God's purpose*, at one with *God's intent*. For these were *country*men, and daily they looked upon the *beauty of His creation*. And thus it was that they devoted their long, hard lives to the *stewardship of His land*. For, humble though they were, they knew in their souls that mole-catching was *holy* work. *Mole-catching was God's work.'*

Revd Bennett-Jones had come from another century. Or indeed another culture. The vigour of the delivery, the dynamism of the gestures, the charisma of the black polo-neck jumper, all spoke to the long-gone days when religion was a roller-coaster ride to redemption.

'Though they *dirtied* their hands, although they *damaged* their bodies, all was at the service of *a higher calling*. And day after day, they plunged their arms deep into *God's good earth*, ceaselessly searching for their prey, for this most elusive of *God's creatures* – their aim always to augment the joyous *bounty of our land.'*

He had the look less of a preacher-man, more of an Old Testament prophet – recently returned from some wilderness. A wildness in his eyes, he boomed out his panegyric like Moses with rhythm.

And all the while, the afternoon sun shone full behind the lectern, encasing his head in an aureole.

After the joyous *bounty of our land*, Revd Joshua Bennett-Jones paused for oratorical effect, perhaps expecting that his audience might want to shout a few hosannas, or chant a few refrains. But this was a Nant audience, and only up for the odd nod.

Whereas Eryl, he was keen on a V-sign.

No stranger to misdeeds, Eryl was rarely comfortable amongst the strait-laced and the God-fearing. Being the solitary soul in the valley who had chosen James Dean for a role model, albeit some twenty years later than the rest of the world, Eryl personally favoured the demi-monde … if only he could find it. But around him here were those with whom he once played hopscotch, men whose mindsets had not moved on since age eight, and who now bought cocoa in bulk and never crossed the county boundary. Theirs was no life lived to the limit. And so, hoping to keep hip, Eryl did his best to avoid the cultural highlights of the community calendar – the harvest festival, the sheepdog trials, and any event where animals wore ribbons.

Admittedly, Ebenezer Chapel was itself no icon of counter-culture. But these obsequies had offered him more than just an occasion to pay his token respects, one drunk to another. They had provided a means of escape.

Life and work at Crug Caradoc, home of Stéfan, the man who would be squire, were not to his full satisfaction. Eryl did not take well to orders, or rising before noon. And neither was he happy as a handyman: his carpentry skills were not what he claimed, he looked upon plumbing as an arcane art, and he had trouble with ladders. But what he did possess – as Stéfan had reluctantly recognised – was the great virtue of being available, which trumped all his shortcomings. Yet this ersatz squire (whose means of making money were a mystery to the valley) struggled with personnel management, and was often confused by how to cope with the unfamiliar ways of his key worker. Only yesterday, he and Eryl had clashed over the length and frequency of the little-known Welsh siesta.

And today, Eryl's choice scheme had been his claim for compassionate leave.

But though this claim might be true, it was not the whole truth. Eryl had another motive for wishing to be in a pew, and absent from his duties. He did not want to be around when the dynamite went off.

He had himself obtained the sticks from Nico – another of the small, unsung services which the antiques expert provided – as a furtive favour. Eryl was not a man much bothered by illegality, for he liked his image as a rogue, and nor was he a man much bothered by blown-up fish, for he was rarely kept awake by ecology. What did bother him, though, was being blasted to bits, for Stéfan was not a boss big on health and safety. His plan for fly-fishing with bombs (the traditions of huntin', shootin', and fishin' being thereby rolled into one easy hobby for busy people) was still at the experimental stage, and Eryl had not been keen. Armed commando raids on trout fell outside his job description, and he had no wish to be known as the gillie who lost his goolies.

Which is why he was now sat in the sunbathed chapel, pretending to pray. It could be argued – indeed, would be argued by such moral men as Revd Joshua Bennett-Jones – that he should have tried to discourage Stéfan, should have explained that angling was an artform. But an appeal to Eryl's sense of duty would not have had a hearing. For any untoward fate of Stéfan would not have been met by his grief.

Because Crug Caradoc was the house that Eryl was born in … on the estate where he once was heir.

2

After Wednesday

Chapter 6

'Best to advance from the rear!' called the colonel (rtd). 'If you want to make it through alive!'

'Thank you. But I think I'll risk the front door,' rejoined the dentist (also retired). 'I've always been one for living dangerously.' Mr Hampton did not like the colonel.

'Joking!' said the colonel, coming to a halt beside the dentist. 'Just joking!' Col. White often found his jokes got lost in transmission, but had no idea why.

No further pleasantries were exchanged. Instead, both of them tilted back their heads and stared up toward the June sky.

It was early evening, and the two men were stood in the forecourt of the museum. Abernant Museum was a fine eighteenth-century edifice, or it had been in the eighteenth century. Now it was wearing a hairnet, some twenty yards by ten.

'Thought it was a leg-pull when I first heard,' said the dentist.

'A hundredweight of loose frieze is no leg-pull. Not if it lands on your nut.'

'Make for an unusual epitaph at least.' The dentist squinted at the gap-toothed frieze. 'Death by architecture.'

The pair continued gazing upward at the council's latest health-and-safety feature.

'Tensile steel,' stated the Colonel. 'Get a lot of it in the Alps.' He liked to boast he was a practical man, and often spoke of his time with the REME Support Battalion, though rarely at relevant moments of a conversation. 'Through mountain passes.'

'Not very neo-Georgian though,' said the dentist.

Col. White had no response to this aperçu. There was a further pause in the cut and thrust of their dialogue.

'Best not be late,' he said eventually. 'Or we'll miss the minutes.' He pushed open the imposing left-hand door with the decisiveness that comes from leadership skills, and the two committee members entered the museum.

Doors, shoes, words, everything echoed in the high-ceilinged, marble-floored entrance hall, which was now empty of the day's few visitors. Signs pointed through the half-light toward the galleries that housed the town's treasures. Here the seminal moments of Abernantian prehistory were lovingly, bilingually, labelled; here five thousand years of farming were celebrated in detail, the highlight a life-size pair of papier mâché sheep, believed to be Victorian.

But on this evening the two men's attention was caught by a new collection of exhibits – exhibits which, in the three months since their last visit, had been placed on display around the entrance hall. As yet in no catalogue, and lacking the aid of labels, these were objects of mystery.

'Pediments,' announced Miss Stevens, emerging from a shadowy recess, and hitting the implosive 'p' with a venom unusual in a curator. 'Swan-neck pediments. *Inter alia.*'

'Of course,' said the colonel, sensitive to the charge that he had led a brutish life.

'Which includes your ornamented tablature –'

'Right.'

'Your sculpted cornice –'

'Right.'

'And lots of frieze. Some of it pulvinated.'

'As you'd expect.'

The dentist prodded a bit of swan neck with his foot.

'So ... roughly what date would these artefacts be?'

'1786. When they built the museum.'

'... oh,' said the dentist. 'Oh. And all this is caused by ...?'

'Council retards,' said Miss Stevens, whose silver hair was kept in a preternaturally tight bun. 'Too stupid to spend any money.'

'Uh-huh. So what will happen?'

'In time? All the outside of the building will have to be kept inside. Until eventually the museum's only exhibition will be *of* the museum, commemorating its collapse as it happens. If that's not a logical paradox.'

Col. White chose this moment not to mention his opposition to any and every rise in the rates, and made a sympathetic noise instead.

Miss Stevens was the town's only practising intellectual (which was believed to be the cause of her failure to breed) and her views were always received with reverence, if not silence. Her current exhibition on the history of pewter had been very highly thought of by pewter experts, though it had admittedly fallen short as a crowd-puller. As indeed had her definitive look at the role of Celtic pottery in medieval warfare. She seemed pleased to have company.

'Still want a classy title,' she said. 'Exhibitions need a hook.'

Both men gazed around at her assorted masonry, which had been laid out like a miniature Pompeii. No name immediately sprang to mind.

'Something to shame the bean-counters,' Miss Stevens added, switching on a spotlight.

'Puns are always good,' said the colonel, though offering no example.

'Perhaps we'll put it to our committee,' said the dentist, adding a mild grin to show he had no such intent. And letting his words remind her that they could not dally.

'Committees!' snorted Miss Stevens.

'Not for you?'

'Not got the choice,' she said grimly. 'I'm on a committee too. Just like yours.'

'Like ours?'

'Full of dead wood. And always trying to stave off disaster. Isn't that what you do in your Naturalists' Trust?'

The dentist pondered the thought. 'Well, yes ... yes, I suppose we do.'

All three stood a moment among the indoor ruins. The conversation had run its course.

Col. White fingered the knot of his regimental tie – a standard reflex when women were at close quarters – and then he headed off for the first floor, with Mr Hampton a couple of paces to the rear.

They made their way up the marble staircase, which curved with imperial grandeur toward the mezzanine. Here the colonel was struck by a new thought, and he turned, and looked back at the entrance hall below. The acoustics carried his words effortlessly down to Miss Stevens.

'Pediments from Heaven!'

The Abernant Naturalists' Trust, or ANT (an acronym that gave a quiet pleasure to the trustees for the way it brought public attention to the unglamorous end of the animal kingdom; indeed, it was to the trustees' regret that no member had as yet published a monograph of this little hymenopteran from a mid-Wales perspective), was noted for elderly pedants. An hour could be happily spent on deciding the date of a meeting ... or the place of the meeting ... or the agenda of the meeting ... or whether there was need for a meeting at all. And, indeed, whether the decision should be deferred. Administratively, the natural world was a minefield.

The dozen or so members always met, with little noticeable sense of irony, in the Neolithic Era. This was, according to the information panels, a period famed for the first farmers and for arthritis – a complaint which, judging by the committee's struggle with the plastic stacking-chairs, had seen few medical advances in five thousand years. Gwyn's charm as chairman secured this gallery almost free of charge and, though an impressive setting for meetings, its sight-lines were easily compromised by the standing-stones. The moth recorder and the geology secretary were making the last of several realignments to the three folding tables when the colonel and the dentist entered.

'Evening, everybody,' said the colonel. 'Evening, Mr Chairman,' he added, with the eye for rank that had marked his rise.

'Evening,' said the dentist.

A chorus of polite responses greeted their arrival. The dentist was pleased to see that the two remaining places were not adjacent. He squeezed past the bat expert (wittily known as Batman) and sat down opposite a giant mural depicting the dawn of farming by hairy trolls.

'I have two apologies for absence,' said Chairman Gwyn, in a tone intended to be brisk. 'Mr Forrest and Mr Dadie.' Mr Forrest was the Trust's solicitor, a post he had accepted in a moment of inebriated weakness, and who rarely attended as he could not see the point of wildlife. Mr Dadie was the council's representative, and used these occasions to visit his mistress.

Unfortunately, there was no apology for absence from Lady Hartbury. She had turned up as always.

Her role was to represent the landed gentry, and put a stop to anything that might interfere with her lifestyle. She was very much against the protection of any species, flesh, fish, or fowl, because it was always possible that she or her husband might be in the mood to kill it. Anything environmental with letters, like SSSI, she was opposed to; anything governmental that spent public money she was against. Like most of the Country Landowners' Association, she was a believer in small government, with a paramilitary wing to deal with ramblers and picnickers.

Almost alone around the table she had no specialism, no esoteric sub-species awaiting her monograph, no lonely plant she wished to save from extinction. She was herself a rare species, with a 1930s Home Counties accent, but any motion to make her the prey of a hunt would have passed *nem. con.*

'If Professor Appleby could read the minutes of the last meeting?' proposed the chairman.

Professor Appleby could, and would. As Secretary to the Trust, he always found this a rewarding part of his functions. Like many of the other retirees, he had once been a man of some authority. Unfortunately that had been in metallurgy, which offered him few opportunities to shine in social settings. But now, belatedly recognised for his wide, if amateur, knowledge of newts, and blessed with the childhood gift of tidy handwriting, he had risen, almost unchallenged, to be the Trust's amanuensis.

'*Item One,*' he said, with a preparatory cough, and looked along the folding tables at his audience.

Sticklebacks, dandelions, micro-moths, pine martens, bee orchids, wood sorrel, each had sent a spokesman. An unlikely lot, they included a chemist, a divorce lawyer, an electronics engineer, and a quantity surveyor, all now with time to spare for private passions and many fuelled by the missionary zeal of the incomer. The calendar of events bulged with offers of recondite slide-shows and talks.

'*Item One*,' he repeated, to hush any naturalist chat. '*Fundraising.*'

Item One was always fundraising. Nature was always on its uppers. The need for rattling tins never ended. Sponsored walks, sponsored swims, occasionally a sponsored parachute jump; standing with a tame owl in the high street, dressing up as a panda at the summer show; and, of course, trying to crack the form-filling code that worked the grant-aid black magic. These variations on the theme of beggary formed the leitmotif of Item One.

'*Fundraising*,' he said again, milking the moment. '*It was agreed by the management committee that the annual wine-and-cheese party will be held, by kind courtesy of our patron, the Lord Lieutenant, on Sunday, 20 September at Pencroesllan Manor.*'

Each member brought different life-skills to the Trust. Gwyn Hopkins, JP, brought wisdom, calm, and an extensive understanding of the bird world. Doug Dykes brought a twitchy nervousness and an unrivalled experience of otter spraints. Miss Lyn Chambers brought an unfortunate sniff and over five hundred drawings of ferns. Edward Vellacott could talk for twenty-four hours without cease if asked about fungi. Whereas Mr Hampton's contribution was his life as a private dentist, because constant contact with money made him *numero uno* for the post of treasurer. And Col. White, he ran the work parties. Digging ponds, building holts, killing weeds, giving orders.

'Only one "l",' said the tetchy voice of the retired head of Greek, whose strength was procedural. And who thought he should be Secretary.

'Sorry?' said Prof. Appleby, but in a taut tone which suggested 'Sod Off!' was his preferred response. (There was history between the two men, much of it grammar.)

'Only one "l". In *Pencroesllan*.' He pointed to his copy of the minutes.

'Oh. Thank you.' Refusing the offer of a pencil, Prof. Appleby moved on. '*Any lady members wishing to help with the preparation of the buffet would be most welcome. There will also be a bring-and-buy plant sale, and an exhibition of three fossils recently discovered by the Geology Group. The finale of the afternoon is to be an auction of items kindly donated by local celebrities, who will be available to sign autographs. The auction to be conducted by Mr Probert, the well-known auctioneer.*'

'On a point of order, Mr Chairman.'

The chairman suppressed his first sigh of the evening.

Three hands had been put up during the course of this seemingly inoffensive paragraph. Points of order were rarely true points of order, being triggered by anything from daftness to deafness, but the favoured tone for these evenings was parliamentary punctiliousness, a self-importance masquerading as nostalgia for a long-gone age of manners.

'What about the croquet?'

'The croquet?'

'What happened to the croquet?'

'Molehills. Long line of molehills.'

'No! When?'

'Late one night.'

'But can't we do something?'

'Not if we're naturalists.'

'Oh.'

'And besides, the mole-men are dead.'

The second hand waved.

'These local celebrities ...'

'What about them?'

'Who are they?'

There was silence, while all looked to young Mr Perkins the herpetologist (and trainee estate agent). He claimed to move in circles where celebrities were to be found, and had promised to provide some. His primary skill was pond-dipping, so his words had been taken on trust, his tendency to fantasy ignored. He went a little pink.

'Still firming up,' he muttered. 'But I will just say the words "orienteering" and "steam traction engines".'

There was a pause while the full showbiz impact of these words sank in around the table.

The third hand waved, a little querulously as it belonged to an eighty-year-old.

'This buffet,' said the expert on upland butterflies, 'will it include sandwiches?'

'I expect so,' said Prof. Appleby.

'What sort?'

'Oh. Well, er ...'

'Only I like egg and cress. Nothing too chewy.'

'I'm sure the choice of fillings will –'

Chairman Gwyn raised his own hand. 'I think that the fillings would perhaps better be the subject of a sandwich subcommittee ...? The governing body's role is to focus only on the broad brushstrokes of buffet policy.' He gave an encouraging nod to Prof. Appleby.

'*Item Two,*' said the professor. '*Recent deaths.*'

Behind him stood one of the menhirs, its ancient stone framing his bald head like a rough-and-ready throne. A runic comment was inscribed above him, and the hand-carved letters helped add a touch of medieval mystery to his presence.

'*It was with regret that the Trust learnt of the death of Edward Morgan, killed in a tragic accident with his bees. A pioneer in the study of the biogeography of bees, many members will remember his invigorating evening lectures.*'

'Detached participle!' exclaimed the one-time head of Greek, unable to hide a hint of triumph.

The retired metallurgist glared furiously at him.

'It's customary to go through the Chair,' he retorted.

Chairman Gwyn suppressed his second sigh of the evening.

'And finally, peregrines.'

The janitor had already been in twice. Next time he would flick the lights on and off and it could get ugly.

Gwyn never found it easy to draw up each quarter's agenda. Like the Vatican of the Middle Ages, Nature seethed with doctrinal sects, each jockeying for position as they tried to get their own angel species on to a pinhead, preferably with grant-aid. When he had been young, and a one-man band, Gwyn's only baggage had been binoculars. Now his hinterland was bureaucracy.

Gradually, the pleasures of observation had given way to the duties of conservation. And with that had come the leaden language of priorities. Trusts had to nurture nature, and had to acquire nature reserves, and had to spread them across county and country like little landlocked arks. Like Bantustans for the privileged. In his darker moments, Gwyn felt he had become a company man, compiling a portfolio of nature stocks, and seldom lying in the sun to the sound of a skylark.

When the damned archbishop had died, and left them a slice of virgin glebe-land, pastures rich in rarity, it had proved a poisoned chalice. Arcadian water meadows, mulched timelessly by Welsh Blacks, fluttered over by the small pearl-bordered fritillary, flown over by the sedge warbler, adorned by the golden-ringed dragonfly: this was a recipe for civil war. In one corner, the marsh lobby, keen to halt all drainage and inspire pond-life; in another corner, the wildflower lobby, keen to make more drainage and encourage wood bitter-vetch; in a third corner, the butterfly lobby, eager to claw back the rampant beech hedges and let in more light; in a fourth corner, the bird lobby, eager to go easy on the beech trees and bring on more branches; and then there were other corners, almost more corners than geometry allows for, arguing for unsung Sphagnum and unseen Insecta.

Like competing generals, the muddy advocates gathered in wellingtons and rain, each to champion their cause with statistics and surveys and quotes from quadrats. Although gentlemen warriors, they were not above a quiet dissing of other, not *quite* so worthy, species, letting it be known that their evolutionary role had, shall we say, been less than glorious. (A letdown of their Latin, so the hint went.) And the arguing continued in the dryness of subcommittees, with much talk of habitat use and abuse, of native breeds, of declining numbers, of gene structure comparisons, of responsibility for generations yet to come … How nature had survived before man arrived was a question that often hung in the air.

Such distractions were why Chairman Gwyn was glad to bring the evening's agenda around to birds, and finally focus the committee's mind on the subject closest to his heart.

'Perhaps we could leave peregrines for another day?' said Lady Hartbury, whose own mind had been on a late liqueur for nearly an hour.

'People have been saying that about peregrines for a long time,' he replied with an unyielding smile. 'Which is why there are now so few.'

Prof. Appleby briefly wondered whether to enter this exchange in the minutes, but then thought better of it. The landed gentry were a dark and mysterious force.

'And I have recently learnt some important news,' continued the chairman. 'Which must be kept secret.'

He had the attention of all three folding tables. The primal urge to make points of order was stilled, the meeting suddenly spellbound.

'A rare pair are breeding – and we need volunteers to mount a watch.'

Chapter 7

Nico reluctantly allowed the large black Labrador to sniff his crotch. The dog was unexpectedly thorough, but fortunately showed few signs of excitement. Nico himself focused on staying ramrod still, much disconcerted by the notice warning him not to be friendly with the dog. (Was it a bitch, he found himself wondering?) Had so much not been at stake, the antiques dealer – usually a man of truculent pride – would have forgone the public humiliation. Instead, he next approached the dog's owner, and compliantly opened his mouth for probing. Then, pronounced drug-free, he advanced into the holding area and waited for the last locks to be unsprung by the warders.

Even now, his mind was on money. Force of habit had caused him to accidentally bring £1,500 in cash, neatly rolled, for any impulse buy. Not easy to explain away, this had – with every other item in his pockets – been taken from him and put in a locker. For security reasons, this was a transparent plastic locker. And now his stash of £20 notes was on display to all those visiting the criminal elite of South Wales, a fact that caused Nico some professional disquiet.

He tried to stand a little apart from the gaggles of kith and kin, whose chat and chewing gum he found uncongenial. Normally, Nico's persona of choice was the unclubbable heavy, a man of mystery, danger, and bad taste in clothes, who liked to lurk on the periphery of groups. But here, faced with low life en masse, he opted for a more middle-class disdain, and tried to invest his distance with moral superiority, as if hoping to convey there was no blood-line between him and the villain he was about to visit.

The women – and the visitors were mostly women, mostly young, mostly fake blonde – were first out the door of the featureless anteroom, fully familiar with HMP routine. They clogged up the corridor beyond, outwardly as cocky as ladettes off clubbing. But their appearance was unusual for ten in the morning, as even Nico had noticed. It was not the tattoos, of which there was excess. It was not the clickety-clackety heels, which undercut any claim to be cool. It was not the mounds of make-up, which hid all signs of strain. It was the décolletage.

In this least sexy of settings, there was more yardage of tit than is found at most operas.

At first Nico did not realise why. But then, when he too entered the cavernous space that the Victorians had laid on for the inmates' brief acts of reunion, he saw the choreography. Across the vast room, made vaster by the raucous clamour, were rows of metal tables. And seated on opposite sides, divided by sterile space as effectively as a sword down a marriage-bed, were lonesome, onanistic bovver-boys and their besotted birds, teenage arms stretched out so fingers could fondle. They had no hope of anything carnal, no chance of any congress, and therefore each Bonnie had brought to her Clyde an unwrapped present: a jailbird's-eye view of bulging bosom. Enough to see him through another week of separation.

Nico's heart, on the other hand, was not beating any faster at the thought of seeing Gareth.

The sheep farmer's natural demeanour was gloom – and a failed marriage, cuckoldry, and public ridicule had not helped lighten it. Discovering his wife *in flagrante* with the bank manager had been a bit of a body blow, but finding a priapic statue apparently erected in the man's honour had been a ball-breaker. Closing his bank account with a shotgun was indicative of his negative attitude, and this had then led on to assaulting the said statue with stolen ironmongery, a crime that had shocked the mid-Wales art world. In court, he had scarcely spoken, and his probation report had said his social skills were best suited to solitude, give or take a sheep.

Nico was not even sure that Gareth would want to see him. Gareth had not responded to his letter, crudely presented as concern, and no one seemed to know how he was now coping as a con. Secretly, Nico hoped to find him in a state of deep despair, and vulnerable to pressure.

Looking for a forty-something farmer in among all the head-bangers and body-builders, Nico did not at first notice him. Always runt-size, he seemed to have shrunk; rarely without a drab, dungy Barbour, he looked at a loss in prison cloth; usually silent, he stood dazed by the din.

'How are you doing?' cried Nico, hitting the false cheery note of two men who had just met on a golf course.

Gareth shrugged.

Hugging seemed wrong. Nico reached over and gave him a rigorous handshake, the same reassuring grasp that he used to seal the deals that dealt disaster. Then the two sat – as required by the signs – on opposite sides of the table, to ensure that no illegal substances missed by Fido could pass between them.

'Everyone sends their best!'

Gareth had no idea what he meant. Even his parents had been little more than lukewarm, sending only a postcard of a castle.

'Your friends are all thinking of you.'

And still he did not speak.

Nico, himself not a man known for light comedy, saw that bonding might not be easy. He wanted to move his chair closer to the table but both were bolted to the floor. He favoured soft speech, but this was a room where high decibels were the only currency. He tried to think what tack to try next. It would have been simpler, he reckoned, to visit an unknown inmate and plan a heist.

'How is Jessie?' asked Gareth.

Jessie …? Not a question that he had expected. But the new caring Nico hid his surprise. 'I talked to her yesterday for you. She's doing well. She sends her love. Promises to write.'

'Jessie's my dog.' This in the flattest of tones. He seemed too beaten down to take offence; perhaps he only expected lies. 'I got her from Hefin when he hanged himself.'

'Right!' Somehow that came out too emphatic. Almost enthusiastic.

'She sleeps in the house.'

'Uh-huh.'

'But don't get me wrong, she's a working dog.'

'Of course ... Is she working now?' Nico saw an opening for mind-games, but it felt too soon. His compassion had not yet had a proper outing.

'Don't know.'

Long pause.

'Coffee?' asked Nico, nodding at a nearby machine.

'Grey and white,' said Gareth. 'A crossbreed.'

'Good choice,' said Nico.

'I know dogs,' said Gareth.

'I'm sure you do,' said Nico.

'They're not like women.'

Nico said nothing.

'You get loyalty with a dog.'

Nico again said nothing.

And Gareth, it soon became clear, also had no more to add. He had made available the sum total of his hard-won knowledge of women.

Nico got up to get two coffees. He was alone at the vending machine. Only his table had run short on conversation. The coffee was far from hot, but complaints did not seem wise. He walked back slowly, thoughtfully, trying to keep his eyes off cleavage lest he be butchered in a love triangle. He needed to open up new areas of dialogue with Gareth.

'Did you know you'd made the papers? And the radio!'

The shrug was back.

'Yes, the most famous hill-sheep farmer in Wales since ...' Nico struggled with precedents. There had not been many famous hill-sheep farmers in Wales. 'You could sell your story!'

'Sod 'em!'

Gareth was not a natural folk hero.

Nico wondered if he knew about the T-shirts. (*Gareth gouges off your gonads* in dribbled red on a white background. Nico had run off two thousand five hundred in three sizes, but had only netted £18 before they fell foul of *sub judice* rules.) He had also briefly entertained thoughts of being Gareth's agent – a line of work he knew – but for a client to have the garrulity of Garbo and the face of a ferret was not a winning combination.

Another long silence fell. As Nico gazed around them, wishing he was visiting a more charismatic criminal, a thought struck him.

'If you're asked what you're in for, what d'you say?'

Gareth looked up from the table for the first time.

'Crime of passion.' A quarter-smile. 'Some people think I'm a killer.' No smile. 'I wish I was.'

He looked back down at the table again, like a man searching for signs of polish.

Nico sensed a line of enquiry to be pursued.

'So, your cell, who d'you share it with?'

Gareth did not bother to reply.

'But it's OK, is it, your cell?'

Gareth shrugged.

'I mean, is there anything you need?'

'Why've you come? I've got no antiques.'

Nico reassessed his strategy.

After several minutes reassessing, he began to wonder whether there might be a way to use truth to his advantage.

'Your farm. Have you asked yourself what's going to happen to your farm?'

'Like what?'

'Well, you're away, right? For the best part of six months. What's happening to your animals?'

Gareth paused before replying, the answer apparently painful. 'Parents are selling them. Going to auction.'

'Too old to look after them now, are they?' The question came with a barb, for Gareth's parents had farmed on until their eighties, a vote of no confidence in only son and heir. As all the valley knew.

'I'll restock. When I get out.'

'Really? What about the land? What state will the land be in then?'

'Could grass-let it, for now.'

'Not easy to start again. From scratch. For a middle-aged man. With a drink problem.' He had several further salient points to itemise but Gareth had regained interest in speech.

'Fuck off.'

'I could buy your land.'

'It's not for sale.'

'You could retire. To somewhere with palm trees and dancing girls.'

'It's not for sale.'

'With pina coladas and no bank managers.'

'It's NOT for sale!'

'Well, I can see that you're still undecided. So why don't you sleep on it, for month after month, and let me know when you change your mind ...?'

'I won't.'

'Try counting noughts jumping over a stile. Always helps.'

And on that note, Nico stood up. This time, his offer of a hand was rejected.

He moved toward the aisle that led to the exit and the personally intrusive Labrador.

'Oh, one other thing,' he said, turning back.

'What?'

'Those genitalia that you chiselled off ... where are they now?'

'No idea. Not seen them since I crashed, going home. Why?'

'Oh, nothing. No reason.'

And with a smile, the wheeler-dealer was gone.

Chapter 8

Stéfan raised the champagne bottle to his lips and swigged the last of the Krug. Then he moved to where Eryl was bent over the snooker table and gargled in his ear. Stéfan always liked to do something witty when his opponent was potting a black.

Eryl wearily stood up again.

'What, lost your concentration?' scoffed Stéfan.

Eryl shook his cue at him, as macho men do, but he somehow did it without conviction. The Friday after-work match had its rituals to observe, and accommodating his employer's braying wit was one of them.

'Ever played with a cue up your arse?' Eryl asked him.

'Ooh, lovely!' squealed Stéfan. 'Extra chalk, please!' And he tossed the cueing chalk at Eryl's chest.

Eryl tossed it back, and made a show of being angry, but again it was the phoney testosterone of a gamma male trumped by an alpha, as seen in nature films. He thought of farting in retaliation, as he had done once before, but Stéfan's urge to triumph in all human endeavours had led him to a grossness which Eryl did not wish to see repeated.

'You're only fit for fucking Morris dancing!' he retorted instead, an obscure line of abuse which left Stéfan uncertain how he had been offended.

Eryl assumed his stance again.

Despite the company, there was a pleasure to playing snooker in the games room. The walls were House-of-Usher red, the mirrors were boudoir tarty, and the table was full-size. Stéfan's homing instinct for bad taste went quite unnoticed by Eryl, though he had questioned whether a jukebox should go in the Louis Quinze dining room.

'Think you can finish before your bedtime?' boomed Stéfan, and whinnied at his wit.

Eryl ignored him, as best he could. He squinted down his cue, checked the line of the shot. It was an important black, one which would decide the game. He was much the better player, with years in bars as back-up, and he liked to make sure nothing untoward could happen.

The shot was inch-perfect, and missed the pocket by a fraction. As intended.

It was over a year since Stéfan had abandoned his Grade 1 house in a huff, driven out by a sea of drips and the absence of artisans. When he returned, driven back by the urgings of his ego, Crug Caradoc was occupied by squatters. Eryl and the bride he had accidentally married in Romania had moved in.

It was, nonetheless, almost a week before Stéfan discovered he had squatters. In a mansion with three storeys and twenty-eight rooms, it was some time before their paths crossed. Had Irina not been so excited by indoor plumbing, she would not have tried out all the bathrooms and Stéfan would not have come across her peachy buttocks bending over the basin in a distant ensuite. (It was the rogue gurgles she had caused in the antique pipes that brought her ablutions to his attention.) Their meeting – her naked, him clothed – was given added drama by Irina's belief that Stéfan was the squatter. A not unreasonable belief, given her husband had always implied – by sign language, since the couple had as yet no common tongue – that this grand and empty house was his.

With Eryl flushed out by her cries, Stéfan soon realised he had squatters à deux. His first instinct was to use the techniques he found so successful with fish. As a man whose genes came from the land that spawned Stalin, he saw no need to mess with legal niceties. Nor was he one to be swayed by Eryl's teary tales of torn-up wills, of a crossed-out heir, of dynastic dysfunction. But his hard line began to bend when he heard the word handyman. Leaks and cracks and rot and damp might just, he felt, have found a saviour. Yet the sits vac of Crug Caradoc called for more than just the one miracle. And as Stéfan pondered his domestic plight, he hit upon a two-pronged solution: he would employ the pair, and give them lodgings. The sweetness of the deal was Irina, because in her he could see a housekeeper, a decision much influenced by the memory of her buttocks. (Stéfan had still to fully research *le droit du seigneur*, but what he so far knew meant wenches, as and when you wanted.) So figures were bandied back and forth, and terms were struck. And Stéfan the squire at last had staff.

Today, the complement of two was down to one. Eryl had swiftly been abandoned by his bride. The revelation that her playboy husband – black bike-leathers were a symbol of Western glamour in rural Romania – was in truth a two-faced pauper had caused Irina to modify her love. She had gone to live in London.

And left Stéfan to share his Jacobean pile with Eryl only.

The two warring men watched the black ball come to a halt on the lip of the pocket.

'Oh what a pity!' cried Stéfan.

Eryl turned away, and went over to the cocktail bar. He helped himself to another bottle of bubbly. There were many unwritten rules to working for Stéfan. Prime among them was to lose at snooker every Friday.

'I guess,' added Stéfan, 'some of us just can't take the pressure.' And he laughed.

His years at an English private school had fused in unconventional ways with the frontier spirit of the Caucasus. Anarchy and despotism jostled to shape his great ego. At the end of every week, Stéfan insisted on a military inspection of the gardening tools in the outhouse, requiring them to be hung and buffed in neat, unmuddy rows. Yet he would also hurl water-filled balloons from the roof, a jape which had rarely amused Dafydd the postman. Stéfan regarded himself as life and soul of the party, but he made sure the guests all knew it was *his* party.

Still laughing, Stéfan moved towards balk and chalked his cue.

No skill was required. He sank the final black and punched the air.

'So, that's one more fiver you owe me!' Betting on the game was another rule. 'Hardly worth paying your wages!' He gave a roller-coasting guffaw.

Eryl reached into his jeans, and pulled out a crumpled note. He tossed it on to the baize. Stéfan let it lie there and opened a box of cigars, which he claimed to be Cuban. After choosing one, he offered them to Eryl.

'Go on, take several.'

Eryl obliged, complicit in the patronage.

Stéfan brought out his lighter, the one he used for dynamite fuses, and clicked it into action. He picked up Eryl's £5 note and, holding the paper between two podgy fingers, he set fire to its far corner. Then, with a boyish glee, Stéfan used the burning fiver to light both their cigars.

Chapter 9

'Have you got the blow-up doll?' demanded Sgt. Griffiths.

'You've asked me that twice already,' responded his wife.

'Well, what's the answer, woman?'

'I told you, yes.'

He grunted, the grunt of a man hoping to find another fault. In his home life, nothing became him so much as grumpiness.

'Well, are you ready, then?' he asked.

Thirty-plus years of marriage had, apparently, taught him little. Barbara was always ready. If Barbara had a vocation, it was readiness. A dutiful, long-suffering readiness.

She sighed in response, as if reluctant to state the obvious. 'I've got my uniform on, haven't I?'

Finding himself, as so often, the flatter-footed in quarrels, Griff chose not to press the point. Instead, he just stared at his wife, once long ago a slender bride, but now, like him, a victim of home cooking, and stretching her XL uniform to button-bursting tightness.

'How long have we got?' he asked.

'About fifteen minutes.'

He looked at his watch, as though distrusting even her capacity to tell the time.

'The booking's for six o'clock.' Barbara's tone added distinct asperity to this information.

'How many are coming?'

'Ten maybe, mostly farmers. Be wanting the usual.'

'Right.' Griff fell briefly silent.

The pair were stood at the bottom of the stairs, a holdall at their feet.

'So,' said Barbara, 'we'd better get started.'

*   *   *

The village hall was modern and brick and dull. Its predecessor had been an attractive wooden building, with character and a century of memories, but the valley had felt obliged to celebrate the Queen's Silver Jubilee.

To qualify for funding, the new hall was required to cater for all known niche activities. So, in apparent expectation of the Olympics being staged locally, the laminate floor was latticed with blue tape and green tape and yellow tape and red tape, to accommodate football and basketball and volleyball and badminton and, some said, water polo. Mostly, though, the place was used by the WI, who did not move about much. In the summer there was a local eisteddfod, but grant-aid had not extended to acoustics and any massed voices produced little more than white noise with a lilt. And in the winter a further funding shortfall meant coats and gloves were de rigueur. Even the knitting circle had lost heart.

It was hoped to knock the building down when the Golden Jubilee came round.

The noticeboard was usually the biggest draw. Here, in the porch, was posted the formal life and times of the valley. Here one could learn of tarmac to be laid, with its threat of three-car traffic jams, and the dates of low-flying bombers, with their power to abort ewes. Here one could read the agenda of the parish council, and learn of all the hopeful plans to put neo-Georgian bungalows in spare fields. Here one could also learn, if one wanted, when the peripatetic Vicar might next pass by with surplus blessings.

Today it was notice of a sale that had caught the eye. Several farmers, gathering in the gravelly dust of the car park, had been drawn to the red block capitals that signified an auction. Squinting in the early evening sun, they were reading the details.

'Quite a few cattle,' said Ben Pritchard.

'Quite a few sheep,' said Bryn Pritchard, his older brother.

'Won't be in good condition, though,' said Brian Pritchard, *his* older brother.

'No, they'll have been neglected of late,' said Brenig Pritchard, _his_ older brother.

The Pritchards were a close family. The four bachelor brothers, too unworldly to woo, and with a widowed mother still holding sway, had never left home and thought of little but farming and drinking, and their dream of getting more land.

'Inevitable with Gareth gone,' added Ben.

'No one to look after them,' added Bryn.

'Bound to go for a low price,' added Brian.

'Bargain!' added Brenig.

And the four brothers laughed as one. Theirs was a family made more tight-knit by all being tall. Baby Ben was five ten, and inch by inch the others each rose, right up to Brenig at six foot four, gangling giants who still went, in single file, behind their mum to chapel.

They were shifting their attention to an ADAS warning about organophosphates when the St John's Ambulance juddered into the car park, just as the village-hall clock reached six.

'Gored in the groin.'

'Bitten by a snake.'

'Struck by lightning.'

'Ripped open by barbed wire.'

'Trapped in a burning haystack.'

'Swept under water in a flood.'

'Crushed by an overturned tractor.'

'Poisoned by ham sandwiches gone off in the sun.'

Superintendent Griffiths (a rise in rank that made first aid so rewarding) now rather regretted asking his audience for details of the farming accidents that they most feared. His small collection of triangular bandages seemed inadequate to the task.

Also laid upon the trestle table by his assistant – as always, he had introduced his wife in terms that suggested a circus act – were a set of splints, with wood and metal joints to be slid together; finger dressings, nos. 8, 9, & 16; crêpe bandages; strips of plaster; scissors; tweezers; water bottle; collapsible metal cup; and notebook and pencil. Pink Annie had yet to be blown up.

The corpulent couple stood side by side at the table, official role-models for the saving of life. Disconcertingly, of all those in the hall, the Griffiths looked the most likely candidates for sudden death. Both their bodies bulged like pods about to burst. His Edwardian whiskers only partly hid florid, sweaty cheeks, and nothing disguised his wheezing; her tumbledown white hair fell across a fleshy face and neck, and although Barbara smiled a lot, she tried to avoid any unnecessary movement. The image that came compellingly to mind was Tweedledum and Tweedledee, grown grosser.

'Triangular bandage, Barbara,' commanded her husband. To the audience he joked, 'Useful for all those who want to tie up their wives!'

The all-male valley audience gave a hearty snigger.

Wife Barbara, smile fixed, handed him the chosen dressing. Husband Griff held it aloft and expatiated on the folding options. And then enumerated the usages. And particularised the alternatives. He liked public speaking.

'We will now imagine that my good wife has fallen downstairs – drunk again! – and has broken her arm. Assume the position, Barbara.'

Silently, Barbara assumed the position: sideways-on to her husband, her (broken) arm folded across her never-ending chest. Less silently, Griff demonstrated how to slide the folded bandage under his wife's arm and over her shoulder. Ideally, he would have liked a dais. (This was not a recognised accessory for first aid, but he had always seen himself suited to a dais.) Instead, Griff grasped his wife's shoulders and rotated her for the audience. His handiwork with knots was best appreciated in the round and he was also able to point out the finer features of his soft padding. As she came full circle, those watching were then instructed on the angle of her arm and the need for her fingernails to protrude. And her bones were named in Latin.

'Now,' said Griff to his group, 'you each need to find yourself a Barbara!' He laughed. 'I'm open to offers for mine.'

Haltingly, the villagers paired off, conscious that straight men only touched when in a scrum. Although long-time neighbours and friends, the locals stood and faced each other without any eye contact, for, however medical the motive, they felt it unbecoming to play at doctors and nurses. And being horny-handed and all thumbs was hardly a help. Unused to the demands of fabric, they struggled to keep the crêpe from slipping; unfamiliar with the techniques of caring, they let their bandages unravel and fall to the floor; unaware of hygiene, they left mud on the patient. There was not a Nightingale among them.

Advice, though, was never lacking. At every moment, Griff was on hand, hands on, puffed up by the mantle of mentor. He commented constantly, his guidance ubiquitous. Because being of help to others was, he always said, what meant the most to him.

Barbara knew better. Were her husband ever forced to confess what gave him greatest pleasure from his work as a humanitarian, the answer would have to be the uniform. Supt. Griffiths believed his personality was best expressed with the aid of a uniform, any uniform. If he could have found any, he would have bought pyjamas with epaulettes. It was to his great regret that the military overtones to St John's Ambulance had recently been muted. The white stripe had gone from the trouser leg, the leather belt had vanished, the metal badges had surrendered to cloth. Pomp had given way to practicality. Strutting had become less viable, authority weaker.

'Ken Hammond fell in his baler,' said Ben. 'The whole arm came off. What knot would you use for that?'

'Oh, that'd be Book 2, I expect,' added Bryn, before Griff could find a riposte.

'Yeah, "How to Assemble the Body from Scratch",' added Brian.

'Personally,' added Brenig, 'I always carry a staple-gun. Just to be on the safe side.'

The group creased up with laughter. Griff joined in warily, uncertain whether it was at his expense.

But, like many a good joke, it was not without its truth. Hill-farmers were often far from home, with no help near to hand. The first responder was oneself. And the know-how to staunch a wound, or splint a break, was no idle extra. Dying in some corner of a distant bog was short on poetic appeal. So there were always takers for first aid at the village hall.

After broken arms, the class briefly tried their hand at wrists and fingers, whilst the better bandagers had a go at trussing up a broken jaw. ('Ideal for keeping the wife quiet! No need to wait for her to break it.') And then, an hour nearly gone, it was time to practise new tricks – on Resuscitation Annie, as she was known in the trade.

Supt. Griffiths dragged her from his holdall, limp and pink and pliant.

'Someone you killed earlier?' asked Ben.

Griff laid the blow-up doll out on the floor, upon her back, a bung in her side. Only the presence of Barbara staunched the flow of other, cruder, jokes.

The class formed a semicircle in the blue goal area, with Annie as their focus. They made an odd tableau, weather-beaten rustics and a shiny plastic blonde. These were men who normally got together only for harvest festival supper, and talked of crops and scrapie.

Now they were looking at a fantasy figure, schoolgirl size, with lips half open and eyes fully closed. The label on her side said *Scandinavian*, so she was probably not asleep but anticipating ecstasy.

As the villagers awaited Griff's next actions with interest, an awkward silence fell. In some, this came from a sixth sense that jokiness might appear immature; in others, it came from a knowledge that they had a doll of their own, but with more sophisticated orifices.

Griff tugged at Annie's limbs, which lay loose and lifeless and waiting for air. Her torso and head were solid, as were her little plimsolled feet and friendly hands. But the rest of her was crumpled and floppy, like a ventriloquist's dummy. Annie was kitted out in a fetching navy tracksuit, and clearly longed to be inflated.

Griff knelt at her side and fiddled with her bung. From the holdall he took a small rubber pump, as used on Lilos. Then he looked up, feeling the urge – as so often – for a public pronouncement.

'ABC,' he said. 'Airway, Breathing, Circulation. That's what we'll be learning.'

He attached the tube to Annie. Then started to squeeze the pump up and down with his hands. And as he squeezed, he said, in a sing-song voice:

'I'm just a first-aid dummy, and I do not like it much,
'Cos I'm pink, and made of plastic, and I'm very cold to touch.'

Barbara rolled her eyes – every day another ditty, or what her husband believed to be educational tools. Recitation at a police social event had led him into the arms of poetry, and he regularly overreached himself with odes. Odes that aimed to illustrate a truth or a fact or a moral.

His agricultural audience, men who rated high on any repression index, crowded closer, aware of the rarity of the spectacle. They watched intently as Griff's pumping grew in force and frequency, but to little effect.

And all the while, as he pounded away, he wheezed,

'They puts me in a suitcase when they've had their little play,
And they folds me up in pieces, to come out another day.'

But eventually Griff was forced to pause, to check on Annie's slow progress.

'I don't think she's well,' said Ben.

'Not a lot of life in her legs,' said Bryn.

'Her arms are still floppy,' said Brian.

'Should we call a doctor?' asked Brenig.

Griff tried to take no notice, though the urge to arrest was strong. He peered at his doll more closely, and soon saw the cause of her continued demise. His surgical scissors had at some time snagged the rubber of the pump, and all his hard-won air was gone to waste. So Annie remained deflated. The kiss-of-life lesson could not yet begin.

Griff, however, was not to be beaten. He bent still lower, reluctantly removing his peaked, white-banded cap, and applied his own lips to the body's bung. In, out, in, out, he breathed, though not with pauses as per the manual. Instead, he just puffed and puffed. And puffed again … And then began to go as pink as his doll.

The bung slipped from his mouth as he gasped for more air. Slowly, sweatily, he eased himself on to his back, alongside his shrinking Annie. And lay there loudly panting, exhausted by his medical exertions.

Barbara spoke, for the first time.

'Anybody want to give my husband the kiss of life?'

There were no volunteers.

Chapter 10

'*I caught this morning morning's minion, kingdom of daylight's dauphin, dapple-dawn-drawn Falcon*,' recited the magistrate as he lay on his stomach in the grass.

Gwyn took the dawn watch by choice. Few places were as remote as the Lynfi Valley, and he loved the purity of the silence. It was a silence that humans rarely heard. It was a silence that let birdsong soar.

From high above the valley floor, from his soft bed of peat, he could see the early light of a July morning spread like water across the land. At first timid and pallid, it would slowly grow golden, and embolden those creatures who took fright by night. And who now knew that Nature's daytime dramas were about to begin.

Gwyn raised his binoculars again. The smaller peregrine, the male, with a mere metre of outspread wing, had stepped off his cliff into space. Languidly the bird glided at idling speed, as if to disclaim any deadly intent. On the slip of a ledge, hundreds of feet above the stream, his equally lethal mate sat on her off-white eggs and waited her turn for breakfast.

Neither bird of the species indulged in flashy plumage, for neither needed to impress. They came as harbingers of sudden death. Sombre birds, their greys and blacks and whites in bars and bands were the grim dress code of avian undertakers. Set against the sky, their anchor-like outline gained instant respect, male and female. Although he perched like a hunchback, he flew like an aerial Ferrari. With eyes that could see food from almost a thousand feet, with wings that could hurl him at 180 mph, with a beak that could dice raw steak, his was the gold standard for birds of prey. And so the peregrine falcon was much sought after, as egg or adult.

This nesting pair had found a rare fastness on the moor. Far from any roads, the secret narrow valley had been scooped deep and steep and sheer. A stand of Scots pine towered on a mound beside the tumbling water, in rugged reminiscence of the Highlands. The further the stream descended, the higher the rock face rose.

Gouged dramatically out of the moorland, this terrain had long been fought over by warring bands of geologists. Substrata had been studied and detailed maps pored over. A conference had even been held, with foreigners, to decide upon its status as a site of international import. Some experts said it was a unique landscape of glaciation and moraine formation. Others said it wasn't. So the conference had broken down in disarray and given up. And left the remote and contentious land to the rule of the peregrine falcon.

Gwyn moved the walkie-talkie and adjusted his position, which damp and cramp had made uncomfortable. Two hours leaning on his elbows, lying crouched beneath a crag, took its toll on bones from the 1930s. He poured a coffee from his thermos and munched a salad sandwich as he shifted his gaze to a fuller panorama, his ears pre-tuned to pick up any rare bird calls. Even in his sleep.

It had all begun with a budgie. Aged seven, he had been given Joey – not a very original name, but budgerigars were known to struggle with polysyllabic monikers – and was expected to tame it and teach it to talk. The birdseed had been bought and the luxury of a cuttlefish acquired. Young Gwyn's response had been to open the cage door and the parlour window, and set Joey free to fly through suburbia. This was almost certainly a fatal freedom, but it was a view of birds' rights that was to last him a lifetime.

Gwyn carefully scanned the length of the Lynfi Valley. Now as a man of the law, he was seeking any untoward signs of human life: of men out and about unnaturally early, of men with bags or bearing egg-boxes, of men bent on scaling the cliff-face opposite. But today, as every other day of the vigil, this hidden haven on the moor was a world known only to its wildlife. Away on the mound (or was it a moraine?), he watched an early rabbit emerge from its burrow, and saw it cautiously, almost cutely, sniff the morning air. And then die.

Like a harpoon gun fired from the sky, the peregrine snapped its neck. In one swift and perfect movement, the grey blur of a bird had hurtled down, wings back, in a screaming stoop. Its talons as powerful as a mechanical grab, it scooped the corpse up without touching down, with scarcely a beat lost from the rhythm of its flight. And then the bird was back in the sky, away to the rock that was his plucking post, to rip off the skin before breakfast.

Gwyn marvelled at the moment, at the skill of the kill, at the drama of the death. He was glad that he had witnessed it on his own, alone with his private thoughts. The watching of birds was for him a solitary hobby, what the soppy would call communing. Yet Gwyn was also rather chuffed that he now had a good tale to tell, for the next watch had fallen due.

The colonel and the dentist were running late. The dentist had not wanted to come at all, not in the company of the colonel. Nor, if the truth be known, was he that bothered about birds, for they were found outdoors, not one of his favourite places. But the colonel believed they were best of friends, albeit from different ranks in life. And had insisted on offering a lift, in a way which civilians cannot refuse.

The first delay was caused by his inability to find any early-morning petrol, an odd oversight for a REME man whose life's work was claimed to be logistics, and keeping an army going. And now, just a few miles up the still drowsy Nant Valley, they had come across a Volvo, oddly parked upon a lethal bend.

'Oddly parked,' said the colonel, who prided himself on observation.

'Abandoned?' said the dentist.

'Suspicious,' said the colonel, who had a suspicious mind. And he stopped.

It was a bend with history. In recent memory, it had caused three broken legs, two written-off cars, one prosecution, a dead horse, and a complaint by a councillor. But to qualify for straightening, it needed a death, and unfortunately no locals had as yet been killed. A chevron board had been put up in the interim.

'It's not near anywhere,' said the colonel.

'And no sign of sex going on,' said the dentist.

'It's not even near a gate,' said the colonel, who had not discussed sex since 1958.

The pair sat in his lower-end-of-the-range Rover while he did a bit of musing. They had stumbled on the makings of a mystery. Life in the valley followed predictable patterns, and a car in the wrong place was rightly seen as a shock to the social system. A bomb could not be ruled out, he reckoned.

'I'm going in,' said the colonel.

'In where?' asked the dentist.

Miffed at the question, the colonel did not respond. He got out of the car cautiously, followed very quickly by the dentist, who felt a bend was a dangerous place to be parked. Together – give or take a pace or two – they went up to the Volvo Estate, and found it not as empty as it had looked. In the back were three vintage commodes, a wooden hay-rake, and a transgendered garden gnome.

The colonel stared up and down the winding B-road, but no one was in sight, nor making a sound. For a moment, and not for the first time, it seemed his Army training was useless.

The dentist meanwhile had wandered over to the warning chevrons, which guarded against a steep drop down to a ditch.

After a couple of seconds, he waved at the colonel to join him, and put a finger to his lips. Then he pointed out a scruffy figure below them, rummaging in the long grass.

The man had his back toward them and was clearly in a strop. Occasionally, he would lash out at the undergrowth and mutter. But, as they watched, he suddenly fell to his knees, and when he rose, he was clutching something.

He turned back to the road before they could depart, and caught them both watching. He did not smile. His face was vaguely familiar to the dentist, like a man one saw round town

– but not the sort with private teeth. He scrambled up the bank, avoiding some broken indicator glass, and heaved himself over the chevrons.

'Morning,' he cried, unabashed.

'Morning,' they replied, with shifty courtesy.

'Bollocks,' he said vigorously, opening his right hand by way of answer to their discomfited gaze.

'Pardon?' said the colonel.

'Bollocks,' he repeated, 'with a knob on.'

And held up a set of larger-than-life-size stone genitalia.

The two men stared at this, uncertain exactly what, in the circumstances, to say.

It was the dentist, the more worldly-wise, who spoke first. 'And what are you going to do with it?'

'Make casts,' replied Nico. 'A special souvenir edition, I thought.'

And he walked back to his Volvo Estate and drove off.

Col. White and Mr Hampton returned to their Rover and, without mentioning what had occurred, drove on up the Nant Valley, and aimed for the hills.

Up the field past the semi-derelict long-house, up the path along the ridge, up the track across the moor, Gwyn monitored (8 × 40; Field 8.2) the progress of the two men in shiny anoraks until he identified their gait. The colonel did a poor man's yomp, all angular and showy, while the dentist rolled from side to side, like a man tacking in a squall. For operational reasons, the colonel walked in front.

The ground was soggy, the air muggy, and the ETA well adrift by the time they arrived.

'Puffed?' asked the magistrate.

'Not at all!' replied the colonel.

'God, yes!' replied the dentist, and flopped full-length to the grass – leaving the colonel to stand looking manly, sweaty, and envious of wimps.

By now the birds had had their raw rabbit, all except for some intestine, and there was a pause in aerobatics to allow for digestion between courses.

'Hope you've not brought meat sandwiches to eat,' said Gwyn. 'Or you could be kebabbed.' And vividly he illustrated how.

It was the first time the others had been on watch, the first time they had seen a peregrine. They took turns to look through his scope, which Gwyn had placed upon a tripod, and examine close up the cause of their cloak-and-dagger ops.

'Fastest-moving feathers in the world,' said Gwyn.

'Don't like the eyes,' said the dentist. 'Wouldn't make a good pet.'

'Unless you're a sheikh,' said Gwyn.

'I've met a sheikh,' said the colonel. 'When I was in the Army. Only pet he had was a tart.'

'Is that who'd steal the bird, rich Arabs?'

'Well, not personally,' said Gwyn. 'Oil sheikhs tend not to shin up cliffs. But they know people who will.'

'Large, violent people?' enquired the dentist.

'That's why you've got the walkie-talkie. Puts you through to Sergeant Griffiths. He'll sit on them.'

The colonel raised an eyebrow or two of doubt.

'Well, he'll send some RSPCA heavies to sit on them. Metaphorically speaking. Might even get a helicopter if you're lucky.' Sixty-two committees meant a lot of unlikely favours could be called in.

'Pity we're not armed,' said the colonel. Speaking as a man who once had command of some heavy-duty paper.

The upper parts of the cliff were coming within range of the sun. The female falcon stood up and stretched her wings, her compact kilo of killing power making all her moves look unmotherly. She shuffled delicately around her prized eggs, and then eased back down upon her unsafe scrape, a fatal omelette always seeming possible.

'Of course, it may not be sheikhs,' said Gwyn. 'It may be pigeon-fanciers.'

'*Pigeon-fanciers?*'

'Oh yes. Pigeon's a gourmet meal for a peregrine. And a lot of folk down the valleys bet their wages on their racing birds. Don't take kindly to them not doing a return journey.'

'Thought they'd be bird-lovers.'

'Oh no. They get up to all sorts. Even send out kamikaze pigeons.'

The colonel laughed, and then realised this wasn't a joke. 'So … how does that work exactly?'

'Superglue.'

'… sorry, Gwyn, you've lost me,' admitted the colonel.

'They stick it on the back of their bird. Peregrine hits the glue at over 100 miles an hour, bonds instantly! Goes into an everlasting clinch, loses all control, spirals about a bit, and then both birds plunge to their death. Splat, splat!'

'Eeugh! … And this really works, a tube of glue?'

'So I gather. Not seen it myself, so far.'

'Well, I've heard everything now!'

'And then there's explosives.'

The colonel paused again. '… go on,' he said hesitantly.

'Well, I've heard some pigeon-breeders in Bristol have developed a bird bomb. Because there were peregrines on their flight path, having pigeon pie every day. So their owners rigged up a little explosive device, to strap to the back of the neck of a pigeon. Their bird flies along perfectly happy, looking like a packed lunch – but the instant it's hit by a peregrine … *boom!* Feathers everywhere!' And Gwyn fluttered his hands in demonstration of dead-bird parts falling.

This was a man whom the court accused never saw, whom the ANT members rarely heard. The laconic public image had suddenly given way – for just a few minutes – to show the passion that lurked beneath the bird-loving surface. It was hard to say what surprised the two other men more, his remarkable array of facts, or the vigour of his delivery.

'Well, I'm on the bench this morning. Better go back and get the mud off. Don't want the Lord Chancellor moaning.'

And with a cheery wave, Gwyn set off across the moor.

'Yes, you always need a vantage point,' repeated the colonel, still rigidly upright, and rotating like a lighthouse beam.

'Right,' said the dentist again.

'That was the Romans' key to success, vantage points.'

'Right,' said the dentist again.

'Yes, show the Romans a hill and they stick a fort on it. The Seven Hills of Rome, that's where they get it from, you know. Vantage points are in their blood.'

'And the dead straight roads, where did they get that from? The way they drive?'

The colonel made another grand sweep of the valley with his bins, as he called them, and affected to be too busy for speech.

The last of the wispy mist had given up, and the land now had full-blooded sun and shadows. Below them, a grassy path wound down through heather to the stream, where a very small meadow did service as a flood plain; behind them, a Victorian-looking crag rose up, in need of a pouting stag; and opposite them, the cliffs stood sheer and scary.

'Hadrian's Wall,' said the colonel. 'That worked well.'

The dentist raised himself up on an elbow, and unpacked a banana. 'You do wonder why they bothered.'

'Why they bothered to what?'

'Swap sunshine and olives and Chianti for rain, wind, and Scots.'

'For posterity, of course.'

'Posterity?'

'Two thousand years on, and their military presence is still here. Still stamped on the landscape–'

'Along with their bones.'

'Real achievement that, to leave your mark on the world. Still be remembered today.'

'There are a lot easier ways to leave your mark on the world.'

'Like what?'

'Like dentistry.'

The colonel almost dropped his bins. He gave a cross between a snort and a laugh.

'Dentistry?'

'Absolutely. Dig up a Roman corpse after two thousand years, and what's its most distinctive feature? Dental records. Because if you want to learn about the past – you examine the teeth.'

This was not a viewpoint that the colonel was familiar with, and he said nothing.

'I could look at a Claudius Maximus tomorrow, and tell you if he had toothache.'

Col. White was losing interest.

'That's posterity for me,' said the dentist. 'My bridges and crowns will last a good millennium or two, *and* I don't have to conquer anywhere cold.'

The colonel raised his bins again, and silently returned to scanning the horizon at the far end of the valley, with the intensity of a man expecting a full legion. The dentist remained lying on the grass, admiring the view.

He was therefore in a good position to see the rope as it was dangled down from the top of the cliff opposite ... and the egg-stealer began to descend.

'Oh dear,' said the dentist. And pointed.

'But ... but they're not meant to do that!' cried the colonel. 'They're meant to start from the bottom!'

'Perhaps they had a vantage point,' suggested the dentist.

'Oh bugger!' cried the colonel. 'Bugger, bugger!' His plans for unarmed combat had become the first casualty of the conflict. 'Give me the walkie-talkie! *Quick!*'

The dentist handed him up the walkie-talkie from where it lay idly on the grass. (It was a walkie-talkie obtained by his Army connections – providing proof of the colonel's value to the Trust – and was his personal contribution to Operation Big Bird, as he liked to call it.)

The colonel pressed on its buttons to summon up reinforcements.

And was answered by static.

The egg-stealer descended further, the rope held firm by an egg-stealer's mate.

The colonel shook the walkie-talkie and pressed again. Only to receive more static. Radio communications had not been his speciality in REME, and the prerequisite of finding a signal had not previously occurred to him. Cut off from base by the rock face, the walkie-talkie was a waste of time.

Except perhaps for whacking the enemy with.

'Shout!' he ordered.

'Shout? Who to?'

Col. White pointed furiously at the man on the rope. Reluctantly, Mr Hampton got to his feet and, resisting the feeling of foolishness, joined the colonel in yelling – in a threatening sort of manner – across the void of the valley. Privately, the dentist blamed his wife, for it was her idea that he get into charitable works, she being keen he left the house more often. And now he was at war on a ledge.

Together, the two men shouted and waved and shouted again … and eventually the egg-stealers waved back.

Gwyn meanwhile was keeping up a steady pace. He had come down the track across the moor, and the path along the ridge, and reached the top field by Pantglas, the long-house now occupied only by the 1957 combine harvester in the lounge. After twenty years of living in the Nant Valley, and of walking its paths at all hours (with binoculars), Gwyn knew more than just natural history. He could have been a social diarist, a rural Pepys.

Both Pantglas and its field had tales to tell. The house had seen two mystery deaths within a year. First the owner had been found dead, hanging in the barn, and then his neighbour had been found dead, lying in the yard. For reasons that had never been satisfactorily explained, both men had their trousers round their ankles. And, not unreasonably, the new owners had fled, probably back to the city. Gwyn, being a magistrate, did not share the valley view that the house was haunted. Nor did he subscribe to the other popular theory, of witchcraft, a gay coven, and widespread human sacrifice. But, as a man who believed in evidence, he had struggled to explain the presence of a Vietnamese pig and an excessive number of acupuncture needles at the scene.

However, as he walked down the wooded dingle that led back to the lane, it was the field that was more on his mind. For this was one of the fields belonging to Gareth – farmer and pervert of this parish, and currently in clink because of Gwyn. The field was now empty as the sheep had been moved to lower pastures, to await the trip to town in the big bad lorry. Fringed with native woodland, bisected by a spring that tinkled past massed mats of watercress, this was grass as God intended, and not force-fed by Fisons. Organic by neglect, species-rich through farmers poor, this newly sheepless land would soon be ablaze with the old-fashioned blooms of a bygone summer.

Gwyn was pondering on the fate of the field when he heard a sound he had not heard for years.

Lu-lu-lu.

He stopped and listened.

Toolooeet.

Unmistakable. He felt his blood run faster.

Lu-lu-lu.

He looked around for the little brown throat that would be singing it, but could see no sign. Its habitat: trees and bushes. Nest: on ground.

Toolooeet.

Six inches and unobtrusive; dull even. *Was it breeding?*

Gwyn looked again to no effect, all the while aware that a case of drunk-in-charge was waiting. He tried to locate the source of the sound, only for the foliage to foil his ears. To find the bird would be a first for the valley, and a fine footnote for his records.

> '*Teevo cheevo cheevio chee:*
> *O where, O where, what can that be?*'

recited the magistrate as he slid his profile behind an oak, quietly delighted to have recourse to his famous namesake twice in one morning.

> '*Weedio-weedio: there again!*
> *So tiny a trickle of song-strain.*'

The call of the bird was indeed growing fainter. And the call of the court growing stronger. Duty would have to trump nature. His search would have to be delayed until a day with more time in hand.

And yet this would not be his only reason to return. Something else had been bugging him since daybreak. Something bizarre and somehow sinister. In the pre-dawn light, in the dead-end lane, his headlights had lit up the oddest of billboards.

What on earth was the meaning of a sign saying *PROFIT THROUGH NATURE: EXPERIENTIAL PROJECTS?*

Chapter 11

A black BMW, only 3-Series but with personalised plates (ROD 1), swerved in through the ornamental gates, revved up the drive that curved around the wide beech-lined lawn, and came to a showy stop at the gravelled area marked *Guests*, a word newly painted on a short white post and indicating half the forecourt of a very substantial red-brick rectory, circa Jane Austen. The driver, a well-built thirty-something, did not at first get out of the car, but took time to take in the setting. When he did emerge into the gathering grey of the evening, he displayed an overdressed informality, the look of a man who had paid an untutored visit to a clothes-rack labelled *Country*. He seized a leather holdall from his boot and strode purposefully into the house, whose front door was open and waiting.

A little while afterwards, an Austin Maestro moseyed into vision, treating the home-made speed bumps with deference, and parking with less aplomb than the BMW. Its driver was a slight young woman dressed in a pro forma business suit, though with unconfined dark hair that hung down her back like code for a different culture. She got out of the car and stretched, a long slow stretch that suggested a long slow drive. She wandered over to a bench that looked out across the grounds, and here she briefly leaned and smoked a cigarette. Then she came back, took a bag from her boot and strolled into the house.

A few minutes passed, and then a small Citroën, winner of a previous decade's What Car? award, hummed in and parked at a jaunty, individualistic angle. The driver was late-twenties, and leapt from the car in a cool kind of way, frayed jeans flapping over designer trainers. He reached for a puce rucksack that lay on the back seat, and then, with scarcely a glance at the grounds, went straight into the house.

Before too long, the inevitable Ford saloon drove in – all features road-tested for the Blandness Benchmark essential to a company car – and took another of the parking spaces, but this time, reflecting the foresight of a driver who problem-solved 24/7, it reversed in. The man was in his forties, the jacket part of his suit on an executive hanger. He swung his legs out on to the gravel, rubbed a cloth over his shiny black shoes, removed a small suitcase with wheels from his boot, and walked at a measured pace into the house, accompanied by a roll of thunder.

Over the next half-hour, four more cars arrived, at different speeds, with different mannerisms. Had there been a ninth car, it would have had to follow the red arrow to the overflow parking on the grass. This sequence of events did not go unseen. Or unassessed. Crouched behind curtains at a first-floor window, Rhys Jenkins had been busily evaluating the visual data of these behavioural patterns, as befitted a facilitator.

'Thirty-two to the gallon.'

'Myself, I always lead from the front.'

'I wonder how much this place is worth per square foot.'

'I began in headed stationery, which was controversial at the time.'

'Cuts nearly three minutes off, the B430. Not a lot of people realise that.'

'Myself, I take no prisoners when I negotiate.'

'Bowls and Scrabble, but that's as far as it goes.'

'I met the assistant deputy head of the CBI once.'

'Thirty-eight mpg out of town.'

'It's a hobby of mine, guessing house prices.'

'Myself, I believe business is a war and you've got to leave some dead.'

'And when I say house prices, I include light industrial units.'

'What's your company's mission statement?'

'Forty-six mpg on a motorway. Less with the air-con on, of course.'

'You should see my secretary's arse!'

'I can't find any name badges.'

Mingling had begun.

The chat flowed in jerks as all were strangers to each other, all of them recipients of the promotional weekend. They had unpacked, freshened up, and dressed down, and now it was time for pre-dinner drinks and bonding. Rhys tried to move silkily among them, aware that on their collective goodwill rested his milch-cow.

'Loved your brochure,' said Alex, a personnel manager in oil.

'Yes, it speaks to the moment,' said Teddy, who was something with a long title in local government.

'Well, I tried to push all the buttons,' replied Rhys, with what he hoped was not a smug smile.

'You certainly pushed mine,' said Alex. 'A couple of days playing Tarzan, it's just what a chap needs.'

Rhys forced a brief, accommodating laugh, and wondered which of his concepts had been misunderstood. Sensing he might be in the presence of an idiosyncratic approach to personnel, he made his excuses and circulated.

Rhys had cast his propaganda net wide. He had aimed not just at executives thirsting to be first with the latest fads of management, and accountants seeking to be funkily creative when writing off tax, but also at PR people keen to puff all the perks their caring company gave to staff, and journos eager for freebies in a fresh format. So it was an eclectic octet, of the corporate and non-corporate, that he had gathered amid the fading plush of his family seat, which once had echoed to the strictures of a rector.

'Did you distress the furniture yourself?' asked Jane, who was young and blonde and wrote for *Country Trends*.

'No, it was old to start with,' replied Rhys.

'Oh, what an original idea!'

As Rhys did the rounds of the hands yet to be shaken, and tried to hide that he too had first-night nerves, he was pleased to note there was no one over fifty. Team-building in the wilderness has many challenges, and he did not wish cardiac infarction to be one of them. Even though retrieval of a corpse did have bonding potential. Admittedly, he had recently done a local first-aid course, but he had had less than full confidence in the instructor.

Rhys was aware that it had been a lengthy cross-country drive for many – indeed several had already recounted their route, and alternative routes, in detail – and so, as soon as his grandfather's grandfather clock began to strike nine minutes to eight, he pulled back the dividing doors of the reception room, and revealed a long and well-worn oak table laid for dinner.

'First test,' he announced. 'Eating as a team. Synchronised use of knife and fork.' This was a joke, and at least five of them spotted it, though he felt unsure whether their laughter was recognition of irony or sign of sycophancy.

He watched as his group approached the table. The absence of a seating plan was, to some, just absence of a seating plan, but to others it was a career opportunity, a chance to gain hierarchical advantage from a three-course meal.

It was Roderick who captured the head of the table, using an unseemly turn of speed. First to arrive at the house, first to descend for drinks, first to be seated for dinner, Roderick clearly hoped to be a high achiever. He had changed his clothes again, from country-carwear to country-housewear, and was now in an Aran sweater; whatever his aims for his image, its creamy-white ribbing left him looking awkwardly short of a yacht.

To his left sat the long-haired Amanda, whose priorities had been noted as perverse. Spurning the joys of networking, she had wandered around the room's recesses and browsed through the books. *With interest.* Now in designer jeans, she also wore an air of detachment and reclined upon her dining chair with a wry smile.

Opposite her was voguish young Greg, the Citroën driver, too modern to sit languidly in any form of furniture. Word was that he only worked part-time, and yet earned enough to live – not information that made him popular. So far, he had changed no items of clothing.

And beside him, currently in corduroys, sat Mervyn the middle-manager, whose small talk had been designed by Ford.

Rhys and his assistant facilitator – a smiley youth whom the brochure claimed had once worked for the BBC (though in an undisclosed capacity) – took up positions mid-table and helped pass the carrot and coriander soup back and forth.

'I'm in the franchising business,' announced Roderick, in answer to no one's question.

Status was the ghost at the banquet. Or, for the less literary, it was the elephant in the dining room. And (to pursue this analogy) there were unwritten rules on how and when you got the beast to blow its trumpet. For one's status was a subtle asset, not easily established. *Assumed* was best; *implied* was good; *alluded to* was OK; and *publicly announced* lost you points.

'Tumble dryers,' responded Mervyn, imagining he felt the warm glow of public interest. 'Transportation requirements of.'

Before he could be restrained, he elaborated. It soon became a matter for wonderment that the daily dramas of his workplace had not been the subject of an epic novel. Fortunately his flow was broken at the far end of the table by Teddy, who had what he believed were seldom-heard observations to make about local government.

'Yes, franchising's the future,' pronounced Roderick, not a man easily rerouted from a train of thought, or limelight, or possibility of money. 'Initiative, entrepreneurial vision, innovation, that's a winning package, and I'm a winner.'

Amanda's wry smile grew wryer.

'Because a franchise can be key to your power base. One of the building blocks of life, for a businessman. The start of an empire – if you've got the skill set, and the get-up-and-go.'

Rhys the host, on the other hand, said little of the world of work, as it had yet to form part of his career path. His own past had been spent in the anterooms of life, gathering up nugatory degrees to serve as a cover story for sloth. So tonight, while others jockeyed and joked for an edge, Rhys opted for a policy of superior silence, and sprinkled it with the sagacious stardust of open questions.

'And who here works within a structure of interdependency?'

'Guess I do,' said Gary, removing what appeared to be several dog hairs from his shirt-sleeve. 'In health care.'

'Doing what?' enquired Amanda.

'Looking after the mentally ill.'

'Is there much money in the mentally ill?' asked Roderick, visibly puzzled.

'Not a lot,' replied Gary, as unhelpfully as he could manage. He had taken against Roderick an hour before meeting him, upon sight of his number plate.

'No chance of a mentally ill empire, then?' said Amanda, moving from wry to sardonic.

'And what do *you* do?' asked Roderick, rather frontally. 'Something in the caring line as well?'

Amanda took her bread roll on a slow journey round the remaining damp patches of her soup plate. She did not wish to respond as if under interrogation. When eventually she looked up, she said, 'That's not exactly how I would characterise the fourth estate.'

'Journalist?' said Gary, his surprise favourable.

Roderick was more wary, perhaps already focused on how best to manage his image for a profile. 'Who for?'

'The *TES*.'

Roderick nodded, as though a lifelong subscriber, and hoped someone else might explain.

'*Times Educational Supplement*,' explained Amanda, her helpfulness a Trojan horse for subtle condescension. Not that his outsize ego seemed to notice.

'Will we be named and shamed?' asked Gary with a grin.

'Oh, you'll all be "anonymous sources".' And she laughed. 'Feel free to dish the dirt! On anything you fancy.'

Rhys forced a smile. She was not the pliable hack he had hoped for. It was possible she knew long words that meant something. She might even have her own views on interpersonal dynamics.

'So, no free publicity, then,' said Roderick, failing to sound like a man who did not care. 'No flyers for the business!'

'Good. I get quite enough publicity in my life,' said Gary.

'You do? ... How come?'

Gary turned his attention to his shirt, carried out a brief examination, and for the second time that evening pulled long white dog hairs off it. Which he then held up for inspection.

Gratifying bafflement ensued, which he milked for a good few moments before declaring, 'That's the downside of the Dulux dog.'

His end of the table fell suitably silent.

'... *you own the Dulux dog?*' said Roderick, trying to quell his incredulity.

'Yeah. My pooch is on primetime.'

'You are joking?'

'No. Canine entrepreneur, that's me.' Gary pulled out a card from his jeans.

' "Entrepreneur" ...?' snorted Roderick. 'That's not a business skill, owning a fucking dog!'

This dog news was also a surprise to Rhys, and it somewhat subverted the profile of the client base that he was hoping to build.

'So, in your opinion, Roderick, what exactly does count as a business skill?' enquired Amanda, in calm *TES* tones.

Roderick looked her up and down before responding, as ever finding it hard to take seriously a woman with small breasts.

(Meanwhile Mervyn, as usual a couple of beats off the conversational pace, turned to his neighbour and said, 'I used to have two of those Yorkshire terriers.')

'Drive. Determination. Leadership. Setting goals, targets. Man management. Vision. Did I say drive and determination?'

Amanda nodded. She wrote nothing on the pad beside her.

'Yes, that's the way to the top in the franchise business. And mine's a growth sector.'

'You're in *a growth sector?*' Amanda let her eyes widen, as if on first sight of the Jesus child.

'Food,' replied Roderick. 'I'm a food entrepreneur.'

'Gosh, I've never met a food entrepreneur before!' confessed Amanda.

'Burger bars,' declared Roderick, not holding back on the pride. 'Wimpy Burgers!'

'Goodness me!' said Amanda. 'Another household name!'

Roderick watched her write down *WIMPY* with two exclamation marks. Suppressing some sense of niggling doubt about her editorial line, he prepared to divulge his big burger plans in bullet points.

But the arrival of pheasants (pot-roasted) signalled a natural break in the socialising, and cue for an old-fashioned feast. The earthenware tureens were butler-size, the shot-filled birds a gamy reminder of how the estate used once to pay its bills. Rhys himself was agnostic on blood sports, less exercised by the principle than by the people, whose zeal for the kill he found unfetching. Still strong were his childhood memories of chinless gun-groups who stood, eyes to the sky, for long, bleak hours in cold and driving rain, desperate for their fun day out to climax with a death. (In man versus pheasant, the result, Rhys often thought, was a posthumous win for the bird.)

That breed was gone. Those around the table tonight were from a world beyond the rustic mindset of his grandfather, who had rarely left the valley. Yet some truths seldom changed. The need for income in Arcady is the economic counterpart of the Fall, and long had the Nant seen schemes and scams that meant much supping with business associates of the devil. And so here, where rural Hoorays once brayed for blood and feathers, there now were found the urban apostles of commerce, eager for Nature to miscegenate with Mammon.

Time passed as they chewed.

'I've never seen so many miles of nothing,' moaned Mervyn, trying to build an orderly cairn of his lead shot by ring-fencing it with unwanted sprouts.

'Scary or what!' mocked Gary.

'Just dull,' replied Mervyn, a man with no irony gene.

'Town parks are more my type of thing,' admitted Teddy from local government. 'Where there's grass, you need street-lights, in my opinion.'

'Ballooning!' announced Jane, the townie columnist from *Country Trends*. 'Best place to see grass from, six hundred feet up.'

Rhys had asked for views on countryside – another open question – and Mervyn had obliged, at length. Countryside was 'a gateway topic' (*a means to examine minds*, according to his index of jargon) and Rhys had hoped it would help him explore any hinterland his guests might have. (Although he prayed it not be golf.) Attitudes and aptitudes were the building bricks of the weekend's programme, and would be key to his developing the inner executive.

His best analytical tool was the wine. A liking for wine was the one common denominator to be found in the hours of babel around the table. Few secrets of note emerged – though one man confessed an interest in Second World War battlefields, before laughter closed him down – but guardedness decreased. A fear of being judged was gradually forgotten, the need to be first mostly fading. Yet Rhys himself stayed sober, observant, his aim a potted portrait of his protégés by the time the Stilton appeared.

The Stilton was the size of a grand biscuit-barrel, its seventeen pounds awaiting attack by a silver teaspoon, and had been warming in the wings. A leading Abernant chef now rolled it into view atop a two-tier tea trolley, an unusually theatrical entrance for a cheese. But it served Rhys' purpose, for much of the chat gibbered to a halt. And he was well primed for the conversational gap.

With his audience replete and setting about the port, Rhys rose to deliver a speech. To some post-prandial surprise, he produced a flip chart from behind the long velvet curtains.

On it was a meta-structural multidimensional analysis of human inter-relationships operating within a global corporate environment, as drawn by a black felt-tip pen. It was the world of work as overlapping circles. As tidal waves of angry arrows. With linking lines. Dotted lines. Subliminal lines. And a pyramidic triangle or two. Plus, of course, a soup of attendant acronyms. It was the intellectual circuitry of management theory, as depicted by the hip hieroglyphics of the age.

Rhys cantered through learning-style concepts and four-stage character cycles, pausing briefly to expound how and where the axis of Processing Continuum intersected with the axis of Perception Continuum, an issue which had not previously preoccupied his audience. ('Are you a personality type disposed to

Accommodating, or Diverging, or Converging, or Assimilating?' was a question that gave them all pause for thought.) He then diverted to touch on man's hierarchy of needs, instinctoid in nature and culminating in self-actualisation, but kept this brief as he thought he saw a bread roll being tossed playfully to and fro across the table.

He flipped forward to his fifth chart, and the goals and roles and processes of team development. Fortunately the rubric rhymed, and he gained a better grip on his guests. 'Forming, Storming, Norming, and Performing,' he stated. More than once. He did not mention the critique that this theory was linear rather than cyclical, and thus possibly suspect. Instead, sensing he had located the level at which to pitch his concepts, he summarised: 'Team Development – think of it as ritual sniffing.'

'I get enough of that at home!' said Gary the dog-man, and raised an easy laugh.

'Now the big question,' said Rhys, moving away from his prop and his felt-tip pen, 'the big question is *commitment*. And I want to know, on a scale of 1 to 10, what is the extent of your commitment to this course?'

Rhys then went down the length of the table handing out Post-it notes and pencils.

It was late, they all were tired, and some were tiddly. What was the correct answer? Was there a correct answer? Was it a trick question? How best to keep face? How soonest to be in bed?

'Write a number down, from 1 to 10,' Rhys instructed. And waited while they each got in touch with their id, or whichever part of them was in charge of commitment. For some, this proved a task of advanced calculus and even crossings-out.

Then, when all were locked into a number, Rhys motioned to his flip chart. He looked first towards Mervyn, the most middle of management.

Mervyn got up and moved uneasily across the room. He had agonised over what would be the least conspicuous of numbers and had decided on a 7. He stuck this up with the self-conscious air of a schoolboy uncertain whether he had the approval of his teacher.

There was then a flurry of 7s and 8s, from people keen to conform, reluctant to overreach. Gary broke the pattern with a laidback 6 and some callow comment about true genius never getting out of bed before noon. Amanda the observer refused to commit, implying some principle was in play. And last to rise was Roderick.

He strode across the room and stuck up his Post-it note with an entrepreneurial flourish. In big and black and bold, he had written **10**. And underlined it twice.

'I always give 100 per cent!' he boomed. 'I'm a 100 per cent person. That's me! That's why I'm a winner. 100 per cent! Every time.' And then sat down as though expecting applause.

Rhys did not sit down. He walked toward the French windows, which lay beyond the curtains. In the other room, the grandfather clock was making a confused and noisy stab at midnight. Outside, a steady, determined rain was beating against the windowpanes. And at the dining-room door, Rhys' ex-BBC assistant was struggling with a bundle of waterproofs, wellingtons, and miners' lamps.

Rhys flung open the French windows, and a blast of cold wet wind raced in through the fug.

'Follow me!' he cried.

A collective shiver of horror ran up and down the table, the dreams of duvets denied.

'But where? Where to?' came their cry back.

'To the woods!' Rhys replied. '*To the woods!*'

Less than a mile further up the valley, Stéfan had been wanking for over an hour. First he had wanked standing naked on his verandah, then he had wanked standing naked in several of his mansion's windows.

But this was where a large estate had disadvantages: nobody sees you.

He had thought of wanking standing naked in his courtyard, but the practicalities of simultaneously holding up an umbrella had discouraged him.

Sex, he had it on good authority, was everywhere in the hills around him, but he could not locate it, and he was not a man who reacted well to failure. His was a penis that liked company on a grand scale. And was not shy of strangers. Which was why the postwoman no longer delivered parcels.

For he was not at all a furtive pervert, but a showman of his private parts. These were parts that were well known on the London scene, and used for many purposes. His party trick was to improvise a swizzle-stick, and give body to an unattended beer. He felt this gave the lie to those who claimed he had no wit. The fastness of mid-Wales had yet to rock to a full-on night of his friends and their fun.

In the meantime, he made do mostly with fantasy. He had mounted the Secretary to the Hunt, but so had everybody. And it was debauch he was after, not the dullness of a solitary bang. He had high hopes that a squirearchical phallus would, when waved, bring all wenches within range to their knees.

In his early days he came as a weekend-only squire, and the vistas of his green and rustic valley, where little happened but hedging, had been to Stéfan the self-evident signs of a somnolent world in which passion played no part. But Eryl had told him different.

He knew now of the pub where tired farmers sat in an upstairs room to watch two barmaids lie on a pool table and misuse the billiard cue. He knew now of the cobbler's where the back curtain hid a Swedish tape collection in which feet were not the only fetish. He knew now of the line of parked cars that bounced at the back end of the reservoir. He knew all this and it made the need for wanking worse.

He also had learnt that marriage in Abernant could bring an unexpected bonus. To be the registrar of births, marriages and deaths in a small market town requires diplomacy, charm and a certain clerical flair. The post-holder Mrs Janet Prothero, a worldly-wise and thirtyish wife of a probate solicitor, possessed all of these attributes, but also concerned herself with the longer-term welfare of her newly-weds. She was a wife-swapper.

This was a service that even the most progressive London boroughs did not yet provide, and the very thought made Stéfan salivate. Did she raise the offer at the ceremony? Was there a third person saying 'I do'? Or did she post a card on later, saying it was a follow-up facility?

Stéfan angled his naked body more to the south as he panted at the starless night, his libido hyperactive, his pink and overfed reflection vibrating in the drawing-room windows.

Up and down the valley, tonight was the night when legs opened for the weekend. Such (said Eryl) were the rabbit-like extremes of local humping, that the greatest danger was unwitting incest. For so libidinous were the seemingly strait-laced natives that their progeny was scattered, like unlabelled seed, throughout every nook and copulating cranny of the parish. The odds of a conquest being kin was cause alone for a condom.

Stéfan whacked away, sweatily obsessed by all these taunting tales. And then, as his lust restlessly searched for a focus, like a radio trying to tune, he caught sight of lights. Not street-lights, not headlights, but torchlights. Lights that had to belong to lovers. Lovers threading through the trees to some secret hideaway. Lovers off to where (according to Eryl) the white witches held their sex-sodden rites in the woods.

Speeding up his strike rate, squeezing out the inches, Stéfan pressed his face and his phallus to the rain-lashed panes, and tried his damnedest to conjure up all the dark details of the night's distant orgasms.

'And there's fungus in the autumn,' said Rhys, trying to put a spin on the clinging wet undergrowth.

'Fuck the fungus,' said someone whose commitment was 7.

They were queued up single file to get across the stile. The lamps on their hard hats lit up random bits of greenery overhead, which spookily quivered and jerked like shots from a home-made horror movie. And the rain dripped deafeningly on to their Gore-Tex.

'I knew it!' cried Gary. 'We're going to attack Nicaragua.'

'It *was* in the small print,' said Rhys.

'I've not got the right wellies for a war,' said Amanda.

'Typical woman!' said Alex from personnel. 'Never got the right outfit!'

'Watch a tree doesn't fall on you,' she replied.

'Won't be picking you for *my* team!'

Everyone laughed.

'And to think my staff were jealous of all this!' said Teddy, water coursing down his grin.

'*Wales* makes them jealous? Where d'you work, Belgium?'

'I suppose it's too late to go surfing instead?' asked a man called George.

'*I've* always wanted to go paintballing,' said Mervyn.

'Why's that, Merv?' asked Gary. 'Mid-life crisis?'

Everyone laughed again.

'*Hi Ho, Hi Ho, it's off to work we go!*' sang out someone at the back.

'I'm sorry, no dwarfs,' called Rhys' assistant. 'They get lost in the bracken.'

The joke, like all dwarf jokes, was a hit. Very soon the song was taken up right along the line. And '*Hi Ho, Hi Ho, it's off to work we go!*' became the group's no. 1 as they marched off into the midnight wood.

(Rhys couldn't help reflecting that all one really needed for good company performance was a good company song. But that was a thought without profit and he kept it to himself.)

The path up through the trees, the path he had trod in the brainstorming days of May, looked an unknown land in the dark. Unknown and spooky. With only the red glint of alien eyes for company. With just the rustling, snuffling soundtrack of creatures who killed by night. Even though he knew the way well, Rhys would have hesitated to come alone.

A few hundred yards in, and he arrived at the greatest of his glades, which he occasionally – and predictably – compared to a cathedral. Now a space with pools of daunting darkness, its arboreal architecture rose up like Gothic excrescences.

Here the older woodland grew, more gnarled and eccentric in its lifestyle, more fantastical in its shadows. Here the branches contorted with age, sprouted ferns in their forks, and reached for the sky in convoluted ways. Here art and nature had almost merged, the beauty of wildwood not needing man. And here his grandfather had often used to come, to sit and sketch the day away.

Rhys had, however, made a few changes.

'What the hell …?' said Roderick, who was, of course, in pole position.

'You've been busy!' said Alex, who liked to see busyness in a man.

'You bastard!' said Mervyn, who was none too keen on a challenge.

'Exciting, eh?' said Rhys.

'For monkeys!' said Amanda.

Because on to nature Rhys had grafted an assault course.

To the ancient bark, he had hammered old and rotting planks; across the venerable branches, he had strung up lengths of rope; and from tree to tree he had tied on shaky walkways. There were tyres to crawl through, nets to scramble over, and bits of ladder to scrabble up.

'Piece of piss!' said Roderick.

'Just two rules,' said Rhys, when the group had regathered after their recce in the rain.

'Rule no. 1 …' said his assistant.

'… the team must complete the circuit without touching the ground.'

'Piece of piss,' said Roderick again.

'Every time anyone touches the ground you all go back to square one.'

For some reason laughter rippled through the group.

'And the second rule?' asked Amanda.

The assistant pointed to a builder's bucket, filled almost to the brim with water.

'The team has to carry this around the circuit,' said Rhys. '… *and not spill any.*'

This time there was less laughter.

'This is a test of group dynamics and your ability to interact in a goal-oriented manner.' Rhys looked around at the various pink towny faces, and wondered what they had learnt from a dinner. 'So your immediate priority is to talk amongst yourselves and decide upon a leader.'

'I'll be leader,' said Roderick. 'I'm good at that.'

*   *   *

Rhys and his fellow facilitator stood in shiny yellow waterproofs some thirty yards apart, aiming their lamps at the aerial crocodile as it struggled, eight strong and a bucket, to advance across the rain-lashed clearing in the early hours of the morning. Progress was slow.

There had been several problems. Or, as is said in the ever upbeat world of management, several challenges. These were, in summary, the people, the trees, and the bucket.

For eight people to advance in single file requires those eight people to agree on who is where in the line. A simple matter, this took twenty minutes of animated exchanges and was only finally solved by pushing and shoving. The language of methodology and prioritisation was little heard upon the night air.

Nor did the trees prove blameless. Repeatedly damned as badly designed, and of the wrong material, this meant the shoving gave way to slithering. The combination of the wood and the wet made wellies an unwise footwear, and the gung-ho dwarf spirit was soon going west.

But the bucket – not a standard tool of management, full or empty – was the cause of almost existential angst. Water only stays still when not being bothered. Lift it and it wobbles. Move it and it wobbles. Nudge it and it wobbles. Even a threatening look can disturb its composure. Water is subject to immutable laws of wobbling that even a chief executive cannot rescind. And water, whether or not it knows it's part of an Experiential Project, can be immoderately, unreasonably wet.

'Well, you fucking carry it, you twat!' shouted Roderick at Amanda, after his third go at carrying the water in a wobble-free way had been received with unsupportive laughter.

Roderick ('my friends call me Roddy', but as yet no one had taken him up on this offer) was standing stranded astride two tree stumps, each a remnant of past pollarding, and was attempting to transfer his body and the bucket to the far stump. Behind him, Amanda had one foot sharing the near stump, her second foot on a long and low-lying branch, which in turn supported the six extras, all standing unstably in an increasingly querulous queue. Ten minutes gone and they had got five yards.

Roderick had tried to bridge the gap by taking the bucket with him; he had tried to bridge the gap by not taking the bucket with him (but then reaching back for it); and he had tried, once more, to bridge the gap by taking the bucket with him as he was a man short of original ideas.

Meantime his team – and the word 'team' is used in the sense of warring strangers – were bonding with little other than wet underwear. As they stood clutching at leaves, several were still absorbing the judgement expressed by Rhys. Looking at their line-up, he had proclaimed, 'No one is where they are by chance.' Mervyn, who was bringing up the rear, had taken this particularly hard. It brought back painful memories of his failure to be upgraded to the 1.8-litre company Ford, and even took his mind off the loss of feeling in his fingers. Whereas Alex, whose self-image was at the swashbuckling end of the male scale, born to be the hero of any action with buckets, felt demeaned at becoming a man in the middle. As head of personnel, he had wanted to play Tarzan and had ended up behind a Jane.

'Further! Further, you useless cow!' yelled Roderick, never one for the methods of a flip chart.

'Drop dead, burger boy!' Amanda yelled back.

He was now stood with both feet on the far stump, and reaching back in vain for her to pass the bucket. His stance was far from stable, and the threat of the weight of the water deterred him from leaning too far. Amanda was small and slight and with arms that scarcely went around her men, let alone bridged chasms. Try as she might – and she could have tried more – the moss and the epiphytes made for a very fickle foothold.

'Dulux man to the rescue!' Gary cried, and edged forward to try and hold her, to give her extra stretch. But soon they too were in danger of tumbling.

'I could have bonded better indoors,' moaned the man from local government, his hand recoiling from a fruiting body.

The canopy of leaves shivered in a sudden gust and a deluge of drops splattered down.

'It's just not the sort of problem I get in my line of work,' said the man called George. 'Not in Oswestry.'

Near by, two ageing branches rubbed up against each other, their bark made smooth by years of contact, and emitted a sad and laboured creaking.

'What time does it get light?' asked Mervyn.

As Rhys stood observing the group interactions, he began to feel that his mission *to generate strategic visions and enhance commitment* might yet need a little tweaking.

'Longer arms! Has no cunt got longer arms?' cried Roderick, flailing with ever greater fury.

But no one, whatever length their arms, could have threaded a way through the people packed along a branch better suited to squirrels, and the contretemps continued. Only young Jane, the blonde from *Country Trends*, stayed quiet, and did so because she was thinking up the headline *High-fliers Trapped in Tree!*. Her magazine was written for the new London loaded, its aim to sell the rural scene as more than dreary farmers and the dullsvilles of nowhere. She had done columns on vineyards and microlights, and how the latest wave of chocolatiers and homeopaths were buying up barns, and putting paid to the pastoral tedium. Soon those retarded by being too long on the land would, claimed her editorials, be swept away by those at the new cutting edge of countryside.

'100 per cent!' cried Roderick. 'I want *100* per cent!'

'Right!' said Amanda. 'You can have 100 per cent!'

And with those words, she hurled the contents of the bucket at him and over him, and then threw the thing a full three feet to the ground.

Rhys now felt the need to facilitate.

At the beginning, it had been his hope and intent that a proactive spirit of co-operation – as per the overlapping circles – would have observed the large and handy stick left in full view, its purpose to enable the builder's bucket to be carried coolie-like around the circuit. But in all the Forming, Storming, Norming, and Performing, this had been overlooked.

Amanda and Roderick leapt from their stumps and squared up to each other, followed by Gary shouting 'Fight! Fight!', and several others jumping from their branch to offer her help.

As Rhys stepped hurriedly forward, moving into new managerial territory, he did wonder whether he had been wise to ignore his alternative business scenario – to open 𝔇𝔢𝔪𝔢𝔱𝔢𝔯 𝔥𝔬𝔲𝔰𝔢 for murder-mystery weekends.

Chapter 12

The trucks came just before dawn.

Their headlights swept across the dark farmyard, and spread a fleeting glow upon the bedroom wall. Old Rhodri Richards clasped his wife's hand and turned his face to the pillow. He did not go down to greet the trucks. He did not go down to help the stockmen. Instead he lay and listened, as he had lain and listened all night long, to the sounds that came from the sheds.

It took an hour, perhaps a little more. An hour to end a lifetime's work.

The noisy, nervous beasts were urged out into the early-morning air. Always wary of a journey, they were wisely fearful of being corralled. They butted and back-kicked to escape the herding, but all their bleats were in vain. Before long, each sheep was clattering up the metal ramps in a loopy panic. They rightly sensed their farm days here were over.

Old Rhodri could see their faces in his mind, could recognise them by their quirks.

The farm buildings gave shelter from wind, but succour to echoes. The clanging rasp of make-do metal gates on rough concrete rang around the yard and ended at the bungalow bedroom. The sound came freighted with years of memories, of pens put up for shearing, of sheep prepared for dipping, of lambs sent off for slaughter. And then came the tramp of muddy boots, the closing of cab doors, and the chugging cough of diesel starting up.

Rhodri did not get up to bid goodbye as the trucks set out on their final journey.

He had begun in '37, hacking back the scrub. He had learnt to ditch and to hedge and to worm. He had helped to make his own farm gates as well as wattle hurdles. He had got to grips with the innards of ewes and cows and tractors. He had come to know when not to call the vet and when his stock were goners. Steadily he had built up his Speckled Face flock.

He had married a girl along the lane, a girl whose world was farming, but a girl less fecund than the sheep. Good with curtains and cushions, she brought soft furnishings into his life. Yet she also was content to lie beside the Raeburn and feed the orphaned lambs upon her lap. And she could tow a trailer. Steadily he had built up his Speckled Face flock.

He started to win rosettes. Local rosettes at first, for the likes of the cuddliest lamb. But then came the Abernant Show, and he got a First in Class. Although bigger and less hardy than the true mountain sheep, his breed offered quality carcasses. Yet they also looked good when live. And so once a year he trundled them over the mountains to the Royal Welsh, a show that was the Barnum's of livestock, and paraded them around the arena. Steadily he had built up his Speckled Face flock.

And then his wife gave birth. So keen was he on an heir that he would, if he could, have dressed him up in baby Barbours. But Gareth was to become a shy and lonely lad, with not much oomph or chat. Late at speech and late at sex and slow to master lambing, his son was little trusted out upon the hills. Adulthood arrived, and yet the reins were let go rarely, his daily toil on the family farm more fit for a hired hand. And so he passed thirty, and forty, before finally permitted to be a full and proper farmer. Only to then fall headlong for Moira, a flighty piece from Donegal, and the talk of the valley. And by the time he reached fifty, flagrante delicto had been the farm's downfall.

Now the Speckled Face flock was no more, off to a fickle fate at auction.

Rhodri gazed up at the Artexed ceiling, its swirls now vaguely visible in the light creeping through the floral drapes, and he tried and failed to keep his mind from the market. Still at the front of his memory was the farewell round-up of the day before. His neighbours had mustered in the fields beside the farm, to help him gather and grade his flock. They had daubed every rump in paint, each coloured according to category – from the prized yearlings to the old and broken-mouthed – as an aid to the auctioneer. It was also an aid to the neighbours – like the four profiteering Pritchard boys – as it helped them identify the bargains.

Even when Rhodri closed his eyes, he could still see the heaving market that he had known for fifty years; he could see the green tin shed, round and tiered like a squalid big top, where the cattle slid and shat as they did their prodded circuit; he could see the open-air pens beyond, where the sheep milled and mounted each other, pissing in the crush; and he could see the rival dealers in their ancient wooden cubby-holes, the peeling signs showing where to count out the cash.

In his head, he could hear the mutter of the buyers, shuffling through the straw and the slurry as they checked for lameness and lice; he could hear the rat-a-tat chant of the auctioneer, florid-faced and in a padded waistcoat, lording it above the pens on a makeshift walkway; and he could hear the constant cries of the penned-in sheep, the fate of each lot settled with a showmanly crack of a cow's old thigh-bone against the metal bars.

Lying, sighing, Rhodri played all this over again and again in his mind, the loading of his cargo, the voiding of his acres, the ending of his dreams.

The day dawned warm, but there was no early rising on the farm. All that was now left in the barn was a set of wooden skittles, once the only hobby of the absent son.

Chapter 13

Puffy Mr Probert, auctioneer and occasional estate agent, braked to a halt and took the *For Sale* sign out of the ditch again. It had been in and out of the ditch untold times over the past few months, sometimes defaced, sometimes broken, always soggy. This was not an organised campaign. No one in the valley had called a meeting and asked for vandalism volunteers. But somehow no one ever saw it happen, nor ever fingered a suspect, nor ever expressed any sympathy to him. Although there was suggestion of a hex.

The Dragon's Head had been the last pub left in the valley, and the *unique opportunity to convert an historic hostelry into a highly individual and prestige family home* had got up a lot of noses, not all of them beery-red. Issues of community, history, principle, and civilisation were each available for invoking. The last chapels and churches had had their innards reworked, their functions replaced, their gods discarded; the last village school had had its pedagogic purpose gutted, its playground turned to car park, its children dispersed; the last post office had been moved to a bungalow back room two half-days a week; and the last home-grown village hall had been reduced to rubble. To lose the landmark that once was the Dragon's Head would be the final nail in the communal coffin.

Or so it was said.

But the man who lurked about in the dark, committing unprintable acts to the posters, was not a citizen driven entirely by concern for social infrastructure. Eryl had a grudge. He was the last of the four regulars – two dead, one jailed – who had stood in boots amid the spit and sawdust, pretending to give meaning to their evenings. Left bitter at the closure, seeing beer as his right, he had set about sabotage. He sometimes even wore a balaclava, though a penknife and a spray-can put him at the low end of alco-terrorism. But to elevate his acts beyond mere wilful destruction, he always placed the *For Sale* signs in the ditch, and always at the same spot. For here died the mole-men, anaesthetised by drink, and Eryl liked to think of his vandalism more as a votive offering, a posthumous promise that pints would continue to flow.

But the truth was less maudlin, the motive less sentimental, the urge less benign.

Stéfan owned the pub.

He had bought it in his early days, on the sound grounds that as landlord he could not, and would not, refuse himself an after-hours drink. His other error had been the foodie makeover, with all the uplighters and poncy pastel tones to better showcase the cordon bleu aspects of the Caucasus, not previously known to be locally lucrative. But with regulars not feeling at home and no passing trade to lure, the exotic menus went unread, the black olives and the bread-sticks died from boredom on the bar. And Stéfan soon became the full extent of his customer base.

'You bought a pub in a poke,' Mr Probert had said to his client, on every occasion they met.

Which was why, when Stéfan went off into huffy exile, leaving his Jacobean mansion leaking like a sieve, he had taken the auctioneer's advice to turn the pub to greater profit as a house. Unfortunately, Mr Probert's area of expertise was cows and sheep, as even Rhodri Richards would acknowledge; the business of bricks and mortar, where nothing lowed or bleated, was for him a world of arcane calculation, of almost abstract mystery.

The latter-day Dragon's Head had languished on his books. Whenever sniffs of interest did come about – and none but second-homers were up for weird and wacky living-spaces – Eryl would mysteriously materialise to advise of downsides. Even landslides. For him, a man serially wronged by life, revenge was a dish which could be served cold or hot or lukewarm, and also as a takeaway. And the pub was personal. So he warned off would-be buyers with tales of nasty neighbours and ferret-filled drains, of sheep-borne ticks and bloody-minded bulls, of erratic rubbish collection and noisy nuclear bombers. Eryl could even wax lyrical on the threat of mob violence when the WI exited the village hall, just across the road.

And all the while he watched Stéfan's money go to waste.

And all the while Stéfan watched his wish to be a well-loved squire go sour.

So, as the Range Rover of Mr Probert came into view from Crug Caradoc, winding through the parkland and bearing more bad tidings, Stéfan got ready to rework his plans for the pub once more – and return it to mole-catchers' retro.

Chapter 14

'*Unobtrusive?*'

'Pretty much. A streaky brown. And rather dull and dumpy.'

Rain dripped from Gwyn's waterproofs on to the flagstone floor of the small kitchen.

'You got up at dawn to go and see something "unobtrusive"?'

Her tone was not critical, not even exasperated, but teasing, a ritual teasing, the sign that such eccentric follies were the – sometimes tiresome – source for a lifetime's love.

'*Rare* and unobtrusive. Well, quite rare. For round here.'

'Porridge?'

'Please. Didn't fly much, though.'

'Probably likes a lie-in on a Sunday.'

It was the August rain that made her just a tad ratty. She had wanted to paint some sedge that was on the turn, a little raggedy and oddball brown, but today was not the day to sit in a meadow. She did not stop if rain came upon her, but to begin in the rain, even with the shelter of a golfing umbrella, reduced the pleasure too close to chore. And the umbrella, a new umbrella, a gift, a freebie, made her feel uneasy. Never a fan of stripes, she was also reluctant to be seen out beneath words of corporate wisdom, touting a motto for a mortgage. She liked her life to sidestep the tawdrier truths of the everyday.

'How's the ink?' asked Gwyn.

'Full to the gunwales,' she replied.

He eased off his waterproofs and reluctantly, a little rheumatically, set about his boots.

She reached up to the Welsh dresser that made the kitchen small and took down two large bowls with abstract cockerels and two little plates with a fish mosaic … or what appeared, from a certain angle in a certain light, to be a fish mosaic.

(Their potter daughter was struggling to make headway in an overcrowded profession.) The cutlery was also odd, in a streamlined and Swedish sort of way. And all the mugs and cups on the hooks were impulse buys, wild one-offs, though the ones Audrey chose for breakfast were hand-painted with funny faces. When the rough pine table had been laid, as if by lottery, few would have said they were sat in what once was the world of a gamekeeper's cottage.

And amid the teapot and toast was a manual Imperial typewriter, black, with a stack of stencils. Breakfast was the side-show.

'Three phone calls. One from your Lady H. But I think she just wanted to complain about the government.'

'Probably wants a licence to hunt them.'

'I do worry she likes me.'

'I've told her you're common.'

'Tell her I'm violent.'

Gwyn smiled but did not reply. Instead he clasped both hands round his hot cup and gazed across the table as he took a long, thoughtful draught of camomile tea.

'There's also a request for you to lead a bird walk along the river. And a primary school wants your talk with the stuffed owl. I said you'd ring Monday.'

But Gwyn was no longer listening. He had reached into the back pocket of his trademark corduroys and pulled out an old red notebook and a pencil stub.

'So … 143!' cried Audrey. Her voice betrayed just a hint of that synthetic enthusiasm which a woman summons up for a partner's passion.

'Yes,' acknowledged Gwyn. 'Could be a new spotting record this year.'

'What's still to see?'

'Need something to escape from a zoo!' He grinned at her. 'Like a griffon vulture, or a pink flamingo.'

'Will that count?'

'*I* make the rules.' He grinned again. And, after writing down *Woodlark*, he entered several observations in a tidy, cultured hand.

She sat and watched, as she had sat and watched his ritual many times before, on the top of mountains, in the middle of moors, by the roar of rapids. For an outdoors woman she was very elegant, even at sixty-plus. She could have been a model had modelling been her world. Which it might have been had she not met him. Unusually for someone in the petite and blonde category, she had aged well, her face giving no foothold for ravaging lines, her hair barely faded beneath her fashionable silk scarves.

Gwyn finished the vital statistics of his sighting and put the little notebook back. He looked pleased. 'I've thought of a good title. "Up With the Woodlark!" Think I'll lead with my bird story. Editor's prerogative.'

'How many articles are there?'

'Eleven. Twelve, if Professor Bloody Farquhar finally delivers on "Phytoplankton Population Changes in Nutrient-rich Waters". But I'm hoping he might die before he finishes it.'

The Abernantian Naturalists came out quarterly or twice-yearly, depending on innumerable imponderables. As no one was paid, there was neither carrot nor stick, no editorial form of tough love. And the subbing was a journey through an eco-psycho-minefield. Naturalists were – despite their pacific public image – no more immune from ego-outbursts than tantrummy actors. Gwyn swore each edition would be his last. He had sworn that for nearly two decades.

As had Audrey, for she did the typing.

She looked across at the dresser top, where a haphazard pile of papers had unsteadily accreted, like a home-made ziggurat. Last month it had been hedgehogs. There were few parts of the house, few drawers, few cupboards, few shelves, where married life had not at some time been shared with something sick, something breeding, something dying. Something baffling. There had been – and her memory majored in creatures short on domestic qualities – a bat period, a newt period, a snake period, a spider period, a stickleback period, a grasshopper period, and, in earlier days, many an unidentified object period. Though she insisted that any contents of a turd be examined in the shed.

Still grasping her toast and gooseberry jam, Audrey tugged at one or two sample sheets, written as so often in an anarchic hand with knowledge overflowing the margins.

'And what will I be learning about this time, my love?'

'Oh, the life of a polecat … red wood-ants … plant pathology … decline of the crayfish … micro-moth records … bat legislation … all good sexy stuff.'

'I think cliff-hanging's the word.'

She fussed about her, prey to all the preparatory tics of a typist, organising *A* piles and *B* piles and a phial of correcting fluid. She pulled the typewriter nearer, the chair further, the tea safer. He meanwhile moved – with reference works – to his deadbeat armchair beside the Aga, a comfort zone of coagulated stuffing and stain-hiding covers. She eased down the little-used lever that engaged the keys that cut her stencils; he flipped open the A4 pad that received the thoughts that engaged his mind. And their work began. If this for her was tedium, it was tedium transformed by the joy of joint endeavour. And by way of return, he framed her paintings, chivvied their friends to her exhibitions.

They had met on a riverbank under a bridge, humpback, stone, eighteenth century, a scene whose aesthetic was Aphrodite's design for romantic encounters, a hidden place with shade where lovers could be launched. He had been searching for otter spraints, she had been sketching the bulrushes. It had rained. They had talked. The proof of otters was left to another day (as was art).

She sat and steadily banged away, for stencils needed banging, whilst he sat opposite and softly, deftly, put his account of local birdlife down on paper. Another shovel of smokeless anthracite was emptied into the Aga. Outside, the rain that had grounded the woodlark poured without pausing.

From time to time, as she typed up 'Botanical Highlights', she would ask for clarification, for insight into the finer points of taxonomic revision. But her questions on such arcana as *many-seeded goosefoot* left them each unenlightened. Nor could he add much to the news of a rare *tuberous pea* found on a disused railway line.

And when, straight-faced, she said, 'Well, I see *hoary mustard* is an established alien,' they both succumbed to laughter. But still she kept on typing, making the best of the poor morning light.

In his turn he liked to try out his phrasing on her. His description of *a liquid, flute-like descending song* went down well. But as he checked his bird bibles he grew quieter, serious almost.

'I think our little friend *Lullula arborea* is a bit of a find. Not often seen in Wales, let alone the valley.'

'Perhaps no one ever bothers to mention her,' said Audrey. 'Being unobtrusive.'

'Not in song, though. Not in song. Thought by some to be a singer second only to the nightingale. *Lu-lu-lu. Toolooeet.* Quite the dumpy little diva.'

'So how come she's visiting us?'

'A good question. Might be down to Gareth's neglect of his land ...? Letting it run wild, and grow long?'

'Wilder and longer since you've locked him up!'

'Yes.' A look of concern crossed Gwyn's face. '... yes. I suppose so.' This was a law he had rarely thought about, the law of unintended consequences. Consequences to his benefit. As he thought about it, he started to doodle at the foot of his article, and an outline emerged of a bat-like bird with too short a tail and blunt-ended wings.

'Right. It's cranking-time!' Audrey stood up, pulled out her first finished stencil. 'Who wants to start?'

'You?' suggested Gwyn, but his attempt at charm collapsed into a giggle. 'OK. Me.' And he set off to the bedroom.

The Roneo Gestetner was the closest the couple had ever come to a marriage-breaker. Dirty and noisy and smelly, its ink lingering like industrial pollution, this ancient hand-cranked duplicator was key to *The Abernantian Naturalists*. But the cottage lacked a study. So the day Gwyn came home with his second-hand bargain, to better spread word of his birds, it had no nook to go in. And with half the house a nature refuge, the loss of the front room to an office was not a popular proposal. Audrey never actually said 'It's me or your Roneo', but for several days it got no further than their porch. Only his promise to spend more time upon the human race, and occasionally, say, go socialising, had won the machine a right of entry.

And now the thing stood at the end of their bed. With its use restricted to the hours of daylight.

Gwyn padded across the bedroom in his socks, taking care not to crumple the 'Botanical Highlights'. A methodical man, he found satisfaction in these manual tasks, in the physical act of printing. Cautiously, precisely, he hooked the stencil to the inked-up drum; loaded on the waiting paper; checked the simple settings; and then started to crank, the handle rotating stiffly round and round. And as he cranked, he let his mind go blank, choosing to hear not the dullness of repetition but the mesmerism of rhythm. It was a rare indulgence: his eyes never left the hand-printed pages as they leapt into life and lay ready for reading, primped in a pile that was steadily swelling. All awaiting the moment when they would be scattered by hand across the county.

If feeling bold, if he had what passed for a scoop, he would run off up to six hundred copies. Copies which he and Audrey would later line up beside a specially laid fire in the front room; and here, wine to hand, they would staple the pages together till long into the night. This was not even local journalism, this was micro-journalism, each issue fitting into barely half the boot of his old banger. Yet the smallness of the scale was what afforded him such pleasure, and sometimes a sense of power. The hours and days of little-seen, little-known work had almost the feel of an undercover operation, and gave him the delicious sensation of being subversive.

As though he were producing a samizdat for secret nature-lovers.

Chapter 15

Griff and Barbara Griffiths led separate lives in the evening. Sgt. Griffiths spent the time in the parlour, lying back on the sofa and listening to his LP collection of male-voice choirs while he polished his boots and read back-numbers of the *Reader's Digest*. Barbara spent the time in the shed.

It was already dark by the end of dinner, by the end of the chicken liver on toast and the steak-and-kidney pudding and the crumble and the cream and the cheese and the digestives. Barbara squeezed into a big bright baby-pink housecoat, took a chunky torch from the drawer, and made her way through the beds of dahlias to the bottom of the garden. Here the night scent of Nicotiana fought for supremacy of the air with the invisible shroud of stale sweat that was Barbara's constant companion.

It was a large garden shed, with an outside lamp that leapt into life on the approach of her sizeable presence. She was briefly floodlit like an escapee from a Stalag, faced with a vaulting home-run across a dozen suburban fences. But she stood unfazed on the shed's little private patio and fiddled the key into the padlock, a trigger for the noise of muffled bedlam.

Beyond the well-oiled wooden door was a boudoir world of shocking pink.

The planks, outside dosed with dark creosote, were inside daubed with a Danny La Rue shade of red; a cavalcade of pink light bulbs cast a glamorous glow in the mirrors above the gleaming white bench that ran the length of the shed; a rocking-chair stood in the corner, a shell-pink woollen shawl softening its wood; and scattered throughout this roseate retreat was an infant's army of cuddly toys, of salmon-pink bears and button-eyed bunnies.

And in wire cages upon the concrete floor there yapped and yelped six shiny-coated Cavalier King Charles spaniels.

'Aaah, my *ba*-bies,' big Barbara gurgled, her voice now that of some secret inner child, boarded up deep inside her body.

From the pink pocket of her pink housecoat she pulled out a titbit purse and extracted a packet of something known as Schnackos. Then she bent right down, her beneficence making her breathless, and let the contents be licked ecstatically from her fingers. To judge by her murmurings, the ecstasy was mutual.

Some Freudians would have put it down to the absence of children. The Marriage Guidance Council would have put it down to the presence of her husband. Barbara Griffiths was too good-natured to explain it by anything but a love of doggies. Though why she should have chosen a breed with a fatal heart-valve condition, degenerative knee-joints, dysplastic hip-tissue, congenital deafness, breathing difficulties, bulging eyes, and a brain disorder that caused the dog to chase imaginary flies, was an altogether more puzzling matter. (History does not tell which of these attributes were also true of King Charles II.) The breed was, she had read, the ultimate in lapdogs, so perhaps she was influenced by having a lot of lap.

All snacked out, Barbara stood up and went over to her pink-lit bench, better befitting the dressing room of a drag artist and bedecked by a multicoloured miscellany of rosettes. She opened up her grooming box, a cantilevered Tardis of dog aids, and began the ritual laying-out of the items within. A bomb-disposal unit could not have been more reverent.

One grooming glove, one grooming brush, one flicker brush, one slicker brush, one porcupine-bristle brush; one medium-tooth comb, one dematting comb, one flea comb; one clipper kit; one aerosol of mousse. Laid in lines. Good hair, dead hair, dirty hair, tangled hair, windswept hair, Barbara was primed.

The hair of the Cavalier King Charles spaniel has sidestepped evolution, unless the dog's Darwinian end is to be a road-sweeper. Long and flowing and silky, the coat drags along the ground collecting dust and debris. As with Victorian ladies, the dog is too well-bred to show an ankle and it moves like an energetic millipede, the means of its locomotion a mystery. The breed's unorthodox design helps explain why, in the days before pet shops, its specialised selling-point had been as a fashionable foot-warmer.

Had her hobby not come with a shed, Barbara's love of dogs might have been more muted. Only in the shed could the pinkness of her personality be unfettered. Only in the shed could she do as her heart desired. Only in the shed could she be loved and well licked. Yet the shed was also a launch pad, propelling her into a public arena where the party tricks of her protégés – trotting, say, in a triangle – could bring a modest spotlight to bear on her existence.

And tonight was the turn of Esmerelda to be titivated, to be fluffed and flossed for Showtime, to be put in the running for a red rosette.

Barbara went over to the cage where she yapped. Her dogs were sensitive and yapped for many reasons: because it was night, because it was day; because they were excited, because they were bored; because they were scared, because they were happy; and because they were born that way. She lifted Esmerelda out of her cage up on to the bench and handed her some home-made liver-cake as a pacifier. It was two days since her bath, in nothing but the safest and softest of shampoos; a full day since removal of her drying-coat, a stylish canine camisole with nappy features; and now was the time to take off her snood.

For, alas, the dog's design faults were not limited to its legs – it also had ill-thought-out ears, dangly ears that dunked in all it drank. Just a sip of water and both the ears turned stringy and straggly, damning the dog in the eyes of the judges (a species much shocked by faulty hair). And thus came the snood, the wraparound earwear and all-purpose protector for any dog with ambition ... albeit with the look of a displaced diaper. Barbara had chosen tartan, with elasticated ribbing, and Esmerelda wore it with a mixture of pride and perplexity. (And was perhaps glad she had been spared the snood with the glitzy pink starburst.)

Barbara placed the dog upon a cerise cushion and set to work with the combs and the brushes, singing as she worked up the sheen that is the *sine qua non* of a contender.

Here, in this shed, she had made herself queen of a girlish world; queen because she was allowed no dominion by her husband, a girlish world because she had known little pleasure as an adult. This was her social redoubt. Her choice of companions guaranteed noisy affection, her coming and going greeted by frenzy. For Barbara, this was her time to be tactile, to whisper her gooey endearments. And perhaps Barbara also sensed some buried bond, formed because neither she nor her spaniels were quite the shape that God intended.

With the last errant hair rounded up and realigned, she held Esmerelda's snub-nosed head in her hands and gave its eager tongue full access rights to her face. Then, these daily devotions done, Barbara dug down to the lower layers of her grooming box, seeking the subtler tricks that make a bitch beautiful. Keeping Esmerelda quiet by cooing, she moussed her droopy ears and powdered her weepy eyes and trimmed her too-tufty toes. No dog part was left untouched.

After which, for her finale, Barbara pulled out a big pink hairdryer.

She fine-tuned its temperature, she moderated its blow-speed, she stood the waiting dog side-on. Like a master chef delicately inflating a soufflé, she set about breathing life and bounce and body into each inch of the brown-and-white coat – a coat given added silk by a diet boosted with butter-pats. From pomaded bottom to snuffling nose Barbara huffed and puffed on any flattened hairs and coaxed them all to rise and curl and shine, the hairdryer getting ever hotter in her hand.

It was near midnight before she felt the transformation from dog to god was complete, bar the sixteen toenails to be clipped and manicured in the hour before the judging. She pulled the plug from its socket and told her Esmerelda that she had now been made perfect, now truly had a body fit for a king. Then, to provide her with the proof, Barbara turned around the dog-god's cushion and aimed her goggle-eyed face toward the mirrors.

And when Esmerelda gazed upon her newly created image she wagged her coiffured tail with a great doggy glee. And yapped.

Barbara lifted up her baby with the tenderest of care and carried her over to the shawl-covered chair. And here, with

Esmerelda *immaculata* wheezing on her lap, a very content Mrs Griffiths was soon lying back, eyes closed, in pinkest heaven – gently rocking, softly singing, and utterly immune to the shed's transcendent odour of urine.

Chapter 16

Dafydd Davis, ex-postman to the valley, stood in the high street, hesitating.

Already 11 a.m., and he had learnt of no family feuds, had been told no rumours of gypsies, had been shown no fresh surgical scars, had rescued no one's cat, had been given the name of no one eloping or rustling, had been apprised of no sheep with scab, had been offered no tea with a tot of rum, had seen no dirty photos nor plans for barn conversions, had heard of no rogue dogs shot, had been advised of no hedges in need of repair, had come across no dead bodies dangling.

It had been a quiet morning, as was the fate of the unemployed.

Two years on, and the memory of his sacking still burned deep, his resentment at falling victim to tyrannous time-management still betraying a martyr's mental weals.

Dafydd Davis, ex-delivery man for Interflora, stood in the high street, hesitating.

Nearly midday, and he had come across no hint of hanky-panky in the sticks, had read no adulterous notelet from a lover, had sniffed out no floral-scented signs of dangerous liaising, had found no clues to the practitioners of same-sex sordidness.

It had been a dull morning, as was the fate of the redundant.

Months on, and the memory of his dismissal – for lift-giving beyond the call of duty – still rankled; a P45 from a woman went against the grain of nature.

It used to be his habit to join the local journalist, Clydog, and the local businessman, Hubert, for a weekly in-depth gossip, but Dafydd could no longer pull his weight in the matter of scandal, and currently gave their company a miss. He was less self-denying in visits to public houses.

Even with a job, even with no drink, Dafydd lacked allure. Lost in the no-woman's-land of the unmarried mid-forties, he bore the additional cross of ginger stubble. His one useful gift had been that he knew things, other people's things, and he distributed that knowledge like neighbourhood manna. Gossip is for some a tool, a way, a devious way, to be a player, and to toy with power. But for Dafydd, gossip filled a gap where his character should be, and it gave him personality by proxy. He rarely spoke of his own doings – for he did little, in or out of his council flat – but peopled a personal void with the lives and times of others. And now others were few.

This had left his social standing on the slide. From the post of postman (a venerable brand in a rural land) to a bringer of fast flowers, from the deep-red livery of the Royal Mail to the poncy pink van of Forget-Me-Nots, his career path had been an all too public downhill journey. And now he travelled incognito, no paid purpose to his miles.

Dafydd Davis, a man in need of a job, stood in the high street, hesitating. Under his arm was folded the *Mid-Walian*, the time-warp paper of these parts, and under 'sits vac' two circles in black had been drawn.

Then, as a town clock struck twelve, he turned out of sight down an alley, following a flickering arrow that offered the prospect of pizza.

Chapter 17

The letter skidded under the door and along the floor until it hit the pile of jagged toe-clippings.

Richie gazed down at it between farts, doubtful it was addressed to him as he could not read, nor indeed had friends who could write. Reading and writing began above the rank of corporal. He also had no friends, but chose not to dwell upon that. He preferred to dwell upon the fact that he now had no wife, that even Lola the stripper, once his lady friend, had left him. He said it was because his weight had gone to eighteen stone, but the constant boozing and the whacks he gave women were also to blame, and of this he was in denial. He ate another fistful of crisps.

On the bunk below him, just to the left of the three dozen cut-price crisp packets, his cellmate stretched down for his letter. It had already been formally opened, its brief contents assessed and approved and replaced.

Gareth stared at the envelope and hoped for a moment of silence, a hope that was, as usual, in vain.

'He had no right not to give me that chicken leg. Fifteen minutes, I'd queued up. I was entitled.'

Gareth had not received a letter till now, had not expected a letter, yet felt curiously detached from its contents. Three months into his stretch, he felt curiously detached from life. What he was most interested in, what he most missed but could have so little of, was sky.

'OK, I called him a tosser. But he was a tosser. A useless fucking tosser.'

Miles of sky.

'But that don't mean he can decide who eats and who don't.'

Sky that told him something of the seasons. Out beyond, the harvest would surely be gathered in, bagged up in black along the river, as though waiting for a dustcart. Rooks would be hopping through the stubble, greedy and gawky, always a cash crop for local men with guns. Which would send the rabbits running, no longer having hay to lie low in. The envelope was handwritten, which puzzled him. His life had only ever intersected with typewritten letters, dull and official and sent to everyone.

'It's an injustice. A blatant injustice. I'm entitled to a chicken leg, same as the next bloke.'

And rain. If the authorities were to grant him one request, one little wish to make the days more user-friendly, he would have asked for rain. The pleasurable companionship of rain.

Gareth lay on his bunk and stared blankly at the handwriting, as if unable to proceed until it were identified.

'Power's gone to his head. Gets given a job in the kitchen and thinks he's Pope.'

Gingerly Gareth pulled out the single sheet of notepaper, white. The address was not immediately familiar. He wondered what he would do if it were Moira asking for forgiveness. Asking if they might start over again. Begging even. He tried to imagine her on bended knee. The bed above reverberated to a belch.

Gareth held the paper at arm's length, attempting to catch the limited light of the urban day outside. This made visible the scrawled name *Nico*. And the implausible offer of his warm regards.

'Fifteen minutes in that queue, I was. Starving hungry. I'm within my rights to slag him off. Man's a lazy arsehole.'

Instinct told Gareth it was not good news. Nico was a stranger to the epistolary form. He would not waste ink on chat.

Reluctant at first to read, reluctant to be party to unsettling thoughts, Gareth raised his eyes from the paper and gazed across the cell. But in his line of vision were the shaven pubes of an exotic dancer damaged by darts, and this was a sight he found disturbing, not being a man of the world.

'I've always liked chicken, ever since I was a kid.'

Gareth went back to his letter, relieved to find it short. And to guide him through its few brief paras, Nico had gone big on underlining. But he had not underlined words, he had underlined figures. And this was how Gareth learnt the sad news that he now was a sheep farmer without his flock.

Nor was it a healthy, happy flock which had ended up at market. To have a shepherd in the slammer is rarely recommended by vets and quickly noticed by parasites, both inside the body and out. And the effect of neglect is a loss of cash per kilo. As Nico, ever the silent witness in the shadows of a crowd, had taken delight in noting.

'Yeah, I'm going to make a complaint. A formal complaint.'

Gareth too could do the sums. He too could see the adding up had fewer noughts than was nice. Nico's earlier performance as Cassandra was now shown to have some prescience. The future of Gareth's farmland was indeed looking troubled, for how could he afford to restock?

But Nico, of course, was on hand as a saviour, as he modestly explained. His offer to buy, and thus kindly stem ruin, was made to sound like charity. He wrote of cash, he wrote of favours, he left a honeyed trail.

Far from the comfort of his fields, Gareth found himself in a quandary. Never astute with people, rarely astute with money, and generally at a loss with life, he felt in need of advice.

The big bloated face of his cellmate, fragments of bacon-flavoured crisp on his chin and cheek, swung into view from above.

'You do reading,' declared his new friend Richie. 'I want you to write a letter to the Governor. About my chicken leg.'

Chapter 18

'Fuck off!' shouted Marjorie Whitelaw to her hens.

As ever, the dozen Buff Orpingtons did little to lessen their noise, and Mrs Whitelaw went back to correcting the excessive use of the colon in the account of the Treaty of Utrecht. It was not her period, the early 1700s, and she needed to concentrate; the author's orthography and his quixotic grammar scarcely made her proofing-rate profitable.

Condensation coated the caravan windows, the fug made toxic by four hours of non-stop nicotine. Percolating coffee, out of an exotic packet, was the smell that arrived second. And a sense of damp, a hint of wet washing, hit the nostrils last. Marjorie Whitelaw lay, or rather, she reclined – with some panache, thanks to the slutty luxury of a quilted dressing gown – upon a boxy built-in sofa, her desirable upper body raised high on scatter cushions with flamboyant yet stylish covers.

She had been working since breakfast, apart from a walk to the phone box, and her brain was on the wane when it came to religious wars. She would like to have gone into the lounge; she would like to have had a lounge to go into. Occasionally, the caravan would quiver on its breeze blocks, tugged and pushed by a gust of wind that needed no chimney for its howl to be heard. Summer seemed to be ending early, the season of Calor gas already here, and hissing.

Once more, Marjorie tried to focus on the Dukes of Anjou and Savoy.

Cluck, cluck!

'Fuck off!'

Knock, knock!

She looked up at the curtained-off door, put her pages aside on the fold-down Formica table, and unsmeared a window. Like the early Roman geese before them, her free-range hens had been warning of invaders. But this time it was a man with a moped. On its pannier hung a sign saying *Barri Bertolucci*, and it stood resting against the derelict VW Beetle that served as her hen shed, in a challenging canary yellow. The moped-rider stood waiting on her breeze-block doorstep, hidden by a helmet, holding out a pizza.

'Your Fiorentina, madam.'

'My Fior –' Marjorie looked at the man more closely. '... Dafydd?'

Reluctantly, Dafydd removed his space-age headgear. 'Morning, Mrs Whitelaw.'

'Probationary week,' Dafydd replied, shifting uneasily on his section of sofa. 'To prove I have the right pizza attitude.'

She probed no further, having a divorcee's sensitivity to decline and fall.

He glanced around the multi-purpose room while the fresh coffee bubbled, as if checking for signs of change. 'Last time we talked, it was a suicide.'

'That's right, yes!' she exclaimed with enthusiasm. 'From a beam!'

The pair had history, all of it postal. Marjorie Whitelaw appreciated a good tale, told over the long slow delivery of a letter. And she told a good tale back, knowing the power of detail. It came, she said, from her teaching of the constitution.

'Much up now?' he asked, no longer the lead gossip.

'Salman Rushdie, so I heard. In hiding up the valley.'

'Never ...!'

'Bit of a first, eh?'

'What, you mean ... *the* Salman Rushdie?'

'Lot of trouble for a look-alike to go to.'

'True. But you've not seen him yourself yet?'

'Apparently goes in that pub on the moors. Old Dolly Price's place. The Wheatsheaf. Sits on his own by the chimney breast. Not much of a one for a chat, it seems.'

'No ... no, I guess a fatwa does that to you. Is he looking well?'

'As far as I know.'

'Not on another of those novels, is he?'

'Couldn't say. I think she's trying to preserve his privacy.'

'Fair enough, I suppose. You don't want him blown up, not in your own pub.'

'No. And business is very slow in that place, especially come the winter.'

Dafydd sighed longingly. 'Salman Rushdie, eh? Here! Who'd have believed it …! We'd better watch out for Arabs next … Yes, that's what I miss about the Post Office, keeping my finger on the pulse.' And, though he did not say it, being first to feed the grapevine.

Marjorie poured him a coffee, which came in a small poky cup. He never understood why this should be, but assumed it had something to do with class. She was of that class which always stayed cheerful in public, even when under mortar attack. She kept animals for the hell of it (including once a llama), she had been known to swim in the Nant, and she wrote on envelopes with a fountain pen. And never allowed her frizzed auburn hair to go lank, a detail that somehow stayed with him.

'And,' Marjorie announced, 'the village school has been sold again.'

'She was always flaky, that aromatherapist.'

'Been bought by a consortium of Buddhists.'

'Well …! We've not had any of those before.'

'Or by a heavy metal band from Swansea.'

'Eh …?'

'Or by a sect of Satanists. Depends whose rumour you believe.'

Marjorie laughed, a very vigorous laugh for a woman, which spoke well of her chest. Hearing her news took Dafydd back to his glory days: he wondered which rumour *he* would have decided to spread. Perhaps all three, as he was a man who liked to tailor his intel to his audience. But any possibility of rape and pillage was a certain favourite, advancing faster up the valley than a horse at full gallop.

'Oh, and I may have to be moving on again,' she added.

'Moving on? Where to?'

'To pastures new. Literally. I may need a change of field soon.'

'Why?'

'Well, if Gareth sells the land …' Marjorie smiled, hands held in the hapless position. 'Another rumour.'

'Yes, this one I've heard,' replied Dafydd, though taking little pleasure in the titbit. Or what it might mean for her. 'That'd be sad.'

After all his years of first and second post, he could fill in the dots of both these people's life stories (and, indeed, the aromatherapist's). Happy endings were rare.

He had first delivered mail to Mrs Whitelaw in the days when she had a house. And a husband.

Hers had been one of the better scandals, from a storyteller's perspective.

Her executive husband, her second, had gone to art classes, in Llanbedr village hall, claiming an interest in still life. Regrettably, no fruit were involved. His subject matter was the sort of life form that was still breathing, panting even. And, after being depicted, she had taken to moving about, and opening her legs in the boiler room. Until Week 6 … when the pair were discovered, in an advanced pose *à deux*, by Dafydd's sister-in-law's brother, the caretaker, who then offered him copyright on the story.

These were to be high-profile events and soon destined to shape council strategy on all village-hall usage. The Nant Valley emphasis on sticky coloured tape and esoteric sport was not just a health initiative but a moral and municipal backlash against the dangers of art, especially where the use of drawing charcoal was concerned. The thought of farmers and the female form was a tinder-box best not lit. And the WI had occupied the vacuum with a speed which was shameless.

A brief silence had now ensued, which Marjorie broke.

'You knew Gareth quite well, didn't you?'

'Not a lot to know.'

'No, guess not – but so much drama from so dull a source!'

'Yeah, hard to credit he could cost you your home – like he cost me my job.'

'He did that? How come?'

'Because I used to give him lifts when I found him wandering the lanes.'

'Oh, I am sorry. That's very unfair!'

He was touched by her sympathy. He had rarely had sympathy from an attractive woman. Or indeed anything from an attractive woman.

'Was that when you were in the flower business?'

'Er, yes, that's right.' He wondered whether her dressing gown was next to bare flesh. Or next to something diaphanous, a word he had learned from girlie magazines.

'Enjoyable job?'

'Good training for blackmail!' he quipped, in a bid to make himself interesting. But he knew a supply teacher was out of his league, whatever her subject.

Marjorie grinned. 'Lot of people sending flowers they shouldn't?'

Dafydd grinned back. 'And a lot of people writing things they shouldn't.'

'Ah, the joy of secrets! You should live in Surrey.'

The allusion was lost on him. But the reference to her secrets, and in so languorous a tenor, had accidentally activated a long-buried memory. It was a memory that caused the ex-postie to ponder, and reassess his chances as a charmer.

But he knew he would need to proceed with subtlety, a feature of his character yet to see the light of any day.

'Surrey?'

'Pony Clubs and privet. Secret home of Nazis.'

'Well, I never knew that!'

'Oh yes. They only do the salute in the privacy of their own homes. Between consenting adults. In fact, in the bigger homes – the Tudor executive housing – they have a special saluting room, just to keep the arm in practice in case there's a Hitler coup on the council. So my father always said.'

'*My* father only warned me about nits.' This got a laugh, and he realised he had made a joke. 'At least, I think that's what he said.'

'Well,' replied Marjorie, 'if it makes you scratch your head, it's not Nazis … probably.'

As she leant back laughing, he saw a bit of leg. He quickly averted his gaze, though there was little choice of vistas in this cramped and steamy space. It was a leg which made Dafydd wish he was absolutely sure of the salacious secret he had once heard. It was Eryl who had told him the story, had claimed it was true, had insisted it was first-hand. But Eryl was not a witness to die for.

'And if it wasn't retired storm troopers, it was stockbrokers. Fat and flatulent, and dead from greed by fifty. And if it wasn't stockbrokers, it was trophy wives, everything plastic including the brain. All living in the sort of yummy des res where estate agents circled the block on the hour. Yes, childhood in Surrey definitely lacked the fairy-tale quality. Even Santa came bearing bonds, or some tax-avoiding venture.'

(Dafydd struggled with his end of the conversation, life having given him few insights into Surrey, or indeed Kent.)

'Niceness, that's what I hate. Always a dead giveaway for something venal and nasty. And God were those people nice!'

'... oh,' said Dafydd, now feeling uncertain. '... I quite like niceness.'

At times he found it hard to tune to her wavelength, and tricky to make sense of her sentiments, which were not commonly heard in the valley. Here, truisms were handed down from generation to generation, not to be messed about with by wayward thought. But Marjorie Whitelaw's views were unpredictable, reducing the rules of discourse to a lottery. And yet she was always welcoming, often laughing, even whilst spraying spleen in all directions. Such perversity of character made Eryl's tale not seem too tall.

'Of course, you won't have been to a private girls' school,' she said, still on a roll. 'Where the pretend curriculum is niceness. And the secret school motto is "How to be a snob when you've got no brains". Oh, if I'd only known then the three ways that make parents rich enough to be posh – drugs, guns and porn! Because I could have certainly stirred things up in class!'

Stirrers were not at all Dafydd's type, but he had seen her feed the chickens in a T-shirt and shorts. Which in turn had fed his fantasies. Fantasies now further fuelled by another buried memory: the fact he had once seen the bank manager – he of marital mayhem and memorialised genitals – discreetly dropping by. As the man was a lech who granted no-interest loans to ladies in exchange for carnal collateral, this tended to give credence to Eryl's claims … and Dafydd began to sense his lust for Marjorie might not need to languish.

'I only went to the village school,' he responded. 'My main memory is the double desks!'

He let the innuendo dangle, hoping their chat might veer toward smut.

It was a strategy that needed more work.

Mrs Whitelaw rose and fiddled with her baby oven, ready to reheat her lunch.

'I guess there's no blackmailing to be done over who orders pizza!' she said, laughing again. 'Hardly a compromising act, going big on pepperoni.'

'True,' he replied, hiding his disappointment on the dirty-talk front.

His coffee (small) was finished. Very soon it would be time to leave. Perhaps he should just come straight out with it. Perhaps he should just simply say, 'I hear you do a bit of prostitution on the side.' And see what reaction he got. Though he did grasp that might be high risk. If it were not true. Or indeed if it were true. Eryl had said – and this was a couple of years ago now – that a carful of soldiers had stopped by the church and asked him directions to 'a tart in a caravan'. But perhaps there were other tarts in other caravans? Though surely as an ex-postman he would know them? And it was unlikely there could be two called Marjorie. In the same country lane. It was not like she was a Fiona.

Or perhaps he could blackmail her. Perhaps he could promise not to tell her secret to anyone – if he got the fuck for free … And perhaps she would smack him in the mouth.

And then again, Eryl – who was a bitter man – could be winding him up.

'Thank you for the coffee,' said Dafydd, placing his cup in the tiny sink and retrieving his bulbous black headwear.

'Any time. You're always welcome.'

The unworldly Dafydd hesitated. Was this a standard farewell? Or was it an innuendo? … was this code for trade? And, if so, what move should he make? What money should he offer?

'... that's very kind ... I wondered if perhaps you'd –'

'Did you hear that rich bastard is opening his pub again?' she asked, casually closing with yet another nugget of gossip.

'Er, yes. Yes, I heard that.'

He had done more than hear that. He had replied to his advert for a barman.

As yet he had received no reply. On this he made no comment.

He stood and looked at Marjorie, wanting to find a memorable way to leave, or perhaps to stay.

'Well, er ...' He wondered again what would be best to say, what would seem warm though non-committal, intimate though anodyne. 'Well, watch out for Arabs.'

And, that said, he went back to his moped.

Chapter 19

Stéfan edged to the top of the ladder and stared unhappily at his eyebrows. Balkan bushy and inky black, they had leached down his cheeks, converting his wide pink smile – too wide, too pink, too smiley – into a smeared and fissured toothpaste ad, circa 1955. The dark tones of his blazer and trousers, on legs spread louchely apart, had gone blotched and streaky. The bottle of bubbly in his hand, the cocky totem of a bon viveur, had grown grungy from the ravages of the rain. And he creaked as he swung in the breeze.

Stéfan pressed his lower limbs against the metal rungs, stretched across, and gingerly unhooked his full-length portrait. He came from a land where pictures of the leader were desiderata for every decor, which was why he hung from a shaky hook above the pub's porch, supplanting the more familiar dragon. And why – upon purchase of the place – he had decided that he would, in the tradition of kings, rename it The Stéfan Arms. Words whose paint had now run, and mimicked the font of Gothic horror.

Stéfan favoured fiefdoms and, a year or so ago, had thought a pub with his name was an ideal start. But the latest market research, in the shape of reported sniggers, had suggested he was seen as a sort of joke gentry. A squire that made one squirm.

'Out with the new and in with the old,' Stéfan muttered, as he and his Dorian Gray double slithered down to the ground.

'What?' snapped Eryl, staggering by with a table on his back.

Eryl was tired of humping tables out of the pub and on to a hire van, all to unmake a makeover. This was not, he reckoned, part of his remit. Worse, these were heavy tables – proper wood, and polished, the sort of tables that put up the cost of eating. Up to a level where no one came. And now they were deep in dust, as was the rest of the pub's only bar, its drinkers but an embittered memory.

'And don't forget to give everything a good clean!' bawled Stéfan.

Cleaning was not his remit either, Eryl reckoned. But he decided, as usual, to shut up and bear a grudge.

'Oh and questions, I need questions!' the squire *manqué* demanded of the squire dispossessed. 'For the interview.'

'What, like "Can you pour a pint"?' retorted Eryl.

'You're the drunk,' said Stéfan. 'Thought that'd give you insights into the job spec.'

Fewer aspirant barmen had sent replies than expected, possibly deterred by the *Mid-Walian*'s lacklustre typesetters, who had told the world the pub was in need of a batman.

'Ask why they want to work for a psycho.' Eryl started back through the porch. 'That'll weed 'em out.'

Stéfan followed him into the pub, struggling to hold his sign-size image at arm's length for fear he might touch himself.

Everything electric was off, the small windows of the alehouse offering an anaemic wintry light even in full summer, and the air was dusty and musty. A long-abandoned, half-empty glass stuck to the stained bar, its beer boasting a growth that could well be the return of yeast, ready for a second go at the brewing process. A puddle of something nasty lay upon the polished flagstones, its cause anything from rain to an incontinent rat. And around them stood sets of ritzy dining chairs, mock-period, possibly Tudor, that had rarely felt a bottom.

'This buyer you've got,' said Stéfan, his speech tailored to the breath available, 'you sure he wants *all* the chairs?'

Eryl nodded as he stacked. He did not give details, he did not name names, just tried to make sure he did not look shifty.

Leaving size 10 footprints in the dust, Stéfan made his way behind the bar and fiddled with the fuse box. Then he opened the trapdoor to the cellar, liberating air that was stale and stuffy, and peered down into its depths.

'Nearly noon,' warned Eryl.

Stéfan ignored him and set off down the stone steps. Here the previous landlord used to hide (before the premises had been a failing restaurant, they had been a failing pub) in the hope that his drinkers would die from the wait. The old bar stools had been stored down these stairs and were now tinged green by the damp. Elsewhere, two boxes of dominoes lay open, sprinkled with enough mouse dirts to make a double six, and a bar-billiard table leaned, back legs broken, against the far wall. Some sort of skittle game, from the days when men were men and played silly games in the evening, had been scattered across the uneven concrete, its ancient rules hard to determine in the dust-encrusted 60-watt light.

'Out with the new, in with the old,' muttered Stéfan again, never shy to reuse an example of his wit. Even when alone.

He rested his storm-damaged features against the brickwork, his usual brutal brio a little lessened by what he saw around him.

Stéfan was not a natural for the service industry. He liked to make money wham! bam! and not be bothered by niceties. And customer relations was a mysterious art to a man who saw even friendship as a contact sport.

Being mine host of the valley was fine as far as it went, a role that meant a ready-made audience, and name recognition from men in their cups. But the beau monde would not drop by. No movers and shakers, only locals and hawkers. And the annual high note was a village-hall eisteddfod.

Even the prospect of new housing near by, of ABs in a landscaped ghetto, would merely supply him the salariat in suits, gifting only an entrée to golf-club soirées.

What Stéfan most wanted was instant social standing, nothing too precious, nothing too cultured, but a lot of back-slapping and booming bonhomie. Street cred in the country. Aristo-packed parties. And a row of *At Homes* on the mantelpiece.

And he thought he now knew the solution. Land. In these rural parts, he had decided, the clout of your calling card was measured by your acres. And his were lower league. He had parkland and more than one lake and a lodge and a walled garden and a river with recalcitrant fish, but he could walk his boundaries (not that he ever did) and be back well within the hour. He was not thinking Texas, with never-ending horizons and the threat of Indians, but land which went out of sight over a hill, with maybe a chance to get lost. Land which perhaps turned purple, and ran the risk of ramblers. Land where sheep might die of a lonesome heart in winter.

'You're wanted!' shouted Eryl from above. '*Now!*' he cried, enjoying a rare peremptoriness of tone.

Stéfan groaned and reached for the supplanted dragon.

His protracted reappearance through the trapdoor, dragon sign first, suggested a man struggling with a magic trick, a sight that brought bemusement to the waiting applicants. Who wisely did not follow Eryl's lead in laughing out loud, rarely recommended at a job interview. As Stéfan reached full height and looked about the bar, now emptied of all but a corner table's chairs, he was surprised to see four people waiting when he had expected just the one.

He had blue-pencilled several names – Daniel, on advice that he was a drunk; Gwynfor, on the rumour that he was a crook; Emrys, on the hunch that he was a prat; and, in the case of Dafydd, because he used to deliver Stéfan's letters late. The valley's gene pool had not been blessed with barmen. Nor, indeed, employers.

Stéfan looked more closely at the four men. They were vaguely familiar, in the way that local farmers often were: weather-beaten and worthy, old-fashioned and uncomplicated.

'And which of you is Mr Pritchard?' asked Stéfan.

'I am,' said the four brothers.

Chapter 20

They met on a bend. Any faster and they would have met in a hedge. Had they not been friends, they would have followed this up with a ruckus. The blame, though, was at no time in doubt. The single-track lane winding through the woods was punctuated by black smears of rubber, all of the same pattern, all from the same car. And everyone local recognised the spoor of what would have been a boy racer were he not within sight of his pension.

Each driver got out of their car, the near-crash a pleasing pretext for a chat.

Gwyn grinned ruefully as he and Rhys shook hands. 'On my way to see you,' he said. 'Sorry about that!'

The two men strolled over to a grass bank, and here they sat and relaxed, confident theirs would be the only cars of the morning. The noonday sun of late summer filtered through the leaves, and even a picnic would not have seemed out of order.

'It's been a while.'

'The family funeral, I guess.'

'Must be.'

'Nearly needed another one!' said Rhys, angling his head at the bend, but in good humour.

Gwyn smiled, imperceptibly letting the conversation pause while his ears scanned the trees for anomalous birdsong.

'I used to go go-karting with your granddad. Many years ago. So he's to blame for my bad habits.'

'That's a side of him I never knew. But then I guess I didn't know that much.'

'Used to take advantage of his telly. I would sneak out and watch all the Grands Prix with him.'

'You?'

'Me.'

Rhys looked surprised, which the older man did not reckon unreasonable.

Gwyn found his love of speed to be a passion that left him more uneasy with every year that passed. The statistics on road-kill had grown in thoroughness and authority, and what they now described was the Black Death of the animal kingdom. In his defence, Gwyn at least knew where the badger runs crossed the roads and where the barn owls dipped to scavenge, and here he would moderate his revs. But not all creatures were so avoidable and he drove in fear of a strike ... and of the possibility that Sgt. Griffiths would pass by. Smirking.

'But you're right,' responded Gwyn. 'Thomas was never one to waste his words. He and I must have spent a good many hours in near-silence, wandering about his woods – your woods.'

'I remember the bracken theory.'

'He wanted to create the model woodland. One-third new trees, one-third mature trees, one-third dead trees. But you need several lifetimes to do that. So we chivvied nature around the edges.'

'Still got Granddad's geese. Like lawnmowers with attitude, they are.'

'Some of them must be, what, pushing twenty?'

'I give good grain.'

'He reckoned you'd a flair for livestock.'

'Did he? Never told me.'

'Oh yes. Patient, he said.'

'Patient and poor. Livestock's no living.'

'Sadly not. So, what's an *Experiential Project*?'

'Oh, you've seen the sign?'

'Hard to miss. Not many capital letters on this lane.'

'It's Outward Bound for men in suits. You take a management theory and try to apply it to real life. Helps you get in touch with your inner barbarian.'

'Oh, I think I've read about this. Though not so much that it makes any sense.'

'It's fairly straightforward. In a bullshit sort of way. It's an Away Day but with acronyms, so that you don't feel you're skiving. Personally, I call it a chance for desk-drivers to bond in mud – but with an awareness of the managerial dynamics. And all done to boost their firm's profits.'

'And does it work?'

'Oh, that's not the point.'

'Oh.' Gwyn was of a different generation and baffled. 'But the countryside itself, how exactly does that help?'

'The *Profit Through Nature* bit?'

'Yes.'

'Makes for a sexy backdrop after the city. And clients like to crash around in the woods.'

'Is that good for the woods?'

'Means I get to keep them.'

'Ah, yes, I suppose it would pay well. I was thinking more of wildlife, like birds nesting.'

'Well, ideally, we'd like to get some extra land, rising up to the ridge. And spread the load. Be a good cause for the last of Granddad's dosh.'

'I see … have you heard anything go *Toolooeet* lately?'

Rhys thought. 'Can't say I have. Why?'

'Oh, no reason.'

'Anyway, enough of work and me, what was it you were coming by for?'

'Just to say hello, that's all,' he dissembled. 'See how you were settling in.'

'That's very kind of you. Yes, things are really working out well. In fact, I have to go soon. I've got eight sanitary engineers coming for assertiveness training. But it's great to see you again.'

'And you.'

'Who knows, perhaps one day the Trust itself might sign up for some group activities?'

'Oh, we're beyond hope!'

The two men stood up, regained the tarmac.

They walked unhurriedly back to where their cars nuzzled nose to nose and shook hands a second time.

'Love to Audrey.'

'Look after yourself.'

Gwyn reversed into a passing space and then, the road clear, he hit full revs and raced down the lane as if still in a go-kart.

Chapter 21

Nico had heard a rumour. Nico could hear rumours beyond the frequency on which the human ear operated. He could hear talk of a sweet deal from a thousand yards, news of a fire sale from a full mile. He could have detected an earth tremor in another country were there a profit to be made.

But this most recent of rumours had travelled a circuitous route, as if on a pre-Beeching line, and he had belatedly overheard it while buying pizza toppings. Had he not fancied extra buffalo mozzarella, a rare dietary whim for him, he would never have dropped into Hubert's health-food shop and the news would have passed him by. He did some spadework on its provenance, and it seemed to be about sixth-hand.

According to this woman called Harpur, who had been choosing some specialist chocolates for her cat, the owner of the flower shop (where she had earlier been shopping for recommended bushes that were evergreen) claimed he was told the news whilst making a delivery of peat-free compost to the suspended Vicar, who, he said, cycled a lot to ease his depression and had come across the part-time caretaker of the village hall having a surreptitious smoke and bursting to repeat what a member of the WI yoga class (briefly resting from her standing straddle, forward-bend pose) had heard from her dentist while her teeth were being whitened. And then the trail ran dry.

Although keen to confirm the key facts for himself, Nico was not free to leave his bric-à-brac shop in a back street.

The hire van was nearly an hour late. While he waited, Nico sat, somewhat incongruously amidst the agricultural cast-offs, upon a Queen Anne armchair with buttoned seat in antique green leather which he had acquired at an advantageous price from a widow preoccupied by recent death, and read up on second-hand pediments. Nico was not sure of correct procedure on how to asset-strip a museum, but suspected the prerequisite was a feckless councillor, and Abernant was spoilt for choice. Nights of frost and loose frieze would do his work, and deliver him a quality windfall.

A few generations back, Nico would have been a sheep rustler, an outcast lurking in mountain mist and luring gullible flocks to an early end as chump chops. He would have been illiterate, probably with scrumpy for wages. Today, such were the advances in social mobility, he could aspire to dispose of the town's top artefacts.

'Deal done!' cried Eryl, entering backside first. Two of the ritzy chairs were clutched to his chest.

'Out back,' said Nico, and wedged open the door.

He let Eryl make all the journeys to and fro. Both men were embittered but Eryl had fewer brains.

And today he was happy.

'Like a kipper,' bragged Eryl on his way in. 'Like a kipper,' bragged Eryl on his way out.

This was the first deal they had done together. It arose not from friendship but shared spite. Whose target was Stéfan.

'So – no problems?'

'Cover story swallowed.'

Eryl was righting the wrongs the world had done him, and his aim was money.

For Nico it was the deal, the buzz of being one up. And being one up on Stéfan was as good as two up. Nico was a great hater, and Stéfan was perfect for hating. With his glad-handing arrogance and his bombast, this pretend-patrician scored maximum points as a class enemy, a species that low-born Nico loathed. Nico had once stitched him up at auction, outbid him on his own mansion's archives, and still had not forgotten his outrage, nor his tantrum. Nothing was better than beating a man not to be bested. And using a sap – his own sap – to do it.

'He doesn't think I've got the IQ to outwit him!' scoffed Eryl, the last of the seating stashed. Feeling expansive in what he thought of as triumph, he looked around and chose to rest by lounging on a Dutch marquetry two-seater sofa.

Nico bridled at his presumption. Indeed, had Eryl stayed standing he would still have outlasted his welcome. Not that there was a welcome. Nico reserved his charm for buyers and sellers, to speed them to their role as victims. For him, the end and essence of business was power play. He was not a man who saw the point to friends.

'He'd no idea it's you,' continued Eryl matily. 'I just said I had a buyer. Said it was top dollar. And of course Stéfan knows fuck all about foreign furniture. Or furniture. And his would only look good in a brothel. So he'd believe any price I told him. And I told him ours.'

'Mine,' corrected Nico.

'Yours,' admitted Eryl.

Eryl wondered when he would get his cut of the scam. Wondered if he should ask when he would get it. Chose to say nothing on the matter. Which was unwise.

'So who is it you've got lined up?' he asked.

'A contact,' said Nico.

'Right,' said Eryl.

He did some more lounging.

Nico had sacked people for less. In fact, he had sacked six assistants in two years. Sometimes for idleness, sometimes for ugliness, sometimes for wanting their wages. Sometimes on a whim. He had moods.

'Not been squire's day,' reprised Eryl, coming close to pleasure. 'He's after a barman. Simple enough, you'd have thought. Honesty and a smile, hardly needs a packed CV. But then all the Pritchards turn up – Ben, Bryn, Brian and Brenig. Or Brian, Bryn, Brenig and Ben. Because they swapped their names around – an old party trick of theirs – so as to have a bit of fun. And they sure ran rings round him.'

Nico's eyes narrowed, a rare sign of interest.

'He kept trying to say he only wanted one barman. And they kept going on about the working schedules of the modern farm, not that theirs is modern. How they had to fit in with the milking rotas, and the after-dinner ploughing, and the hedging by moonlight, and the need to bottle-feed their lambs and babysit their mother. Everything except watching out for wolves. Of course, it's all bollocks. Their game plan is one to serve the beer and three to drink it – with no money changing hands!'

'So how'd it end?'

'He's now got four barmen! Coming and going all hours. Giving new meaning to a free house.'

Nico almost smiled.

And then he remembered that he had still to check the rumour that Gareth had been seen – freed, so it seemed, some two months ahead of time.

Chapter 22

The colonel always began his day with a run, weather permitting. He drew the line at actual rain, and sometimes at the threat of rain, and occasionally at heavy rain which had just finished, and he had also been known to balk at wind. But in principle he always began his day with a run.

Where many runners prepared by limbering up, Col. White prepared by ironing. There was little in life that he didn't iron, and white shorts were no exception. He used to claim, in jest, that the quality of their razor-back crease gave him an aerodynamic edge. And he liked to think (but kept this claim quieter) that his lower legs were set off in a way that might appeal to ladies. For similar reasons, he also ironed his underwear, though as yet there had been no opportunity for feedback, either in REME or retirement.

His was not a random run, not a wind-in-your-hair, great-to-be-alive run. Nor was it aimed at any of his endorphins, eager though they might be for release. It was more a blank-out-your-mind run, a fill-a-gap-in-the-day run. A stop-if-you-meet-anyone run.

The route he took was always the same, up one side of the Nant and down the other. The distance was 7.61 miles, according to the pedometer which hung from his belt like a back-up phallus. So far this month his average recorded time was 59 mins 46 secs, which included twelve stiles and was seasonally adjusted for September brambles. There was a Variant Section, more mud, more puff, more views, but he had not run there this year. Col. White was a man who greatly valued routine, describing it as roughage for the mind, and he always left on the last of the 9 a.m. pips.

He lived amidst the final dribbles of suburbia, in a built-by-numbers house which eschewed all claim to character, and from his bottle-glassed front door he had to start out down a crescent where a running man risked laughter. A right-of-way then led across a field where two lethargic horses awaited the clumsy nervous knees of Pony Club children. The grass was a dingy yellow, its strength sapped by a constant fear of developers.

And then he would reach the river.

Medium-fast but fordable by stepping-stones on the good days, the Nant was here the width of a fallen middle-aged tree. Its slew of rocks created an obstacle course for the current, and served, for fleeting splashy moments, as a base for bobbing dippers. And, in times of clear light, salmon could even be seen lying low in the pools. At first the grass path followed the bank, trodden smooth by dog-walkers from town and crushed by courting couples in search of alfresco sex.

But soon both riverbanks got much steeper, tamed only by plant life and trees with goat genes, and had to be bypassed by the path as it clawed up packed clay to follow the fields above. A bluebell walk in the spring, a badger track by night, its joy now was early autumn's turning leaves. And the wire fence alongside, source of solace for itchy sheep, was decorated by tufts of wool waving in the wind, like poor Welsh cousins of Tibetan prayer-flags for the dead.

Not that such things were ever noticed by the colonel. When running over rough terrain both eyes must be kept on the footholds ahead. Besides, he thought of this as cushy land, with none of the rewarding rigours of the hills. The farmers in the valley filled out their Barbours better, and had faces that went fleshy. Whereas on the uplands, midwinter was known to shrink-wrap the features, and harden the soul, and develop a sub-breed of ascetics.

The farmer here was close to town, and ruddy and jolly and drunk. He conformed to type and leant on posts, and made a welcome interlude for any runner. Or any walker. Or any other kind of passer-by.

But this farmer's greatest claim to fame was for being a man without principle. His fields were high profile because they lined the route into Abernant, a road which, come election-time, was the perfect spot for placard posters. Hammered in beyond the hedge, these made public his politics for more than half a mile. All subject, however, to one commercial condition – each time the canvassers came calling, he would sell his allegiance to the highest bidder. And thus the shrewd old man had, like a hyperactive Vicar of Bray, belonged to all known parties in the course of one day.

The path wound back down to the river, still wide enough to have islands – albeit long and narrow and prone to move about. Here in the holidays, barefooted children would picnic round fire-blackened stone circles and build brief-lived tree houses for resting pirates. Too small to farm, too fickle to tame, these strips of damp green were home to the oldest woodlands of the valley, their survival due only to the disregard of man.

Next came a sometimes squelchy stretch, the nearest mid-Wales got to mangrove swamp, and here the path had to make its way across a tangled web of tree limbs, of transversal trunks that had fallen in the fight to reach the light. Faced with dirt which clung, the white-clad colonel would come over all dainty, loath to be besmirched, and through here he moved at a very picky pace. This was not the type of path favoured by planners, not the type of amenity suited to signage – this was nature to make a bureaucrat despair.

But after these sodden scrublands (the sort of scrub he loved to clear, as colonel-in-chief of a conservation party) there came a serene water meadow, and his mph could be cranked up, as long as there were no Welsh Blacks to be spooked. These were the ageing commodore's lands, looked out upon from a Queen Anne house, where generations of gentry had gently declined. This was where they fished and died. This was where they set the valley standards, or did in the days before new and nasty money. This was where the true squire regnant held befuddled sway.

Here the river made a languid curve, allowed itself a sandbar, and only a man of very mean spirit would have been untempted by angling. Here, the colonel knew from memory, he was 3.62 miles from his start-point.

Ahead lay the waist-high remains of St Brynnach's, the graveyard washed clean of its headstones, the vault swept bare of its bones. The flood of three years ago would not be quickly forgotten. The bell tower had cracked, the nave had departed downstream, and centuries of worship were wiped from the record, all between a dusk and a dawn. Although no one had drowned, several had been reburied in unknown deeps and Christ had been relocated.

And it was as the colonel was cautiously crossing this unhappy holy ground, on the Friday of the week just gone, that he saw the figure standing on the humpback bridge. This was the bridge where the bats came snacking, the bridge where his run turned homeward.

The colonel had never seen the man before, but recognised him instantly. The special *Mid-Walian* supplement had captured him from every angle, showing him in multiple action shots and leaving no mad stare to the imagination.

He looked even runtier now and his hair was institutional, but there was no mistaking Gareth Richards. Celebrity shepherd.

Col. White instinctively glanced down at his stopwatch, but in that moment of memorising the time as 9.31 a.m. he caught his foot on a memorial plaque. He struggled to stay upright and keep his shorts clean, but his momentum kept him going and he toppled forward into a coffin-free grave, chipping his tooth upon a plank. By the time he had pulled himself out and reset his pedometer, Gareth was gone.

The colonel's response had been to run to the dentist. And tell his best friend the news.

Chapter 23

The discharge money had not been enough to make it back home, and the taxi had abandoned Gareth part-way up the valley. His parents had been reluctant to venture as far as the prison, his father having a working knowledge of just one traffic-light and a phobia of roundabouts ... and, were a psychiatrist allowed to probe for home truths, a dislike of their only son.

Gareth was in two minds about the last lap. He wanted time for long, slow breaths of the valley air, but also had the urge to avoid the eyes of all his neighbours. He paused briefly on the bridge, and gazed glumly down upon the water. Part of him wished it was deeper, deep enough to sweep him to the sea. At some moment – he was unsure when, unwilling to think of when – the water would close above his head and he would drift along in a dream. The change of state from life to death would thus be smooth and blurred and painless, no act of volition needed. He would go, literally, with the flow.

Seeing a stranger coming, running, he turned and hurried on up the hill. His breathlessness surprised him. He had never lived so long without hills. Exercise had been available for him, but in a bleak and grunting way, and in an airless gym. Gareth set no store by anything but walking outdoors, thus saw no sense to pull-ups and push-ups, press-ups and push-offs, and squats and hops and bar-bells and dumb-bells, all for worship of a body disfigured by tattoos. So he lay on his bunk and ate crisps ... and dreamed of an early release for good, if sullen, behaviour.

Like many men in cells before him, he had made his mind pretend he was home. Closing his eyes and ignoring the crunching, he had kept on winding and rewinding rural memories, always giving himself the director's cut. It felt to him a victory that he had a mental microfilm which no guard dog could sniff out.

He heard a car coming and branched off up a track, a sunken green lane whose neglected hedgerows had bolted into trees, offering erratic shade and a toothy profile. Only used now by local children, and the odd walker in the know, it had the sponginess of compost in progress. Once the lane used to go from A to B, but both these places had been wiped from the map of collective memory, part of the rural past that had no further value. But it went vaguely uphill, and it smelt as land should, and this was all that he asked.

Gareth had missed much of two seasons, an event unique in his life, and a disconcerting jump-cut in the year. He was not a great fan of autumn and its leaves, regarding it principally as the season of blocked gutters. And the sun of summer brought him out in blisters. What he always preferred was the new life that came with the spring, the start again of the cycle. His greatest regret was not seeing his lambs go to market, not following through on the work of the tup. Not being present at the births.

And now there were none of his animals left on his land, young or old, sick or healthy, fruitful or sterile. Nothing to give life even a modicum of meaning.

He tramped slowly up the boggy lane in the black shiny shoes he had bought for prison. He carried a small suitcase – also shiny – of unremarkable belongings, a suitcase that had never seen service for the purpose it was bought, away-day trips with his beloved. Where those trips would have gone to, what he and she would have done when they got there, were typical of the details that had defeated him.

To see his land again was to remember his dilemma, though dilemma implied choice, and he seemed only to have a choice of poison. He had not the vigour – or was it the stomach, or perhaps the heart? – to start anew, to rebuild the flocks of the family from scratch, to winnow the weak, to breed the strong, to do the daily grind. But for how long could he bear to grass-let his land?

From time to time the trees met overhead, their branches intertwining, and the morning light became softer, almost mellow. As Gareth trudged along beneath these golden-brown drapes, along what once was a thoroughfare for hay carts, he wished he could trudge for ever. The view ahead of him, of the deep mossy banks and the ancient arthritic hawthorns, was the same as the view behind him, a continuity almost mesmeric. Twenty minutes of steadily trudging, twenty minutes of old-fashioned flora seldom seen, twenty minutes of a vista that did not vary, and he felt the world around him was wrapped within a time warp. And, his plans uncertain, his plight best forgotten, he found some comfort in the delusion that he, like the lane, was on a journey back to the past.

Chapter 24

Stéfan was short of a theme for the orgy. His latest thought was something rural, maybe Welsh Transylvanian.

He put another coin in his 1960s fruit machine, a gaudy mechanical model, one of four that lined the opulent entrance hall, and pulled down on its handle. Like a chiropractor versed in manipulation, Stéfan applied variable pressure, teasing and toying with the one arm of the bandit. But even though he owned it, even though he fed it, even though he had saved it from the scrapyard, the thing still did not pay up, and so he kicked it, hard. Each of the machines showed signs of his footwear, curious conduct from a collector. Whilst reasonable that a punter be disgruntled in defeat, an owner has merely to unlock the brightly painted innards and that which is lost is refunded. But Stéfan required subservience from his machines, a loyalty and fealty for keeping them in happy working order. He had a similar attitude to women.

His mind had been on the details of the debauchery for some days. He wanted the quality and quantity of fornication to do justice to the Jacobean backdrop.

Stéfan gave up on the attractions of his opulent entrance hall and wandered into his opulent inner entrance hall. It was mid-morning, midweek, and he was bored. He was not a man who enjoyed his company, a feeling shared by most who knew him. And though his ego argued that twenty-eight rooms was commensurate to his squirely qualities, he had yet to silence a dissident whisper deep in the night that he was lord and master of a mausoleum.

He had more bedrooms than he had beds for. He had more rooms than he had names for: breakfast room, reception room, dining room, sitting room, lounge, library, games room, music room, study, and still he had rooms whose purpose was a mystery lost in history. He had rooms that it took several attempts to find. He even had rooms with rooms. To take a tour of his rooms – and guests had little choice – was to set out on a journey that sometimes needed sandwiches.

Stéfan was not a restful host. He filled the days of any guests with must-sees and must-dos, and all on his own terms. Be it business or pleasure or hobby, his only known aim was to be the main man, to lord it for plaudits, to play it with chutzpah. And group sex was no exception.

Since Sunday his mind had been seized of a plan for ceramic nameplates, chintzy but with an inventive twist. So far he had thought of Dyke Room, Blow-job Room, Anal Probe Room, Big Tits Room, Vibrator Room, Bondage Room, Slave-girl Room, Spanking Room, Wanking Room, Voyeur Room, Gang-bang Room, Spanking Room 2, and that was just the ground floor. He felt this covered the bases and did it with the gift of humour. It was only the area's shortage of ceramics craftsmen which had led him to reassess.

'Eryl!' he bawled, moving on from his inner entrance hall. 'Eryl!'

Previously his groups had groped amid the nouveau riche furnishings of a Pimlico penthouse – the pad where he did the deals of which he never spoke – but that had been your basic orgy, your free-for-all model. Your market economy model, as some City participants called it. And it had certainly had a similar structural flaw: only the strong and the pushy managed to get their rocks off in the mêlée. But in time Stéfan, always sensitive to insinuations of not being top-drawer, had come to feel that wall-to-wall bouncing bums might lack sophistication. So now he wanted an upgrade.

'Eryl!' he bawled again.

His next idea had been a medieval dungeon, with shackles and manacles and walls in black leather, and a role for him as ring-master. Sex by proxy, but under his command and choreography, was the ultimate vanity trip for Stéfan. The image of copulation to order – as the hired bull to the tethered cow – gave out an aphrodisiac with the strength of ten thousand oysters, and an orgasm that was instant. This was the final frontier for seekers after impersonal sex. For the true lusters after power.

'*Eryl!*'

This wet dream had hit the buffers of his builder, for Eryl was proving difficult. Not that Eryl was opposed to sex. He had lived for over a year with the bisexual aromatherapist at the converted village school (now believed to be bought by a horse-whisperer) and she was up for threesomes. Though not with him. He had long been a dogged partygoer, leaving with the coming of the milk van, and was known around the county for being the lay of last resort. So to be employed by a provider of mass pussy would appear a big plus.

But Eryl had issues. His role as house handyman was not being given the expected respect, the duties doled out with disregard for his status. Misused – and in public – as a supplier of suspect explosives, as a furniture removals man, as a pub cleaner, the ex-heir felt he had been the butt of serial indignities. Of unreasonable demands. And now a demand too many had been made. Never would he agree to be a naked doorman.

'... yes?' sighed Eryl, not very hotfoot from fixing a plug. 'You shouted?'

'I've been thinking about the orgy again,' said Stéfan.

'I'm not doing you a dungeon.'

'No. OK. You said. But have you –'

'No way is that routine maintenance. Handcuffs on a cross! Nipple-clamps attached to the wall! And besides, this is a listed building.'

'OK, agreed – touchy! But have you had any thoughts for a theme yet?'

'And I am *not* meeting-and-greeting with my bollocks out. Even if it is a giggle for your guests.'

'All right, all right! You can keep them under wraps. Both of them. Probably too small to be noticed anyway.'

The truce was agreed with a glare.

'Walk with me,' said Stéfan, a phrase he had picked up from a presidential movie.

The pair walked in tetchy silence, through what was believed to be the breakfast room, and on through the great folding doors that revealed the sunlit drawing room(?) with high French windows that opened on to the terrace and the ornamental gardens. Stéfan was in a rare conciliatory mood and did not mention the small shoulder-charge needed to reach the outside world, the warped wood being but one of many items not yet crossed off Eryl's worksheet.

To those inside Crug Caradoc, whatever weather was outside always came upon them by surprise, and today it was an Indian summer. Even the wind had gone elsewhere, and left the warmth unchallenged. Although the scent of the garden was fading, the aura of a decaying idyll remained, a floral watermark of long-dead gardeners.

As if drawn by a need for some colour, they walked down and around the beds of delphiniums, where the last of their purple was making a stand. Stéfan brushed his unsubtle fingers through their petals.

'I reckon on fifty coming to fuck.'

A more classical age had scattered the route with urns, their carvings an elaborate indulgence, their once-white stone muted by lichen. An occasional statue, of the usual distracted Greek, gazed into the middle distance. And a sundial on a plinth unhurriedly told the time, with the confidence that comes from no clouds.

'That's a lot of fucking,' said Eryl, after he had given the matter some thought.

'Exactly,' said Stéfan. 'And it needs organising.'

They paused beside an ornamental pond, a little fountain splashing just a foot into the late-summer air. Surprised by their presence, a water snake slid off the stone surround and jackknifed sinuously across the surface, a masterclass in rhythm and speed. An unseen frog gave up the shade of a frond and plopped abruptly into the weed-green depths.

'Organising how?'

'I don't know. Teams?'

'What, time trials?'

Stéfan glared at him. 'Be serious. Something rural.'

'Rural? … You mean, like a fertility rite?'

'What would that involve?' asked Stéfan.

'You all march round the garden carrying a six-foot prick,' replied Eryl, who was enjoying the power of being unhelpful.

'What?'

'Dressed up as peasants, spilling your seed on the ground. Singing a lot of rude songs and sacrificing virgins. So as you can get a decent loaf next year.'

'Oh, like on old Greek vases! No, that's dull,' scoffed Stéfan. 'Everyone does that in Georgia.'

'Oh … right.'

The two men stared down at the water, the only sign of life a lone goldfish nosing round the pump.

'Besides, I've not got the phone number of any virgins!'

And he guffawed. The fish took fright and went to a lower depth, leaving the pond empty of interest apart from an eroded naiad. The pair resumed their walk along the narrow gravel path, heather now creeping through the edging hoops.

'Thought perhaps we could fill a room or two with hay,' Stéfan ventured. 'Pretend we're all fucking in a barn.'

'Why not add some cowshit? Make it really authentic.'

'Oh, do shut up!'

'And you could play some moo music!'

'You got any *sensible* opinions?'

'You mean about having hundreds of bits of razor-sharp straw sticking in your flesh, slicing the end off your hard-on?'

'Jesus! … are you sure about that?'

'What, not on any of your old Greek vases? Of course I'm sure! Some of us had a misspent youth.'

Stéfan was briefly subdued, his urge to provoke in abeyance.

'Nor can I see your rich snots being any too chuffed at thrashing around in a barn all weekend,' added Eryl. 'Getting treated like yokels.'

The pleasing sight of doubt clouded his employer's face.

'No. No, perhaps not,' he conceded.

The inner Stéfan was a zone in need of conflict resolution. He was both bent on global dominance and in search of social acceptance. Unaware of all rules except his own, he found this an uphill task. Were he indeed to succeed, he would surely be that mythical creature, that unicorn among men, the lovable sociopath.

He headed off the return of silence, fearing that it came with an overlay of failure. 'Seems the pub's doing well.'

'Yeah?'

'Yes, those Pritchard boys say the beer is really shifting.'

'Oh, good,' said Eryl. 'Good.' And smiled.

They wandered on, moving beyond the formal gardens, and rounded the corner of the Grade i house. Here, clippings from the topiary lay underfoot, another of Eryl's tasks still to be completed. Yew was too slow for Stéfan, too stately a bush for his tastes, and he had first favoured the axe. Only photographs of grander estates, their pruned menageries a proud and public display, had been able to dissuade him. His plans for objects more striking than cockerels and cats had yet to grow to fruition.

In front of them lay a sunken lawn, precise in its proportions, perfect in its tonsure, gleaming in its green. Almost too good to walk upon.

'Of course!' cried Eryl. 'Croquet!'

'Oh, I never play,' said Stéfan.

'No – a croquet orgy!'

'A what?'

'A croquet orgy! On the lawn. It'd make for really classy fucking! And probably be a first!'

'Yes … yes, that would be classy, I agree,' mused Stéfan. 'But … but how would it work?'

'Well,' said Eryl, trying to think on his feet, 'you'd need to adapt some of the rules …'

Chapter 25

Nico was muddy for the third day that week. He had mud on his right shoe, mud on his right knee, mud on his right arm. He had left a smear where he had slipped down the bank. And it was a bank he had climbed in vain. He had climbed several banks in vain that week.

His mood before had not been good but the fall in the mire had also done damage to his psyche. It brought back memories of his childhood, memories he almost never mentioned. He had begun life in a hovel with a smallholding, where mud had been all he could call a cultural influence. Mains water had been a pipe dream, the yard a playground from the Somme. With feral parents who rowed drunk or sober, dirt had been his default setting, always the cause of derision on those days he made it to class. Mud, for him, now meant mockery, and signified the trigger for contempt. Which all added to his anger at the fruitless search.

Old Rhodri Richards had said his son was somewhere on the hills, though knew not to what purpose. He had said this three days running, with a generalised wave of his arm. And three days running Nico had acted unbothered, then driven his Volvo hard to where the tarmac ended.

Here stood the wooded dingle with the track that led to the moors where the peregrines now pined. This was the field that Gareth had bought from the late and hapless Hefin of Pantglas, the long-house still left empty and half-ruined on the ridge. That purchase had been the only entrepreneurial act of Gareth's working life, an attempt to be the son come good by enlarging the family farm – and impressing the wife. Here was where he had once had hopes.

But Nico could see him nowhere, not on the ridge, not in the woods, not by the stream. He had scrambled up banks, he had stood on knolls, he had even called out Gareth's name. The lonesome shepherd made no appearance. With his footing regained, but his vexation still growing, Nico peered one more time among the trees, and listened for any sound of Barbour movement. But all he could hear was an annoying *Lu-lu-lu* and the faintest ripple of water.

His prey had gone to ground elsewhere, to some other of his hundred-odd acres. Nico wondered if he might even be hiding at home in his farmhouse, crouching from the world and his father. He set off back down to his Volvo, placing his feet with more care.

Gareth watched him go. As he had watched him come and go on each of the previous days, while staying hidden in the barn up at Pantglas. The ancient stone walls had long and narrow gashes – that architectural hangover from the days of archers – and from here Gareth could survey all invaders. And everybody, or so it seemed to him, now was an invader of his life. But up here on the hill with his dog he still had some peace.

He knew why Nico had come. He had come as a saviour, come to seal the deal. For Nico had smelt blood. But Gareth, too, smelt weakness. A winner holds back his hand, and Nico was too eager. His life was built on bargains, on bouncing the vendor. But Gareth, albeit now a failed farmer, knew the facts of life of land. And Nico was serving to prove its value.

Nico meanwhile felt in need of a lunchtime drink. A five-point turn had not helped his temper. Dropping back down to the valley road, he drove past Gareth's other fields, and resisted the whim that he should perhaps nail cash to his trees, and flush him into the open.

Five men were sat drinking at the Dragon's Head's back-to-basics bar, three of them barmen.

'And if a nut of yours got stuck in my throat?' asked Eryl.

'Yes!' replied Ben.

'And if I tripped on your Welcome mat and broke my leg?' asked Dafydd.

'Yes!' replied Bryn.

'And if I accidentally set fire to myself with my matches?' asked Eryl.

'Yes!' replied Brian.

'And if I smashed Eryl in the face with my glass?' asked Dafydd.

'Yes!' replied Brenig, pulling the fifth free pint. 'No need for 999 in here! My brothers and I are from the Florence Griffiths school of barmen. Heart attack, and the four of us could give you the kiss of life, for eight hours, in relays.'

'I think I'll pass on that,' said Eryl.

'Pass on what?' asked Nico from the door.

'Three!' exclaimed Ben. 'Never had three customers before. Not at lunchtime.'

'Must be the makeover,' said Nico, noting the decor had returned to grot. 'Where do I spit?'

Eryl put his hand over his beer.

'Burns, breaks, bleeding, bad breathing,' continued Brenig, 'sprains, strokes, exploding spots, we can fix 'em all.'

'Should have opened a hospital instead,' said Eryl.

'I'll just have a pint of best,' said Nico.

'On the house, as it's your first with us,' said Brian.

Nico allowed himself a nod, gratitude not being a forte.

'Another ten weeks of old Griff and his wife,' went on Brenig, still waiting on the froth, 'and we could have offered brain surgery.'

Nico took the last stool, regretting he had come in. He had not expected chat, nor indeed company. And neither had he wished to see Eryl, a man to whom he owed money. Nor indeed Dafydd, a man whom he found too fond of gossip. One pint and he would leave, maybe try the farm a second time.

His presence slowed the cascade of conversation, as though the others feared that speech might make them victims of a deal.

'Pizzas going well?' asked Eryl.

Dafydd wondered if this was a jibe. Did Eryl know he had applied to be barman?

'Yes, thanks,' he responded.

'Oh, that your moped out there?' enquired Nico, who led a sad pizza-centred life.

'That's right,' said Dafydd, flinching at the question. 'Been delivering near by.'

'Will *you* be doing food?' Eryl asked the brothers.

'No way!' said Ben.

'We're run off our feet just doing the bar,' said Bryn.

'We'd need more brothers if we laid on food,' said Brian.

'Been delivering to a rather nice woman, actually,' resumed Dafydd.

'A woman, eh?' said Eryl, with the emphasis on tits.

'Very educated. Historically astute.'

'Really?'

'Yes, knows about foreign wars. And the constitution.'

'In a caravan?'

'Er, yes.'

'Get your leg over?'

Dafydd did not answer, feeling both 'yes' and 'no' were wrong.

'Reckon she's still active, our Marjorie?'

Again Dafydd did not answer Eryl. But this time he was puzzled by the tone. It seemed more than nudge, nudge, more than just shared smut of the sexually thwarted. Floated as jokey enquiry, it almost had the timbre of an availability check.

'We've not had a woman in here yet,' said Ben.

'There's a lot of things we've not had in here yet,' said Bryn.

'Not had a townie. Not had a stranger. Not had a tourist,' said Brian.

'Not even had a drunk,' said Brenig, handing Nico his pint.

There was a pause for some in-depth drinking.

'Of course, the trouble with the last landlord, Gwillim,' said Eryl, as though it were his specialist subject, 'is that the man wasn't customer-friendly. A landlord who comes into the bar, nine o'clock at night, clutching a hot-water bottle, is not going to be the life and soul of any party. If you asked him for anything but a beer, he'd say you were a troublemaker. If you didn't keep hold of your glass, he'd confiscate it. If you ever suggested Twiglets, he'd call you a ponce. *And* he'd be gone for days in that cellar.' Then Eryl added, as a very casual afterthought, 'Anyone know the rules of croquet?'

'… could do you skittles,' said Ben.

'… or dominoes,' said Bryn.

'… or gin rummy,' said Brian.

'… or Morris dancing,' said Brenig. 'Welsh version.'

'Has to be croquet,' said Eryl. 'Technical reasons.'

But he drew a blank, no one even claiming a working knowledge of a mallet.

'Well, I'll be off,' said Nico, standing and draining his glass. As he turned to go, he too had a casual afterthought. 'I gather Gareth's back. Anyone seen him?'

'No, he's not been in here,' said Ben.

'Not been seen anywhere since he got out,' said Bryn.

'Don't think anybody knows when they'll see him again,' said Brian.

'Guess not,' said Nico, turning again for the door.

'Unless he goes to the auction,' said Brenig.

'Auction?' said Nico, seeming to stop in mid-air. 'What auction?'

'Old Rhodri was here yesterday, said his son plans to put the farm up for auction.'

'No, he's eighty-two. He's got that wrong.'

'He hasn't. He says Gareth's been advised to sell it. By some expert.'

'What? Man's an idiot!'

And Nico turned aside, hiding his expression from view as he hurried on out.

'You been in a fight?' called Eryl.

'Not yet!' Nico paused at the door. 'Why d'you ask?'

'You've got mud all down you.'

3

An Autumn Weekend

Chapter 26

It was the lichen that had made Gwyn late.

And now he was trapped at tractor pace. As the clods of mud flew over his head, fired with the force of a trebuchet, he almost wished he had kept his submission shorter. Dusk was upon him and he had miles to go before the canapés.

He had been the last to speak, the day eaten up by slicker suits than his, by men who would be back in the city tomorrow, never to see the moors again. Hired hands with hollow words, caring only for their fee. A rural arsehole of a place, they would privately say, where a bomb would be a blessing. Where their quarry would improve the landscape.

The objectors had been all the usual suspects, talking sense on a shoestring. Five desks of Davids, and still the smart money on Goliath.

Soaring into the air of the remote and rickety village hall were the pleas of heritage, the values of beauty, the desirability of diversity, and the necessity of nature – and dragging them back down were the virtuosic interpretations of planning acts, the legalistic constraints of subclauses, and the citing of villainous precedent as far back as vellum. The climax to three years of verbal warfare, this dusty legal appeal was played out against a noisy chorus of locals, whose contribution was the power of righteous rage.

If only the lichen were sensate, if only the lichen knew. How it would no doubt laugh, in a damply fungal sort of way, to learn of the fight for its fate. Sired by the ice age and now the last of its kind ('allegedly', according to the slurs of the quarry-owners' highly paid hit men), it was unknowingly making its final stand – in a metaphorical sense, of course, for lichen's PR problem is that it clings to the ground, completely unnoticed.

Gwyn put the window-washers back into action as his impatience had again smeared the screen a muddy brown. He eased off once more from the tractor's big back wheels, left with few options but swearing. Its driver was, he saw, of the cussed flat-capped type, who trundled the lanes with intransigence, giving no quarter to cars.

Gareth got little pleasure out of life now. Blocking the path of his magistrate and pelting him with mud was a comfort sent from heaven.

He considered there to be several candidates for the Nemesis role in his tragedy (e.g., his wife; his wife's lover; the sculptor; the editor; the photographer; the mayoress; the arresting officers; his father; his mother; his neighbours) but Gwyn Hopkins, JP, ranked high in this ungodly pantheon. Gareth was of the view – though never expressed, not even in court – that cuckoldry was an extenuating circumstance for any crime, up to and including parking. He had therefore regarded his sentence, and his consequent plight, as an injustice unparalleled since Dreyfus (or he would have done, had he heard of Dreyfus). He made sure he missed no puddles.

Gareth now lived in limbo. Grass-letting brought him a pauper's living wage, and animals of others were source of scant satisfaction. The deal was that every day he hedged and ditched and did all the things that made grass-eating tenants prosper. He was keeping his farm sheepshape for a profit that went elsewhere. A profit that went to his neighbours – to the four laughing, joking brothers.

The choice had been made by his father, while Gareth was bonding with cons. But this was an act about more than mere farming, in Gareth's fevered thinking. This was a wistful wish for a rerun at paternity, for a new start with superior genes. The Pritchard brothers were the sort of sons his father had always wanted, the sort of adults the farm had always needed. Each the sort of man that Gareth could never be. And now their animals were roaming his land, their chops growing lean and tasty on his grass. As Gareth walked the fields, his fields, he could hear the flocks, their flocks, bleating with derision behind his back. Mocking his failure and his future.

A summer and a winter and a spring, that was the length of the lease. Any longer, and unpleasant rights would accrue. But short-term though it might be, there was little to lift Gareth's spirits. Soon he would be out in the worst of the weather, day-labour doing its dull duty. And then, in spring, when the birthing was over and the gambolling was done and the grass was new and green, the land would have to come under the hammer. And his life on the farm would be finished.

The thought of the money from the sale somehow deepened the void that would follow. Already a recluse, his world growing smaller, his speech growing rarer, his mind growing stranger, Gareth struggled to imagine how best to buy back his happiness. All he could think of was an extra dog. And he was far from sure that would work.

He aimed for another muddy puddle.

Sick of second, Gwyn kept his hand clasped on the gear lever, but with his thoughts still in overdrive.

He kept wishing he could have afforded an expert, a lifelong lichen-lover, to make his case with the weight of heavy-duty degrees, to explain exactly how the loss of limestone pavement was a habitat tragedy. And thus bring a bit of anguish to the finely balanced mind of the government inspector.

Planning law was a perverse process, he reflected bitterly, his temper and temperature rising. To have the uniqueness of life subjected to nitpicking and pedantry was abdication of any rational – or inspirational – world view. To adjudicate on the wonders of nature whilst sitting in a room made deadly drab by man was in itself a sign of failure.

Gwyn looked down again at the clock in his car, and it told him the art- and grass-lovers would already be gathering in the museum, his wife with her one good dress on.

He risked a blast on the horn. But even if Gareth heard, he was in no mood for the prissier points of the Highway Code. Still shorn of his licence, he was left with a tractor as his only means of transport – and delaying the magistrate his only form of grim fun.

Gwyn gripped and ungripped the wheel in rare frustration. He could, at a pinch, see the irony of his situation. If the quarry were enlarged and the road-stone liberated, they could widen all the single-track lanes and leave him room to pass any recalcitrant tractor.

Forced to potter along the lane, Gwyn had time to look about him. Below, in the lengthening shadows of the valley, he could just make out the great pond that he and Audrey had years ago created, the Trust's very first reserve. It had been the source of an early and valuable lesson.

Aware that frogs had little road-sense, he and his wife had gone to their aid with a sign and a torch and a bucket. For there comes a time in the sex life of a frog when it rushes en masse to the water, like a hopping lemming playing road-kill with the traffic. Eager to minimise the murderous impact of man, Gwyn and Audrey had patrolled the grass verges in the dark of the evenings, signing up frogs for the bucket. And then, with almost parental care and concern, the couple would carry their squelchy cargoes across to the pond and gently tip them in the water, there to turn their minds to breeding and a fulfilled aquatic life.

The couple had saved scores and scores by these interventions, and by their home-made road sign saying *Danger! Frogs Crossing!*, when Gwyn's eye was caught by the sight of bubbles.

Shining his torch upon the black surface of the pond for several minutes, he was eventually able to detect a carp, a very large carp. Made very large by feeding on frogs.

Today had been another of those days when Gwyn had got to pondering on Nature's view of man and his meddling. He found himself wondering what the woodlark would want him to do, when suddenly the tractor turned into a field without signalling, and left the road clear.

Gwyn reckoned he had five minutes, at most, until the exhibition of his wife's latest sedges was officially unveiled. He accelerated hard. Almost unnoticed, the last of the woodland light had now gone and the high-banked lane was in deep shadow. It was in the split-second before he turned on the headlamps that he saw the creature cross in front of his car.

Gwyn braked, but the mud made him skid an extra yard. Uncertain what damage he had done, or what he had done it to, he leapt from his car, the engine still running. But of the animal there was now no sign. Except that on one front wing there seemed to be small smears of blood, although the dark made it hard to be certain.

Gwyn waited a few moments, listening for any sounds of pain, but the incoming night was silent. There was no aid to be given. He was still not even sure what animal he had seen. A fox, maybe ... or perhaps a pine marten. Something that moved fast, and hopefully fast enough to escape any motorised harm.

A little chastened, he set off for the museum once more, but at a more sedate speed.

'I feel greatly honoured ...' began Miss Stevens, who had failed to get the new mayor to open the exhibition. As usual, the man and his mace had had too busy a day meeting and greeting the coach parties of Japanese tourists, all eager to photograph each other in front of the town's iconic loinless statue, now the Abernant companion to *The Kiss* on the cultural trail.

Miss Stevens had an audience of perhaps thirty in the spotlit bright white lecture room, nibbling cheese and saying yes to Chardonnay. Not quite the tight-tie type of earlier events, with small talk that needed cattle prods, but invitees who had just a faint hint of arty. Who felt that levity was permitted in the presence of paintings.

'... to be here tonight, for such an unusual – indeed, perhaps, unique – collection of one of the most familiar – yet, paradoxically, least-known – features of the natural world which we see – or, more commonly, ignore – all around us in our everyday, often urbanised, lives ...'

It was a difficult exhibition to open, grass. Twenty-seven paintings of grass. Grass in different lights, in different weathers, in different seasons. In different fields.

The artist stood slightly to one side, almost anonymous among her guests. More women than men, they stood loosely gathered as if for a birthday party. Small knots of the Trust stood nearer the drinks. And in one corner, as always, an elderly man with pince-nez peered closely at the brushstrokes.

'Audrey Hopkins is to grass what Cézanne was to Mont Sainte-Victoire,' announced Miss Stevens. 'Albeit on a smaller scale.'

'And in worse weather!' called someone at the back.

'She charges extra for rain!' shouted another. Cue laughter.

Miss Stevens began to relax. Mrs Hopkins wished she were in a field somewhere, wet or dry. Occasions without wellington boots made her uneasy.

'Hers is a remarkable achievement. I gather that we can see before us tonight,' and here Miss Stevens referred to her notes, 'sheaths, stamens, stigmas, stems, tufts, tussocks, florets, spikelets, panicles, ligules, glumes, nodes, nodules, bracts, and blades.'

'Bravo!' A vigorous round of applause broke out among the naturalists present.

'And grasses of both sexes!' added Gwyn, who had that moment slipped through the door.

Audrey turned round, smiled, and gestured him to her side.

Miss Stevens continued, 'Most artists only have to keep the landlord at bay. This one has to fight off cows.'

Gwyn squeezed her hand with pride as the room again gave in to laughter.

'I'm told this labour of love has gone on longer than it took Michelangelo to do the Sistine Chapel. And *he* had assistants.'

Gwyn's wife stared at her feet, helpless in the face of hyperbole.

'But these paintings are more than works of art, they are matters of record.'

'Hear, hear!' cried Gwyn, making amends for his lateness.

'Audrey has done for grass what Audubon did for birds,' concluded Miss Stevens, her use of rococo grammar hiding her fears that yet again she had failed to mount a blockbuster.

It was a much appreciated reference among this audience, and more '*Hear, hear*'s came with the handshake that she offered Audrey.

'So, not such a bad Friday night after all!' said Gwyn when the well-wishing had abated, and they had taken a private moment for a warm wine.

'No, I guess not. And free nuts.'

'So sorry I was late. I went home to put on my best cords and then I got … oh, I'll explain what happened later.'

'Lovely grass,' said the colonel, almost clicking his heels as he halted.

'Thank you for coming,' said Audrey.

'Wouldn't miss it for the world,' replied the colonel, and then moved swiftly on.

'Wonder what's on *his* walls,' Gwyn muttered. 'Prints of tank-resistant plants?'

'Not a bad turnout,' Audrey admitted, looking round the now animated room.

'A woman who can do eighteen shades of green? You're a star!'

'I see there are four red dots already!' said the dentist as he passed. 'Well done.'

'Four?' said Audrey, surprised and delighted by his news. 'Four!' she said to Gwyn.

'I'm so pleased,' replied Gwyn, giving her a kiss. 'It's all down to the framing, you know.'

'Of course it is, my love,' said Audrey. 'Come on, then, let's do some quality mingling!'

And she took him by the hand, and together they went back into the small welcoming crowd.

Midnight, and still old Mrs Harpur had not gone to bed.

Like many solitary people, she had come to live like clockwork, and ten was the hour she was in bed with a book. Eleven was the hour she put it aside. Midnight was the hour when the radio went off and then she would be snoring.

But tonight she was awake and moving from window to window. From room to room. She was not just looking, she was listening. And what worried her was that she could hear nothing.

She had heard nothing all evening, nothing when she had cut the fish up, nothing when she had put the fish down. And fish was a winner, fish was a five-star treat.

She opened the back door again and looked out into the garden. There was only the stillness of the night, and the faint scent of a summer's hard work.

Then, as she turned to close the door, she heard a distorted version of the sound she attended. Either distant or weak.

She moved out on the patio where the last of the roses still bloomed. And here the cry grew stronger. And more frequent. Until, by the light of the new moon, she came to the cracked teak bench. And saw beneath it Arabella.

Arabella barely raised her head, and looked like a cat no longer interested in fish.

Mrs Harpur uttered a moan, then sank to her knees and gently stretched out her hands. The cat was wet. The cat was covered in blood.

Chapter 27

'Oh, we love the countryside!' said the young woman with close-cropped hair.

Mr Probert, the auctioneer of animals, looked across his desk at her. This was the second time she had said that, and it made him want to slap her. He hated people who said they loved the countryside. Especially on a busy Saturday morning.

He handed the couple details of a second barn, a chi-chi conversion by incomers.

'What's the story here, then?' asked the man, who was nasal and Northern.

'Another failed marriage,' said Mr Probert, with gloomy relish. 'The lifeblood of estate agents.'

'… er, no, that's not what I meant,' said the man, who had had in mind the dry rot of buildings.

'Has it got good views?' asked the woman, who loved good views.

'When the mist lifts,' said Mr Probert. 'Which isn't often.'

There was, in Mr Probert's opinion, a scientific study to be done on the life cycle of the incomer. Just like salmon struggling upstream to spawn, with the reward of near-certain death, the go-green incomers set forth on a path that led, as if by social design, to disillusion and despair.

'And we wanted somewhere for a goat.'

He thought of suggesting a cliff. Mr Probert was just back from a testing morning, shot through with sadness and unreason, and his mindset was lacking the sensitivity needed for house sales.

'Because we love the idea of animals.'

He smiled with wan indulgence – resisting the urge to suggest they start with cardboard cut-outs – and handed across a cottage with a small wilderness area, inside and out. It was in need of the extensive renovation which is such a spiritual part of the countryside experience.

'Another failed marriage?' asked the man wryly.

'Don't know. Death from damp, more like.'

Damp had been on Mr Probert's mind all morning. Mustiness was a worrying smell in a house, but even more so on a man. And the whiff off Gareth, of clothes left in a stagnant puddle, of a body left out overnight, was the hallmark of a farmer from yesteryear, too long bonded to the hills and losing interest in the niceties.

'Been abandoned long?' asked the man.

For an instant, Mr Probert thought he meant Gareth. But then reality returned.

'Owners left last year.'

The couple read through the sales details, a brief purple patch on potential.

'Londoners!' added Mr Probert. 'Get too far from a disco and they go to pieces.'

The urban couple laughed, as was only polite.

'We're vegetarians,' said the woman, laying down a marker of moral seriousness.

Mr Probert nodded sagely at this unwanted news.

'And we'd like to grow our own food,' concurred the man.

Mr Probert continued nodding. It was not serious homes such people sought, but adventure playgrounds, and this was where their lives went wrong. In his opinion. A childhood dream … a weekend break … a rural soap … a mid-life crisis … a pre-menopausal whim … and the 'grass is greener' fantasies kicked in.

'One hundred acres be enough?' he asked, as if this was not disingenuous.

He had walked the land alone, Gareth too blue and moody to do the honours. All the key questions of access, and water, and neighbours, so vital to the value, produced little but a disconnected shrug, and grunts that told one nothing. Yet like every other hill-farm it came with history: the horror of stillbirths in snowstorms, the nightmare of tempests upturning grown men, the chill factor of winter days when all running water went rigid, the perversity of parching summers when grass turned to dust on the tongue. Such trials built character like few other lines of work, and made of the land a living partner, sometimes hard to love, but so often hard to leave.

'Just a big garden,' replied the young woman. 'But unusual.'

Next out of Mr Probert's file came the converted village school, open-plan and piny.

'Adapted for an aromatherapist,' he explained. 'Also unhappy in love.'

The couple pondered the photo, checking out the spatial possibilities.

Mr Probert wondered what work the pair did, what work they could do in a rural world. In his experience, incomers had a flim-flam lifestyle, of no obvious benefit to the Gross National Product. They were prone to unusual and exotic needs, needs only understood by other incomers, who by chance were usually the providers of unusual and exotic services. Should mid-Wales be sole survivor of, say, an asteroid impact, the wide availability of acupuncture and foot massage would be a great holistic comfort.

'Been on the market a while,' concluded the man, raising an eyebrow of doubt.

'Probably the fifteen months of rain a year. Some people don't see the attraction.'

And still the couple did not waver from their Arcadian quest.

Mr Probert handed them an erstwhile chapel or two, his mind again reverting to the auction of Gareth's land. Though the sale was certain, a date had yet to be fixed. Never a decisive man, Gareth was reluctant to be severed from his past, to say the final farewell to his acres. He passed most days hedging and ditching, blank-faced but dogged, with the rhythm of a man refusing to cease compressions on the chest of a corpse beyond recall. 'Soon,' was all he would say of the sale. 'Soon.'

'They seem a bit pricy for chapels,' complained the young woman.

'Supply and demand,' replied Mr Probert, his matter-of-fact tone hiding a bitter bewilderment.

He had lived all his working life in this backwater, beautiful and under-populated. Year after year, he had seen the council pour away the rates on PR promotions, praising the landscape and the wildlife, the culture and the history, the churches and the architecture. All in the hope of making people outnumber sheep – and failing.

And now a minute of madness and a stolen chisel had trumped all their lures. Abernant had been made a fashion hot-spot by the midnight maiming of a statue. The place that time had wisely chosen to forget had been noisily remembered by every stand-up comic who loved a cheap cock joke. The mood of the moment had descended like a fickle incubus over this unworldly rural land.

The back of beyond had suddenly become the in-place to be ... but not for Gareth.

Chapter 28

'I only do donkeys.'

Gwyn Hopkins turned his head. The old lady had come up on his blind side.

'I only do donkeys,' she repeated.

He gave her a carefully calibrated smile, courtesy without encouragement. Shaking a tin in the street sometimes had odd effects, acting like a dog-whistle for human strays. And being a JP, he had to be careful whom he told to get lost.

'I only do donkeys,' she said a third time, standing her ground like a fixture.

'Yes, I've fond memories of spending my school holidays at Tenby,' responded Gwyn, 'and taking donkey rides along the beach.'

'*Spanish* donkeys,' the old lady said severely. The lines on her face tautened at the thought.

'*Spanish* donkeys?'

'The ones they throw off clock towers.'

'Oh those ones. Yes. Dreadful.'

'Not even into a net. Though that wouldn't much help a falling donkey.'

'No, I guess not.'

'And it's not just clock towers. Could be any high building. I've got leaflets.'

Gwyn dreaded leaflets.

'Of course, you're an animal-lover. *You'll* know what the Spanish do to donkeys.'

Gwyn nodded, watching her index finger quiver with condemnation. Did he really seem so kindred a spirit, he found himself wondering.

'They get a donkey drunk, they put the fattest man in town

on top, and they ride the poor animal round and round until it drops dead. That's a fun afternoon out for the Spanish.'

Gwyn, whose interest in donkeys – British or Continental – was at the low end of the register, felt obliged to purse his lips and share her pain.

'I'd make it illegal to go to Spain,' the old lady said. 'That would stop it all!'

'Good point,' said Gwyn, fearing she had a petition. 'Good point.'

The council licence to shake the Trust's tin was quite specific re time and place, and this trapped Gwyn outside the ironmongers, leaving no room for manoeuvre.

'Because donkeys will soon be extinct in Spain,' she insisted. 'Which is why they need a sanctuary.'

'A sanctuary?'

The short and forceful old lady immediately rummaged in one of several plastic bags. A short chaos later, she pulled out an elastic-banded bundle of photocopied flyers, each covered with black-and-white images of depressed-looking donkeys. With names like Pedro and Franco.

'They need asylum,' she announced. 'And three square meals a day.'

Gwyn tried hard to keep on smiling as he reached for his wallet and pulled out his smallest note. It was only 11.10 a.m., just minutes into his fundraising shift on the high street, and he was already £4.86 down on the day.

As he watched her stalk into the Victorian market hall, fizzing with donkey drive, Gwyn could not help reflecting on how the world might, in its turn, see him. Was he maybe known as the mad bird-man …? Or perhaps the naturalist nutter? Or Don Quixote even, fruitlessly charging from one animal crusade to another? Did people pass by on the other side of the road, muttering about the bearded obsessive with binoculars?

He gave the tin a shake. It rattled with failure.

Every third Saturday of every third month the diehard all-weather wing of Trust volunteers would commit to their cause in the centre of town. Only the Salvation Army, with the added bonus of heaven, mustered a more frequent presence. Occasionally a member would display the tame owl, or an injured bird of prey in rehab, to soften the heart and the wallet, and show that conservation could be sexy. But today was just the cold turkey of the tin. With a cuddly animal picture on the side.

He gave the tin another shake, and a little girl relieved her mother of pennies.

Mostly, though, Gwyn went unnoticed. He would have liked a loudhailer, but the small print of charity laws meant no show of salesmanship, no selling by showmanship, no sign of unsubtle hustle. Like the early nudes at the Windmill, he could do little more than stand and smile. And sometimes shake. For a man who laid down the law in the week, to be at weekends the subject of others' rules was an irksome role reversal. And worse, his allocated pitch was against a backdrop of tin baths, Mr Bufton's loss-leader for the week.

'D'you have any spare puppies, mister?'

'Puppies …? No, afraid not, son.'

'But you're the man who looks after animals?'

'Er, in a way, yes.'

'Like puppies?'

'Why is it you want a puppy?'

'… dunno, really.'

'You need a reason.'

'My mum says I'm bored.'

'And how would a puppy help?'

'My friend, he had a puppy.'

'Why don't you play with his puppy?'

'He drowned it.'

Gwyn frowned. Children and pets were always a delicate area. Be it hamsters or rabbits or budgies, pets too often fell short of their allotted span.

'And why did your friend do that?' he asked.

But the boy had by now written him off as a fraud, as a man lacking clout in the animal kingdom, and had disappeared amid the morning shoppers. Their averted gazes betrayed a similar – and familiar – lack of interest.

Too much countryside here, Gwyn always blamed it on. Too easy to look at and take for granted. The Ramblers had their biggest membership in Central Cardiff, where half the population lined up to explore beyond the high street. In walking boots. So, too, were wildlife-lovers at their most prolific in urban Penarth, where the grey squirrel was as good as it got. But wraparound 'wilderness' – and he flinched at the phoney word – made most locals blasé. Provided the view stayed green, all was well with the world.

'Not enough leg, Mr Hopkins.'

A broom brushed by his ankle.

Gwyn looked round. A grey man in brown overalls, worried by life, and probably some ten ironmonger's years from death, was tidying up the pavement, which needed no tidying.

'Morning, Mr Bufton.'

'No call for a tin bath, I suppose?'

'Don't remember it on my shopping list. What's this about my legs?'

'It was Colon Cancer last weekend. About twenty-five, the young lady looked. I swear it was a gymslip. Miles of upper thigh. I could hear money going into her tin all day long, like an avalanche. Needed help to carry it home, I reckon.'

'So you have doubts about my sex appeal?'

'Just saying you could do with a gimmick, man of your years.'

'Like …?'

'Well, I used to stock artificial limbs. Gets the sympathy vote every time. Possible war hero.'

'And your second idea?'

'Uniforms are always good. Any sort of uniform. Bit of braid, polished buttons. Suggests a class act.'

'Perhaps I should hire something from *The Mikado*.'

'St John's Ambulance always goes down well. That Griffiths, he's everywhere. "How to avoid Death", it's a very popular message.'

'I could give the kiss of life to a badger, that would draw the crowds,' said Gwyn, his joke not without a bitter touch.

'The truth is,' said Mr Bufton, a man knowledgeable of truths, 'it's a dog-eat-dog world, the charity line of business. I see it through my shop window every Saturday.'

'So much junk, I'm surprised you see anything.'

But it was a truth that Gwyn knew well. There was an excess of charities about. Community spirit was a feature of the mid-Wales hills, with everyone on alert for any new disease in need of a committee and a poster at the library. The widespread presence of Raeburns was conducive to warm meetings in winter and a desire to do good. Mills with no roof, bells with no rope, players with no pitch, bums with no bench, the social shortfalls were endless, and the waiting list of citizens keen to try shaking a tin would not have disgraced a rush-hour urban bus stop.

'Not junk now,' said the ironmonger. 'I'm on the up. Got a lot of quality stock.'

'Especially chisels, so I hear.'

'Collectors' items, I call them.'

Mr Bufton, first name unknown, was from the prelapsarian dawn of commerce, when items came singly and packaging was a paper bag. A latter-day Aladdin, he had a widget wonderland kept in a wall of wooden drawers. And piled up on the floor lay a cornucopian collection of arcane hardware from Aluminium to Zinc, a lifetime of wet dreams for handymen. Such old-fashioned customer care was, of course, a recipe for bankruptcy.

'I was saved by the riot,' said the ironmonger. 'Gareth was a godsend.'

He lived above the shop, in a flat that overlooked the square and the statue. It was his window which was smashed, his stock which was stolen, his chisel which did the deed. A key witness, he had even held it up on local television, to give colour to the action. And had seen the lifelong decline in his sales be reversed, and his profits turn up towards the light. The fading image of ironmongery was soon being restored by celebrity.

'I gather you now give autographs,' said Gwyn.

'Oh, mainly to the Japanese.'

'Perhaps I should be asking *your* advice on raising money.'

'My advice?' said Mr Bufton. 'Very simple. Nothing legal pays.'

'Thank you. I hear that every Wednesday,' said Gwyn.

And gave his empty tin another shake.

*   *   *

Mrs Harpur did not much like the vet. He was not her usual vet, who dealt with animals called Fifi and Tiddles and gave advice on fur-balls. On duty today was the vet for farm animals, big buggers like bulls, and he had little bedside manner. George Cankrey had an unkempt black beard and was a Leninist.

His greatest job satisfaction came on cattle-market days. Just occasionally the smell of fear and shit would cause some truculent beast to bolt for freedom, kicking over hurdles and farmers. The only route to freedom was the inner ring road, where a clattering cow was a traffic hazard in any weather, even to advanced motorists. Pursued by stockmen and breeders and buyers and passing pedestrians, often keen to re-enact Pamplona, the runaway would soon collide with something sharp and hard. And the cry would go up for a vet.

And George Cankrey would be there first. For this was not just healing, this was not just theatre, this was power to the people. By the time he arrived with his get-well kit, loopy Daisy would be a crime scene, her mooing irregular as she lay udders agley and garishly lit by blue lights flashing. It might be a case for the killer syringe, it might be a call for the harness, or it might just be a traffic-jam trauma. But here and now he was the lead agency, the man who called the shots. What happened next and who moved when and where was down to his medical say-so. And the police – the police! – were obliged to obey him. He, George Cankrey, had charge of the fascist bastards, had power over the capitalist state, had authority over the apparatus of repression.

Little old ladies, tearful and fearful and sleepless, came a poor veterinary second.

'I think she's had it,' said George.

'Had it?' queried Mrs Harpur.

'Broken back leg. Internal injuries. Little to be done.'

'Oh …'

'Best I put her down.'

'Oh …'

'Will you want her body back?'

Mrs Harpur laid dead Arabella down in the trug again, as gently as the rarest cut-flowers from her garden. The small body was wrapped in the shawl that spread round her owner's shoulders on days when the air grew chilly. Now it was covered with blood. And soon it would be covered with earth.

The old lady stepped hesitantly out of the surgery where she had sat in doomed hope since early morning. She found it hard to catch her breath, so winded was she by the shock.

Arabella was twelve, the second cat since her late husband. Until her days of widowhood she would have held the companionship of a cat to be a fanciful thing. She read books, she played music, she crocheted, she gardened, she sailed. What need had she for purring?

The walk to her car proved a test of endurance, and went by in a haze. She looked to neither left nor right, and wondered if she had passed friends who thought her rude. She tried not to think of what would happen when she got back home. She tried not to think of the spade. But still these fears made her sweat.

When her first cat died she had a few romantic dreams still remaining. And looks that were not yet old-maidish. But with the death of Arabella, more had somehow died than a cat. Something had happened to her future, something that not even her garden could quite make good. Once she had thought she would sail the world, but today every journey seemed too far, too much trouble, too little purpose. Life was closing her in, shutting her down, a fate that left her weak and sick at heart.

She reached the paying car park, and at first could not remember where she had placed her car. The Saturday-morning shoppers had filled up the rows of spaces, leaving no sign of its presence. She toiled up and down the tarmac slope, almost forgetting what she had lost.

Then sight of the standing caravan jogged her frazzled memory. A recruiting venue for would-be first-aiders, it stood on flat land near the toilets, her car tucked just yards beyond. Dreading the drive home, Mrs Harpur slowed her pace still further, her stomach knotted as if with indigestion. And then she fell to the ground.

Supt. Griffiths was in the middle of demonstrating a gauze dressing to an audience of two, both yet to reach the sixth form, when he saw the woman collapse.

She had not collapsed as in his training videos and at first he thought she had tripped. He was also distracted by the dead cat, which had bounced out of its basket and seemed to be the victim of cruelty. But he took off his peaked cap and puffed his way to the woman's aid, both the boys gleefully urging him on.

He wheezed to his knees beside her, and her pallor soon became a signal it was serious. His first instinct was to puff to a phone box and ring 999; but his second instinct was that action needed to be immediate; and his third instinct was that his finest hour had come. For despite his many years as St John's emissary on earth, he had till now saved only notional lives, had never seen a real person show the textbook signs of mortal trouble.

Griffiths managed to rearrange the legs, which had bent at unnatural angles, and laid the frail featherweight body on its back upon the tarmac. He could see no sign of breathing and nothing in the airway. Hand under the neck, hand on to the forehead, and tilt. Hand on to the chin and push up. Airway open, still no breath. Pinch the nostrils, open wide, and lips to the mouth. No response. Check the chest, adjust the airway, repeat the action.

His exertions made him sweat, the noonday sun no friend to bending double.

Griffiths checked the carotid pulse again, but still he found no heartbeat. Heel of the hand above the heart, fingers locked together. Arms straight, and press, and pump. Again, and again. And again. Fifteen times.

Now back to the mouth. Tilt the head, reopen the airway. Two more breaths.

And back to the chest. Counting *one, and two, and three*. Fifteen times.

And check the pulse, and two more breaths.

Griffiths looked again at the chest, willing it to show some sign of life. And then he saw it rise and fall, albeit feebly. The old biddy had been kick-started. By him. A surge of adrenalin ran throughout his body, dispelling all exhaustion.

Keep the breathing going, keep the oxygenated blood flowing. Blow, blow, blow.

And bit by bit, blow by blow, colour began to come back to the cheeks. Mrs Harpur began to come back to the living.

A huge sense of relief – and of pride – coursed through the corpulent body of Supt. Griffiths. He had just saved his first life. His years of first aid had finally paid off. His years of public service had at last been a triumph. He might well be due a medal, perhaps one he could display – and prominently – upon his person. For he had now become a hero, possibly a folk hero.

He pressed his palms on the ground to raise himself up, ready to receive the plaudits of any passing shoppers. But he could find no strength, no upper-body power. He pressed a second time. And then, suddenly, in his puffed-up chest, he too felt a terrible and savage pain. Squeezing him, crushing him, spreading to his back, to his stomach, his arms, his neck, his jaw, his face.

His eighteen-stone body keeled over, poleaxed by the pain. And he fell full-length upon his patient. The two little boys tried to tug him up, tried to drag him off, guessing his position was not procedure, but a lifetime of Barbara's dinners had made him a deadweight. A very dead weight.

And thus it was that Supt. Griffiths ended his days in the line of duty, crushing the last of the life out of the little old lady beneath him.

Chapter 29

'Darryl ... F. who?' replied the editor, already irritable.

'Darryl F. Zanuck.'

'... no, new one on me. Is he local?'

'Hardly,' said Nico.

'So the reason I should know him is what exactly?'

Nico sighed inside. '... *All About Eve*?'

'Eve who?'

'It's a film. A famous film. The man made films for fifty years. He was a Hollywood mogul. Head of Twentieth Century Fox.' Nico was tempted to ask the editor if he had heard of the twentieth century, but as Nico was the one seeking the favour, he stayed civil.

'I've never been keen on films,' replied the editor, as if artistic curiosity were distasteful. 'In gold, you said?'

'Well, gold-plated most likely.'

'But why would *anybody* put a replica of his own ... penis ... on top of his desk?'

'Things are done different in Hollywood.'

Nico sensed he was losing the argument. When Clydog, the senior reporter (indeed, the only reporter), had balked at writing up his news on grounds of propriety and taste, Nico knew that the forces of parochialism were ranged against him. He had appealed to the ageing editor – a person rarely seen in public as his journalistic strong point was righting split infinitives, not tangling with life – because he had once bought up a job lot of knick-knacks belonging to the man's late mother and he hoped this might constitute a bond.

Shifting a hundred of his penile reproductions, albeit quality items, albeit locally iconic, was proving a bit of a challenge, even for a man who saw the free market as a form of magic wand. First, the classified ads department, which would tout all types of semen, provided it were animal, had drawn a blue line through simulacra of genitalia that belonged to bank managers. Next, Nico had tried to generate a feature article, to place his cock-and-balls story in a wider cultural context, but Clydog, lifelong wordsmith of the *Mid-Walian*, had the nous to know a plug, however well transmuted.

'Your point being?' persisted the editor, who had felt short-changed when his mother's lace doilies had later tripled in price at auction.

'It's part of a showbiz tradition,' improvised Nico, 'sculpting your reproductive organs for public display.' (A collector of Hollywood trivia, he also knew that Clark Gable used to show off a hand-knitted penis, from his wife Carole Lombard, but Nico chose not to muddy the waters with this information.)

The editor's lips pursed tighter. 'It's not a tradition in mid-Wales. I keep a photo of a collie on *my* desk.'

It was an almost monastic desk, in an almost monastic office, as though the man brought the paper out yearly not weekly. It was hard to gain purchase on his personality.

'What I'm trying to say,' Nico tried to say, 'is it wouldn't be gratuitous, the article. OK, the subject might be penis replicas, but it would be full of social and historical perspectives.'

'And include the retail price.'

This was a low blow, a confidence betrayed by Clydog.

'Y-es, that's true ... but I don't think of this as a commercial venture,' said Nico.

The editor raised an eyebrow, not inclined to bother with speech. The visitor's sales pitch had till now confounded all his expectations.

'I think of it more as a commemorative medal. A souvenir of the most famous moment in the history of Abernant.'

'To be worn on the chest?' enquired the editor.

Nico was almost caught short of an answer. He rarely received mockery.

'As a pendant!' he retorted, a jest that lost touch with the social and historical high ground.

His unplanned Saturday visit had perhaps not been wise. Pique had pushed him to promote these very public private parts before his tactics were properly prepared. He had held off sales in order not to alienate Gareth, not to spread reminders of his cuckoldry like bomblets through the valley. But on confirming that his schmoozing had gained him no advantage, on learning that his scheming to graft a done deal had been derailed, Nico had gone straight to revenge mode. Without awaiting any auction.

'Could become a fashion accessory!' he added, to turn the tone to humour.

The editor had an austere face, more bones than flesh, and it showed no sign of movement. No twitch of interest, no curve of encouragement, no nod of approval.

Socially, he was more adept with dead people, and spent his spare time trowelling into the past. Author of sixteen monographs on local archaeology, nine to be viewed (by appointment) at the library, he passed his working days regretting his career path. But he found an eccentric solace by keeping to the Victorian layout, by staying with the archaic typeface, by resisting the crass daemons of modernism, be they gossip columns or star signs. The editor had within his head an ideal edition of the *Mid-Walian*, and it would have been in Latin.

'We don't do fashion,' he replied.

Nico bit his tongue and played his last card.

'It'd boost your circulation, my penises. Even more if you ran them as a Special Offer.'

The editor's glazed eyes made a final effort to focus.

'Perhaps,' he suggested to Nico, 'a stall in the market might be more appropriate?'

'Oh, fuck off, you prat!' cried Nico, undermining his negotiating position.

Chapter 30

'Money?' said the Lord Lieutenant.

'An appeal,' said Gwyn, in his best magistrate's voice.

'Hmm,' said the Lord Lieutenant.

Gwyn had backed the Queen's Representative into an arbour of his best hibiscus.

From the lower lawns rose the chintzy chatter of the soft-core membership, couples who had joined the Trust for the social perks of nature. Perks like Pencroeslan Manor (with one 'l'). These members were not the type to dig out ponds for newts or cut up wood for holts or saw down trees for glades, but they liked a light lecture with slides, and they loved wine and cheese with the gentry. This was not a day for hoop-la or guess the vicar's weight, but a chance to chat with a hat on. A Royal Garden Party *sans* royals.

One Sunday a year, the members came to gaze at the lake, to gawp at the gardens, to guess at the cultivars in the greenhouse. And of course to partake of refreshments. The official word was Open House, an invitation so casually grand as to cause an outbreak of inhibition. (Much like the carte blanche of free love.) Such liberal hospitality presumably extended, in theory, to a game of doubles on the tennis court, but no one was known to have dared. There was, though, a little rowing boat, and some committee members had one year inspected the artificial Victorian island. But that was as far as the lese-majesty had gone.

For the trustees, that quirky collection of cognoscenti, the visit to their patron's estate was more like a field trip to check the man's credentials. Cream scones scoffed, most would wander his woodland taking note of bird-boxes and bat-boxes and eco-piles, and trying to expand their species lists. The fungi and fern experts usually had the forethought to bring a pocket microscope to liven up the party. A naturalist is not unlike a trainspotter, but more sensitive to aesthetics, and even the cushiest recliner and unlimited Pimm's are no match for the thrill of taxonomy.

This year the weather was helpfully good, delaying the parting of swallows, and all the fun and the food was al fresco, with no need to chat in the crush of a Tudor mansion.

Which was why Gwyn had chosen an arbour.

'Hmm,' said the Lord Lieutenant again. Sir Gwynfor Llewellyn-Lloyd, CBE, was formerly of the diplomatic service and had gone a long way in his career by saying 'Hmm'.

'Would that be a yes or a no?' asked Gwyn eventually, sweetening the probe with a smile. '... or a maybe?'

'Hmmm,' said the Lord Lieutenant, adding an 'm'. Possibly for mystery. Occasionally, in his role as patron, he would attend a Trust meeting, and would sit for three hours being gnomic. Even his nods were non-committal. Supposedly his plus point was that he knew people. Who these people were was not clear.

'Hmmmm.'

Sir Gwynfor was a tall, thin, bony man with a leathery face, possibly the price of overseas postings. Young Mr Perkins the herpetologist said their patron was half-man, half-lizard (though he said it at those meetings the Lord Lieutenant didn't attend) and Perky reckoned he probably had an extra-long tongue for flies.

'An appeal?' Sir Gwynfor repeated, his brain having apparently been away on a journey.

'Yes,' said Gwyn. 'That's right.'

'A public appeal? To raise funds? To buy a reserve?'

'That's right.'

'For a bird?'

'Yes.'

'Aren't you taking your hobby a bit far?'

Gwyn counted to 3. He had always found their patron too much of the old school, too much from the comfort of old money to comprehend the post-Edenic world. Tumbrels would have to come calling before the man spotted a malcontent yokel. And, he liked to say, whilst nature must be nurtured, there was no need to nationalise it.

'It's not just the bird –'

'We've already got a pond; and a wood; and that marsh thing of the Archbishop.'

'It's also a rare habitat.'

'What makes it so rare?'

'Benign neglect, the best.'

'And what does Lady Hartbury think?'

Bugger all with *her* brain cells, thought Gwyn. But counted again to 3. This was the all-too-familiar bugbear, the axis of aristocracy. God had given them the land and only they understood it, only they had its interests at heart. Biology and botany were latecomers, as were all the sciences, and likely to make a mess of management. Best leave the blue-blooded to hunt the land to health.

'I don't think she's expressed an opinion on *Lullula arborea*.'

Sir Gwynfor's skin tightened. 'How big is this bird?'

'I'm not sure size is the issue.'

'Will be for the public. They'll want a big bird for their money. What colours does it come in?'

'It sings. Beautifully.'

'The Abernant Male Voice Choir sings beautifully, but we don't try and save them for the nation.'

'No one is likely to destroy their habitat.'

'A lot of pubs are closing.'

Gwyn sensed the colloquy was not going well. And the fact that his bird was small, brown, and a little paunchy did not aid his case. Most previous attempts to mount appeals had foundered on the rock of unsexiness. The higher-ups were hard to pin down, but if they were to save anything for the nation it seemed most likely to be a panda with wings. This giant chimera would fly from roof to roof as it stir-fried bamboo and waved.

'And you say it's going to auction, this land?'

'Yes.' Gwyn nodded. The information was hot from the mouth of Mr Probert, here to bang his gavel for charity. 'Heard today. So any campaign would have to be quick out the blocks.'

'Hard to raise money when you don't know how much money to raise.'

'Oh, I'm sure we could get a pretty good idea of –'

'No. I'm sorry. Won't fly, your Lulu bird.' And with that the Lord Lieutenant turned away to admire one of his trumpet-like blooms. 'Lovely colours, the Lilac Queen. Hmm?'

And Gwyn knew then that the subject was closed. In his bleaker moments, he feared that feudalism would outlast all but the hardiest genus.

He gazed about at the carefree figures enjoying the warmth of the sun. He felt adrift from the jollity of the day, where all was right with the world. He felt the world was fraying at the edges, each new generation with less and less to celebrate. Some did not care what they had lost, but some did not even know.

He watched a grey heron, sent aloft by faint voices on the water's wind, as it slowly flapped overhead. He always found it a bird of paradox, so trigger-sensitive to intrusion yet conveying such languid unconcern as it searched for safer shallows. But then that same bird would also stand transfixed in Buddhist contemplation while it waited one-legged to make a brutal killing.

'**Good morning, Vietnam!**'

The dovecots emptied in a frenzied white flapping and a black cawing cloud rose out of the rookery as Mr Probert struggled to moderate the mike, his little DJ joke booming at deafening decibels.

To a casual observer, Mr Probert was stolid and middle-aged. To his colleagues, he was a man whose stolid, middle-aged exterior was a front for workaday dullness. Yet in private he could, and would, reel off reams of word-perfect jokes from the *Goons* (with funny voices) and re-enact many a scene from *Monty Python*. He also had the full Captain Kirk kit, and the previous month had attended the first-ever *Star Trek* conference in Merthyr Tydfil. The only hint of this rich inner life was the multicoloured blazer he wore on weekend outings.

Like any auctioneer, his voice was his living; and like many an auctioneer, he did guest-spots for good causes. It was as a favour to his employee, young Mr Perkins, with whom he shared an interest in lizards, that he had offered his selling services. A marquee had been put up as a failsafe, but, like the badger-suited person with the raffle tickets, he had gone for the flagstoned terrace, to give a view of would-be buyers beneath him in the gardens.

'**Good morning, Vietnam!**' he cried again, the microphone now tamed.

Alas, it seemed that he alone had been to the Abernant Agora to see the latest release of Robin Williams, and his impersonation – and indeed its purpose – caused bemusement for a second time.

Gwyn watched the guests drift up along the sunlit lawns and garden paths to within bidding range, like agnostics tepidly obeying a muezzin's fuzzy call to prayer. Near by on the terrace, the bring-and-buy plant stand – that social grease of any successful village – was stripped to the last of its leaves, though the three rare fossils on the geology stand constantly outnumbered those showing interest in them. Further along, outside the French windows, ladies in summery frocks bustled about the tea-laden trestle, highlighting the esoteric merits of their cake-fillings.

A downcast Gwyn could not quite decide whether all this was a pastoral scene which had the charm of the timeless or the tedium of the predictable.

'Lot 1,' announced Mr Probert, after posing for a photo beside the Lord Lieutenant and his dog and both his guns and his wife.

Mr Probert had a dozen or so items to auction, all of a nature new to his repertoire. Twenty-three-year-old Kevin Perkins, the Trust's only link with the modern world, and hip things like PR, had promised a dose of stardust. But behind his horn-rimmed glasses he was prone to fantasy and, despite his begging phone calls, the big names of orienteering and steam traction engines had, apparently, found better things to do. This had left the Trust facing a Fun Day thin on fun. So instead, the young man had gone to something he called Plan B. He had written to the top tier of Abernant's movers and shakers: the Chamber of Commerce.

He had not wanted to overreach himself, to risk a further rebuff. So any request had had to be simple. He could have asked for photographs; he could have asked for mementoes; he could have asked for underwear. Instead, the young man had gone to something he called Plan C. Doodles. He had asked them each to do a doodle.

He had read about this idea in a style magazine at the dentist. (*Power Naps, Power Walks ... and now Power Doodles!*) Everybody doodled, it seemed, busy people, powerful people, bright people, dull people, inartistic people. They doodled on blotters, on letters, on napkins, on newspapers, on sandy beaches, on lovers' bottoms. The doodle was the great leveller, no cause for shame, no test of integrity, no loss of face. It took little time (unless you were weird) and it used little effort. In short, it was the perfect new currency for charity. The magazine had said.

Mr Probert looked hard at Lot 1. It taxed his powers of description.

'Lot 1,' he repeated. 'By Mr Bufton, the ironmonger. Wire wool ... or possibly woodsmoke.'

Mr Probert had riffled through the doodles over tea and a sponge-cake, and had struggled with these works of the imagination. Most had no title, some could go any way up, several were open to suggestive interpretation, and one now had loganberry jam on. Few gave one confidence in Abernant's business community.

'... or maybe a wig.' He looked around for a bid. 'Do I hear £10?'

He supposed some of them might be Freudian, and wished he knew what that meant. Camp Mr Devonald, the boutique owner, appeared to have drawn a line of high-kicking matchstick men in skirts. Mr Armstrong, the off-licence owner, had gone for a bee-style swarm of overlapping cuboids, which Mr Probert took to be beer cans. And Hubert, the delicatessen owner, had drawn a picture of a butcher, pierced by as many arrows as St Sebastian, but this was more private vendetta than art.

'Do I hear £5? All in a good cause. To help look after Mother Nature.'

From the shade of a Scots pine, Gwyn watched the auctioneer's attempts to magic money out of the balmy afternoon air. The upturned faces of the well-fed crowd stayed blank, failing to react with either interest or offers. No pockets were about to be dug deep for a potage of squiggles.

'£4? Who'll give me £4 to start? Very artistic man, the ironmonger.'

Mr Probert was also having doubts about the running order. Where should he put old Mr Beavan the bookseller, whose depiction of very long socks on a washing line was a literary allusion that escaped him. Or, indeed, the owner of Celtic Militaria, who had gone big on zigzags, in a blitzkrieg sort of way.

'£3? Surely worth £3? An original work, a Bufton! In Abernant High Street since 1854.'

One hand went up, and a giggle rippled through the crowd. Perhaps a relative, perhaps the potency of Pimm's. But the gesture was not catching, and Gwyn was none too surprised. Financial frivolity was rarely a feature of mid-Wales life, nor indeed was frivolity itself. Loose money only flowed near beer. Gwyn fell reflective. He wished he knew how to make it flow near birds.

'Any advance on £3?' called Mr Probert.

Gwyn gazed at all the members scattered amid the flowerbeds. They had done their bit, they had ticked direct debit. They now slept easy at night. And probably never read what he wrote and Roneoed. Nor hardly ever came to the AGM, the only time he had a captive audience for his thoughts and his plans and his fears. What more was there he could do? He wondered who to ask about woodlark T-shirts.

'Any advance on £3?' called Mr Probert a second time, his gavel raised.

'Four!' bid Sir Gwynfor the one-time diplomat, very loudly and publicly doing his duty as patron.

'Twenty-five!' counter-bid Gwyn, a provocation that caught even him unawares.

Chapter 31

Mrs Whitelaw was pleasantly surprised. There were more naked bodies than she had expected. Even in the hall.

The sex was a welcome sight after her trouble with the chickens. Two hours she had been delayed, and still not found their heads. She had had to shower a second time to be sure she was rid of the feathers. The loss was all the more personal for she had known both birds by name. More than mere egg-makers, more than just pretty cluckers, these were classy chickens. The Buff Orpington is much prized by the trade for the plumpness of its body, for not being bred as a bird of bone and feathers. Presumably this fact made it a fox favourite, and had shortened the odds on carnage at the caravan.

After she had hosed down the leftovers and soothed the squawking next of kin, Marjorie looked upon an afternoon of multiple coupling at a mansion as the ideal way to unwind. Orgies brought back her only fond memories of Surrey.

She and her first husband had been swingers in the days when it was called something else, when its status was subterranean. It was not that she had thought their neighbours were sexy – indeed, there were few that she liked – but she had had libido going spare. And the advantage of blindly banging one's neighbours was that all need to talk to them was neatly avoided. Occasionally the sex had had to be preceded by the social niceties of strip poker, by the tawdry protocol of tease, but mostly it was clothes off and heads down. And a race to be the most outrageous.

'Good afternoon!' announced Mrs Whitelaw as she moved on in to Crug Caradoc and lithely, blithely, stepped around a threesome where no mouths were free to reply.

This was her first time inside the valley's grand house, for so long a borderline ruin, but the name and noise of its owner were known to her as their paths had crossed before, at village fêtes. There he had done his dummy runs as lord of the manor, loudly admiring biscuits and babies and (here he got it wrong) big breasts. She had been reminded of old B movies, where an alien is sent to earth in human form and must master the natives' habits – but their funny little ways confound it time and again, and it is revealed not to be an earthling. Sheep kingdoms are particularly tricky for the outsider. Winning respect is not best done by bombast, and being squirely is not just down to bank balance, so these two baffling truths of the valley had sometimes left Stéfan like a thwarted day-visitor from Mars.

The call for her body had come via Eryl, odd-job man and pander, so it seemed. Quite how he knew that on occasion she took cash for her flesh, she was not sure, but Marjorie had in no way been unwilling to make up the numbers of the naughty. She classed it under iconoclasm, perhaps the more so as she was a pound or two past her prime. Besides, caravan walls could be very confining, and it was a while since her loins were last used.

She kept an eye out for his ponytail, a useful marker amid the monochrome of nudity, as she walked through the heart of the mansion. For puzzling reasons, presumably pretension, a Beethoven piano concerto was playing in the background, tastefully muffling most of the panting and grunting. Classical music and wood panelling, circa 1700, gave to priapism an unexpected aura of respectability. And this, perversely, made it more erotic.

Eryl appeared, not at all an erotic sight. Still partly clothed, he had little to distract from his acne.

The two were acquaintances, in the rural sense that no one is a stranger, and they laid claim to little more than nodding in the lanes. She knew of his scattergun lusting, knew of his failure as an *homme fatal*, and she favoured a barge-pole as their minimum distance for intimacy. Too quick to be tactile, too thick to be tactful, he magnetised few babes. So although Marjorie was happy – indeed rather keen – to get naked in front of strangers, she was glad that her hello to Eryl was not complicated by their private parts.

'Afternoon, Marjorie.' He kissed her cheek, but like a man whose mind was elsewhere.

For a leching loser at last in touching range of totty galore, he seemed subdued, and less than cheerful. Instead of gleefully ogling those around and under him, he kept glancing at his hand, a hand that held something odd in its grasp.

He took her elbow with his free arm.

'Come into the garden,' he said. 'We thought you might be someone with a history of croquet.' He led her through the drawing room and out on to the terrace, now aglow – and possibly aghast – in the warm afternoon sun.

The garden of Crug Caradoc looked set for a rerun of Eden, but on a slightly more industrial scale. Drifting through the grounds in twos and threes, with the giggles that are attendant on near-nudity, were the rest of the guests who had come from Stéfan's world, whatever that was. Odds-on they were urban. Nature clearly came as a new and puzzling concept and few could think of anything to do with it but cavort. So carefree was their cavorting that the shrubbery was superfluous as a venue, redundant as innuendo.

'*Pas comme Déjeuner sur L'herbe!*' joked Marjorie, who had done art history at evening class.

'What?' said Eryl.

'Nothing,' said Marjorie.

Eryl and Marjorie made their sex-free way through the ornamental gardens, past the urns and the sundial and the occasional nude, strolling about like a Greek statue on the make. She loved the matter-of-factness of the debauchery, the casual disregard for decency, the freedom to not give a fig about a fuck. But she was too worldly-wise a woman to believe this was any liberal counter-culture, or some laidback love-children born of the dope-dazed Sixties. These were hot-shot money-makers, high on power and poppers. These were the new young thrusters, whose ego was all and who lived rule-free in the fast lane, in the sod-you club of the hardnosed Eighties.

Marjorie paused by the bog garden, where the last of the mimulus was struggling to impress.

'Any other valley people coming?' she asked, more as a tease than a question.

Eryl shook his head.

'Thought not. Not an easy invitation to put on the mantelpiece!'

Eryl gave barely a smile. She wondered if he looked so sour because in another life he might have been the emcee.

'What's he like to work for, your Stéfan?'

Eryl shrugged and pulled a face. 'He likes to win. So my job description is to come second. He says I'm perfect at it.'

Marjorie struggled, but failed, to disentangle the irony from the self-pity, and they moved on toward the topiary. The most serene of greens, all the ancient yew bushes had bulked out, narrowing the path to the croquet lawn, softly brushing their bodies as they passed by. In need of an end-of-season trim, the cockerel and the cat had grown more ambiguous, less confident.

'D'you know Nico?' asked Eryl suddenly.

'Not to speak to. Not that I'd want to ... why?'

'Oh, no reason.' And then he gave a reason. 'Just don't buy anything from him. Or sell anything to him.'

'Right,' she said. '... why?'

'Oh, no reason,' he repeated. But this time he stayed silent.

Embarrassment had got the better of bitterness. He had spent weeks impatient for the proceeds of his little pub scam, the proof that he could be a player, that he could best his boss. He had tried hints, he had tried demands, he had tried complaints, but the cash somehow never came, for Nico saw in him a sap. A much smarter move, his wheeler-dealer would-be partner kept insisting, was to go for goods in exchange, the streetwise way to make a killing. And so finally, yesterday, Eryl had succumbed to these siren calls to his greed, and his great need to be big-time. He had gone for what Nico claimed to be his hottest items, his Bargains of the Month.

One hundred penis replicas.

Eryl's big idea – his first idea of any size in many years – had been to cash in on Stéfan's hardcore party. Like an usherette with ices, he would come round with penises. And for the last few hours, odd-job Eryl had been trying to tempt the London libertines with his repro bits of off-cut statue. He had touted them in various high-concept ways: as souvenirs of a dirty weekend ... as historic memorabilia of Abernant ... as sex symbols of

Crug Caradoc ... as Oscars of the orgy ... as Welsh works of erotic art. Sales to date were nil.

And so, in a final phallic gimmick, he had attached a set of these genitalia to the mansion's great front door, like a coat of arms for the kinky (to Stéfan's lewd delight), but there for use as a funky knocker. And had tried out a punchier sales pitch. *What every horny house had to have! Begin your visit with a bang! The ultimate in entries!*

Alas, just one knock and it had shattered. As had the second. And the third. And with them went his pay day and his triumph. Cast-iron knockers these were not, despite all of Nico's deal-sealing words. Indeed, they seemed likely to go limp and soggy in rain. Now, lost for a game plan, beaten by his bartering, Eryl was left clutching a jigsaw of cheapo penis pieces in his hand. The sexual mystique of the rampant bank manager had at long last run its course.

Eryl found this all too hard to explain. He tossed his useless parts into the topiary and pressed on to the croquet lawn. Where a group of sporty guests had gathered.

The big bare backside of Stéfan – a rare view of referees – was the sign that new rules now applied. He strode amid the hoops like a circus ring-master in charge of his own wet dream. Champagne bottles lay dribbling in the grass while the players stood around stripping. No polite applause, no traditional whites, just a bit of whooping and a jiggling of tits. In a further break from tradition, the heavy roller was laid with lingerie.

Marjorie, forty-one, felt herself tingle with a teenage excitement. Just by her presence she was declaring and sharing a secret, admitting to much more than the masons. This left no need for subtlety and she stared greedily across the grass at what was in the Y-fronts. She was due a toy boy and now she could stack them in racks. In a sexual free-trade zone, the sex was about more than possibilities, it was about permutations.

'Your attention!' bawled Stéfan, wishing croquet came with a whip.

Marjorie looked in more detail at his bottom, which was not taut enough for her taste; indeed, there were the first signs of wobble on his chassis. Big-boned enough for a medium-sized bear, Stéfan's body had been made soft by sybaritism. And why a man of his wealth should let it stay white was a mystery.

'We are playing to Crug Caradoc Rules.' (Also known as Eryl's rules, but only to Eryl, thus adding plagiarism to his complaints.)

Stéfan gestured imperiously – or was it imperially? – at the mansion behind him.

Marjorie was not impressed. On her route from riches to rags, she had always found the downside of wealth to be the men who came with it. It took more than a listed building to bring her to orgasm.

'Two teams – one for men, one for women.'

Partisan cries came from both camps.

'Dress code, informal …' Stéfan paused for his punchline. 'Birthday suits only!'

He guffawed at his joke and a raunchy cheer went up from his house guests. All laggard nudes were given vigorous help with their buttons and there was a brief delay for horseplay, that soya substitute for humour.

Marjorie had come in a loose gingham dress, the sort that drops to the ankles with a shrug of the shoulders. She shrugged them. She hoped that her vestigial underwear was feather-free.

Stéfan leered around the lawn and caught her in his sights.

'For every fault there's a forfeit.'

His eyes followed her as she strolled across the court, ranging free like her late hens, to add her available body to the others.

'One. Hit the wrong ball and it's a blow-job!'

There was an enthusiastic response to the rigour of the penalty and a scrabble soon began to be first to the off. Or whatever the technical term was. For *croquets, roquets, bisques, peelees, carrots* and *continuations* were not tripping off any tongue. And nor were the wine-bar wannabes showing any sign of a ball-hitting history.

Yet the game could still be played with some period style. Long wooden coffins of croquet equipment stood open and empty on the newly Eryl-mown grass, and around them lay the mallets, and the balls in four colours, and a spare dowel extension for the peg. Venerable hand-worn objects, and all found stored in an outhouse, they had come with the mansion as light bulbs come with a semi. So even though the time-honoured traditions had turned tabloid, each player had the aid of antique weaponry.

'Two. Lose the ball and it's a fuck!'

Possibly a first for croquet, this penalty had the deterrent effect of a pep talk. Two noisy rows of randy men and bawdy women lined up naked with their mallets – more mob-handed than under Association Rules – and got ready for the sweaty joys of battle.

Stéfan advanced on them like a four-star general at a passing-out parade. He strode up and down the ranks of well-moisturised flesh and inspected the turnout of nipples; he stood sideways on and examined the hang of the breasts; and he marched along at the rear and got an overview of the buttocks. And instead of medals for merit, he awarded the women a lot of lustful pats.

'Three. Damage the lawn and it's a gang-bang!'

Words which were taken as the starting flag.

As the first wayward clunks of blue and yellow balls echoed around the court, and the white metal hoops stood fast against threats of violence, Stéfan's mind went back to Marjorie. He remembered her breasts from a jelly-bean stall, where he had briefly bantered about her cleavage with the Vicar. He had sensed a sexual something in the air, as so often was the case with women. He had made an offer that she join him for hoop-la, but she had demurred, clear proof of his view that she was playing hard to get. And now here she was, naked.

He bounded over – there was a certain puppiness to his extra flesh when he moved at any speed – to where she stood awaiting her shot, and watching the roll of the balls. He turned on the full Stéfan charm.

'No using your mallet as a dildo!' he boomed, going for the sure-fire winner of humour.

She took her time to respond. She took her time to so much as meet his gaze. And she left no room for doubt that the laughter was arriving not late but never, that the joke had withered till it fell off the vine as a fully paid-up corpse. She did this lest she be thought to collude in the rat-a-tat-tat of chat-up.

'Is that the national slogan of Georgia?' she eventually enquired.

But by now his leer had shifted to her loins, to her freshly showered and puffed-up pubic hair, and the power of her riposte got lost.

'You've got a great body for your age.'

'You don't know my age.'

'I was trying to pay you a compliment.'

'You've just failed.'

'Feisty, I like that in a woman.'

'Patronising, always a bummer in a man.'

Beyond them the first of the croquet couplings had already begun, the frustration of failure at a hoop leading straight to fornication, a game whose entry point offered easier access. And around them numerous nudes, with boaters bought specially for the occasion, went on striking their balls past the copulating couple, and so creating a tableau both sensual and surreal. With a stately mansion behind, and giant topiary to the side, the setting for the fucking would have won a thumbs-up from *Debrett*'s. All the scene lacked was a Victorian brass band in the background, waiting to give *oompahs* in time with the *ooh-aahs*.

'You come from a long line of wenches and I claim my *droit du seigneur*!' declared Stéfan, and squeezed her inner thighs as the clincher.

'Not a chance! Not even if you were Sir Bloody Lancelot and I was Guinevere on the rebound. So that's a no.' She did not sugar the pill with a smile.

But his hand stayed where it was and by now he had a hard-on. Which he waved around, and then pressed against her hip.

'But you've not met my miracle-worker. Everybody loves him. He'll change your mind.' All said with a syrupy softness.

Marjorie looked down at Stéfan's unprepossessing penis, snuggled up to her side.

'I wouldn't leave it there,' she said. 'It might get broken.'

But Stéfan was too priapic a man to recognise even the unsubtlest of hints, let alone take notice.

So she took hold of 'it' between forefinger and thumb, as if it needed dusting for prints. She looked at it carefully, doubtfully, from several angles, and then, like an unwanted fish, let it go.

'Not quite squire-size, is it?' she said, with dismissive disdain. 'Eh?'

'More serf-size, I'd say. Probably suffers from lack of exercise. And an unhappy home life. I should stick to pissing with it.'

'Abuse of the referee. Free fuck! Rule four.' He tried to disguise his annoyance.

'No means no. Even at croquet orgies. Rule five.' She did not try to disguise hers.

And she turned away to watch the hot hoop action.

'I don't think that attitude's very wise,' said Stéfan, all joshing suddenly gone from his tone.

Marjorie did not initially look round.

'Oh really? Meaning what? Off with my head?'

'Meaning you don't understand your position.'

'Oh? And what position would that be?'

'My tenant.'

Marjorie looked round.

'Your what …?'

Stéfan smiled like a man with a trump card about his naked person.

'That land your caravan's on?'

'Yes . . .?'

'I'm going to buy it.'

Chapter 32

'Walkers?' suggested Ben.

'Lovers?' suggested Bryn.

'Lost?' suggested Brian.

'I thought I heard the words "on the run",' said Brenig.

A bit baffled, the brothers gazed across the bar some more.

'If they're lost, they don't look very bothered,' mused Ben.

'If they were walkers, wouldn't they look a little pinker?' mused Bryn.

'If they were criminals, shouldn't they look a little shiftier?' mused Brian.

'And they're certainly not my idea of lovers,' said Brenig.

They gazed again.

'Couldn't we just ask them?' said Ben, the youngest and least worldly.

'Oh, how would that work exactly?' enquired Bryn.

'*Hello, and what are you up to round here?*' mocked Brian.

'Plus a questionnaire with their next drink!' added Brenig.

The four barmen-farmers returned to their gazing.

The couple in the corner were the first strangers they had seen in the pub for weeks. And the woman was drinking Bacardi and Coke, which had further attracted attention. Yet she was not dressed for Bacardi and Coke, and she had surprisingly sweaty armpits, revealed on removal of her pristine urban anorak. He had a tight Pringle sweater and a paunch, and twenty years more of life's wear and tear. But this did not stop him pawing his young companion's body. Who giggled a lot as he talked.

'I could offer to wipe their table. Again,' said Ben. 'And see if I got any leads.'

'Or I could distract them,' said Brenig, 'and you go through her bag for ID.'

Bryn and Brian laughed, and Ben was forced to grin, and all went back to the certainties of beer.

Then the outside door of the pub porch banged open, bringing the heady promise of another customer. And into the bar came Dafydd, his thirst a first here for a Sunday.

'Evening,' he grunted.

He had spruced himself up (in Dafydd terms) and almost looked presentable, with a 1960s tie, a shirt with no wavy pattern, and trousers in which he had ironed several creases. He had even polished part of his shoes. Unfortunately his crash helmet, with its multicoloured pizza insignia, suggested he might still be a saddo.

'Evening,' replied Brenig and brothers.

Dafydd looked around the bar, in a sort of disappointed hope, then he eased himself on to a stool like a man whose bottom was weary at heart.

'A pint,' he said, 'and a whisky.' This was the second rare order in one day.

'Trouble?' enquired Ben.

'No!' said Dafydd.

'Your moped OK?' enquired Bryn.

'Yes!' said Dafydd.

'That guttering of yours stopped leaking?' enquired Brian.

'It's fine.'

And here enquiries ceased. The brothers sensed that something was amiss, but they were a breed whose caring, sensitive side had yet to find a language for matters non-mechanical.

When the beer came Dafydd let the froth lie unbothered on his upper lip. He sat in semi-silence, spreading no rumours, a sure sign of malfunction. And all the while he ruminated on the ill-luck of his love life.

It had not been a date. It had not even been a provisional date, put down in pencil. He had simply said he might drop by on a Sunday … if he happened to be passing. He had prepared for this vague happenstance by buffing his body for a week and buying men's style-magazines. He had even found a hair dye that claimed to cure ginger.

She was always in on a Sunday, she had said, but apart from some bloodstains and the odd gizzard there was no sign of anyone at the caravan. He knew her social life to be very dull and empty, and had ridden up and down the lanes for over an hour, hoping to effect a chance meeting and bring some zing to her weekend. To complete his charm offensive he had come with a freebie pizza, plus extras. But Marjorie was nowhere to be found, and in his fantasies he feared there might be another man, plying her with tea and buns and sharing a knowledge of the Tudors.

'What do you reckon to a jukebox?' asked Ben.

'Sorry?' said Dafydd, his mind halfway up Marjorie's thighs.

'Hits of the '60s,' said Bryn.

'I don't think you can drink *and* listen to music,' doubted Dafydd.

'It'd get the toes tapping,' said Brian.

'Beer's got its own rhythm. It'd spoil your concentration.'

'It'd bring new life to the pub,' said Brenig.

'The Yellow Cockatoo had folk singers once. Their barman was off with tinnitus for nearly a month.'

'Was he insured?' asked Ben.

'You can't insure against folk singers.'

The thread of the conversation petered out, karaoke unspoken for fear of derision.

The sound of silent men drinking, that cultural quiddity of pubs through the ages, returned to centre stage.

And then a chair scraped across the flagstones, and the Bacardi and Coke lady went off to the outside toilet.

The Pringle man, urban to the touch and balding in parts, carried both their glasses back to the bar. He gave a polite smile as he stood about and waited.

'Hello. What are you up to round here?' asked Dafydd.

'Us? Oh, we're dead.'

The Dragon's Head struggled to match the draws of the bright lights of Abernant. Seventeen pubs and a curry place made this the Mecca of the Nant Valley, the Shangri-la of the drunk. The market days meant drink without end, the quiz nights meant pints as prizes. And there was the added attraction of fights. Modern young farmers no longer wanted just to be bucolic.

Time was, according to the historical stats of Miss Stevens, when there had been 151 pubs, approximately one per front room, and inebriation was the norm. In Victoria's day, Abernant was one big beer bank, with all the locals overdrawn. Town boozing had now been so long in the blood, it had become heritage boozing, and possibly eligible for a tourism grant.

But out in the sticks, Stéfan's hostelry had less of a history and few for a fan base. The bar had begun as add-on to a forge, where red-hot heat gave a boost to a thirst, but even then was seldom a money-maker. For years under Gwillim its specialist appeal had been to the solitary drinker: always male, often curmudgeonly, and frequently defeated by the land and the life he led. And now its new ownership blunted any enthusiasm from the valley, as locals with money to spend saw better coffers to put it in than those of Mr Crug Caradoc.

This meant that Sunday evenings were often on the dullish side.

'... you're dead?'

Dafydd and the brothers waited for help with the joke.

But Pringle stayed kinda smug, milking the moment.

'Dead ...? As in ...?' prompted Dafydd.

'Blown to bits. Both of us.'

'... but not fatal?' said Ben, who easily tired of existential subtlety.

Pringle did not like people upsetting his timing. He was a man to whom excitement rarely happened, and he wished to make the most of his public pronouncements. So he allowed his enigmatic pose to last several seconds longer.

And then went, '**Boom!**' And added expansive gestures depicting a Second World War depth charge.

Pringle waited, like a teacher with slow-stream children, for pennies to drop.

'... no,' said Ben.

'... no,' said Bryn.

'... no,' said Brian.

'... no,' said Brenig, albeit reluctantly as he was the oldest and claimed to be the brightest.

'Bomb disposal. Melissa and I were dismantling a bomb.'

'Oh. Right.' The brothers gave the matter some thought. '... why?'

'Management training.'

'A real bomb?'

'No, of course not!'

'What do you do for a living?'

'I'm a VAT systems administrator.'

'D'you have much problem with bombs?'

'It was an *exercise*,' explained a piqued Pringle. 'To learn new methodologies.'

'And does dying mean you've failed?'

Pringle tried to ignore this. He was not at his happiest under questioning. As when telling a joke, he expected his audience to stick to their function as listeners. Pringle came from that band of middle management where independent thought in others was not to be encouraged. This could have been a contributory cause to his untimely if fictitious death.

'So I guess you came to the pub to get over the shock,' said Ben.

'Not exactly,' replied Pringle, with a slightly adolescent smirk.

'This "bomb" ...' said Dafydd, still struggling with the visuals of the depth charge scenario.

'It was in the middle of a swimming pool.'

'... aah. But not a real swimming pool.'

'Oh yes,' said Pringle. 'That was the problem.'

The brothers looked at each other, and then looked again at the plumpish, pinkish Pringle. These were men who rarely had to wrestle with methodologies, new or old, and were wary of conceptual bombs; they were also distrustful of any customer who spent Sundays in weird forms of management. It all bore out their deepest suspicions of VAT.

'I don't think we'd ever have guessed this one right,' said Bryn.

'Damn true,' said Brian.

'They give you things,' said Pringle, intent on savouring the drama of his derring-do. 'Things to help you get the "bomb" from the middle of the pool and out on to the side. Which renders it safe. All to a tight deadline.'

'"Things"?' repeated Dafydd, revived by the prospect of gossip as good as the best of yesteryear. 'What things?'

'Well, a length of bailer twine, a bar of soap, a safety-pin, a bicycle pump, a sheet of greaseproof paper ...' Here he became vague. '... and a half-brick, I think.'

'But what do you do with all these things?' asked Dafydd.

'Think creatively,' said Pringle. 'That's how we died.'

'I'm very sorry to hear that,' said Brenig.

'Oh, don't be!' said Pringle. 'Good excuse to slip away.'

'Slip away?' enquired Ben.

'Oh, yes.' Pringle leaned closer. 'Nudge, nudge, wink, wink.'

'Pardon?'

Pringle jerked his head in the direction of the toilets. 'It's not *all* management.'

'It's not?' said Bryn.

'Oh no. Wouldn't waste a weekend here if it was!'

He gave the conspiratorial smile that men give to other men, and tapped his nose.

'That's why they've got a waiting list, these courses. All of them oversubscribed. My department is chocker with admin execs wanting to bond better with their staff. In a wilderness setting. With bedrooms.'

'Oh. I see,' said Brian uncertainly. 'This Sunday is full of surprises.'

'Twenty of us here this time, unlocking our potential. Adapting to new situations. Persevering and overcoming obstacles. Pretending to be open and honest.'

'And Melissa ...?' asked Brenig.

'My PA.' Pringle smirked. 'She's hoping this course could give her promotion.'

'And will it?'

'Might need a few more courses.' Extra smirking.

Dafydd surreptitiously studied the middle-aged paper-pusher beside him, his unlovely body looking homeless without its suit, and struggled in vain to understand the sexual magic of power. A moped was no match. He wondered what lessons to draw. Should he and Marjorie go on courses, and what could they be?

'So you'll be back again?' asked Ben.

'Definitely,' replied Pringle. 'Lot of interpersonal development still to do. And, of course, the centre will be expanding next year.'

The brothers exchanged glances of surprise.

'Expanding?' said Dafydd.

'Yes. It's buying more upland. More bracken to get lost in – and lie in!' The nudge-nudge tone gave way abruptly to a dopey smile as he caught sight of the door, where Melissa had reappeared, freshly powdered and looking subserviently sexy.

'Well, *that* will depend on whether their bid or ours wins at auction,' said Brenig.

'Centuries of sheep-grazing history on that land,' said Brian.

'Providing prime cuts of lamb for the public,' said Bryn.

'And a living for hard-working farmers,' said Ben.

Dafydd said nothing, the sight of Melissa making him wonder what to do with the cold pizza in his pannier.

4

Winter Turns to Spring

Chapter 33

'That's strange!' said Gwyn, halting unexpectedly.

He let drop his wife's shopping and stared at the dead fox cub on the end of their kitchen table.

Audrey moved up to his side and stood sharing his staring.

'What's strange?' she asked.

'He's moved!' said Gwyn. 'He was dead when we went out, and he's moved.'

The month-old cub lay motionless on his back, his stomach so distended that no normal posthumous posture was possible; his legs were stuck awkwardly upward like a resident of Pompeii caught short by Vesuvius.

'Are you *sure* he's moved?' asked Audrey.

'I left his body in the middle of the table, next to the butter dish.'

'And you wonder why I left home?' said Pauline, their daughter, as she followed them in with her weekend bag.

Gwyn went down the table and bent over the bloated brown body of Aristotle. (He gave classical Greek names to every animal he rescued, sometimes even called them after gods, for reasons he had never fully made clear.)

'He ate a pound of raw liver,' Audrey explained to her daughter. 'Lamb's liver. Which was meant for your lunch.'

'Took us an hour to find him,' said Gwyn. 'He'd dragged it under the dresser.'

'He knew he was naughty,' added Audrey.

'Wedged, he was,' said Gwyn. 'Wedged tight.'

He put on his reading glasses, his face just inches from the putative corpse, as though to check for written clues.

'We had to move the dresser. Your father had to lift it up.'

'The most bizarre sight,' said Gwyn. 'Like he'd been crossed with a balloon!'

'He'd even swallowed the greaseproof paper with the blood on. Daft creature!'

'Eyes closed, not moving. Dead to the world. That's why I laid him on the table.'

'Without so much as a wreath?' asked Pauline, and got her neck squeezed.

'We were running late for your bus,' said her mother.

Gwyn rested a finger upon the cub's abdomen, a test that left him puzzled.

'He's still warm. I think he must be in a coma.'

'What?' said Pauline, her own concern now showing. 'Can you get a coma from overeating?'

'Perhaps if you're a fox ... Who knows?'

Gently, Gwyn lifted Aristotle up, let him lie briefly in the hollow of his hands, and then set him back down in the middle of the table, the huge liver-laden stomach still uppermost.

'Guess we can only wait and see.'

Pauline blew softly on to Aristotle's tranquil face, but to no visible effect.

'Abandoned and blind when first we found him. That was another palaver.'

'Why don't you two light a fire in the front room?' suggested Audrey. 'While I make some tea?'

Gwyn gave the unconscious cub one last look of bemusement, and then, after lifting the shopping bags on to a chair, he and Pauline took away a copy of the *Mid-Walian*, always best when torn into strips.

The front room, although warm and cosy to look at, was always slow in shaking off a chill. Winter ended later on the hill. Once every month Gwyn would order a pick-up's load of logs, enough to keep the shed a quarter-full, and make claim to be an axeman. Standing on their sward, the axe above his head, his woman needing warmth, he oftentimes found the sight of logs around his feet was quick to provoke some primitive emotions. Shifting them and splitting them was a ritual rich in rural imagery, evoking a life defined by hoar frost and robins and lived by frontiersmen. A morning of hewing would leave Gwyn unfailingly proud of his wood basket ... and trying to deny he felt faint.

Pauline sat quietly behind her father and watched his expertise as he knelt next the hearth, inserting each crunched strip of paper with the precision due a detonator, and adjusting each twig as if it belonged to a hairdo. He had no truck with firelighters, the tool of the idiot and the arsonist, but relied on the flickering subtlety of a match. And with a single match he set alight all sections of the sports page, sending small red flames racing through the rugby, the cancelled canoeing, and a report on bad bowls etiquette.

'Apple,' he said approvingly, as he laid the first log on the kindling.

'Not again!' said his daughter. 'It was apple last time.'

'Well, if you're going to fill the room with smoke it might as well be flavoured.'

'One of my earliest childhood memories, smoke. I wonder if that's normal.'

'If we could have got you up the chimney, we'd have solved the problem.'

Then, as the minutes burned by, her father laid on each new log with exactitude and timing, knowing just when the flames needed feeding, knowing just when the flames were full.

When all was aglow, he leant back on his heels for a long moment and gazed intently into his fire, like an artist checking the brushstrokes on a finished painting.

'Pull me up!' he said, holding out a hand and pretending to be old ... and trying to hide that this was no pretence.

He flopped down beside her on the sofa, a sofa that had come from a second-hand shop shortly after Suez and the cash crisis of parenthood. Like their kitchen, this was a room of whim and bargains, with a rug from the Crimea and a jug from Corsica and a chair from a Cardiff craft fair. Nothing shiny, nothing matching, nothing for the Joneses to get. When young, Pauline had hesitated to bring home her friends, so odd and unaspiring had seemed her surroundings. Yet now, all these years later, nothing had dated and the hotchpotch had harmonised.

'Did you bring your boots?' he asked her.

'Dad ...! You should know better than ask that. I was brought up to keep them with me even in bed. In case you announced an emergency walk.'

'That was only the once.' He looked hurt. 'Glow-worms.' He rallied. 'Part of any rounded education.'

'I wasn't complaining … So, what is it you've got in mind for me this time?'

'Fancy a boardwalk? Just laid down, beside the lake? Through the reed-beds.'

'With ducklings?'

'Not yet. Although I have got a tape somewhere of juvenile quacking.'

'I'll pass on that, thanks.' She grinned. 'But otherwise you've got a yes.'

'Splendid. Tomorrow morning, nasty and early? With a bit of mist rising?'

'You've sold it, Dad. Sounds perfect.'

'Not quite perfect. You've got to walk past a load of logos first. Some bloody bank pretending it cares. Thinks it's in partnership with "the natural world". The bank of choice for swans.'

Pauline was familiar with this refrain. The world was changing too fast for her father, who should have been pre-industrial (give or take a high-speed car). With little prompting, he would still quote chunks of Clare lamenting the first lost idylls, and insist he knew what had driven the peasant poet mad. For him to see the world of business muscling in, trying to draw a dividend from what they were despoiling, was always the spur for a hobby-horse moment.

'Any other news? Have you and nature done anything else I should know about?'

'Sadly not. Nature's been very quiet lately. Very quiet. Very … uneventful.'

He sighed and gazed into the fire again. She glanced across at him, at his grey-bearded profile. Just for a moment it had sounded to her like an old man's sigh. She was going to tell him jokes about her clapped-out car, about how her dance lessons had given her blisters, about how she was learning to cook curry.

But she changed her mind.

'Tell me about the fox.'

'Ah, Aristotle!' He beamed with a storyteller's excitement.

'Abandoned and blind …?' she said to start him off.

'And wet and cold, and in the middle of a ploughed field. He had to be less than eight days old. Not a great start to life for a fox. We almost didn't notice him amid all the dark earth, him still being black. And by now very earthy.

'I didn't want to touch him and leave my scent, but we looked round everywhere, could see nothing, and I reckoned his mother had been got by the hounds. One of Lady Hartbury's fun days out. So we decided to bring him back here, see if we could save him. But we were miles away, and it was pouring down, and he was already shivering. I wasn't sure he'd make it. So, age sixty-three, your father became a surrogate womb for the first time. I put him inside my shirt, and pressed him against my heart, so that he could feel it beating. Made it all very dark and warm and motherly for him. And that's how we got him back home and still alive. Which was when the first of our troubles started.'

'I seem to remember you having a bit of trouble with young of the human kind.'

'At least I never had to feed you through a condom!'

'What?'

'I had to go down that awful pub, owned by that foreign prat, slip into the toilets unseen, and buy a packet of condoms. And then slip out again. I was after an artificial nipple, you see.'

'… right.'

'To fill up with milk, and then pierce with a pin.'

'As you do.' Living away from home now, she sometimes forgot her father was not a normal father.

'I was rather pleased with my plan. A lot of lateral thinking. Very inventive. Didn't work, unfortunately. So greedy, the little brute just bit straight through it, and I got sprayed with a condom's worth of milk.'

In her entire adult life, she had never heard her father use the word 'condom', and she had not expected to do so before she died. And certainly not in a fox context.

'And he locked on to my finger instead. Three times, I tried it. Always the same result. Milk everywhere. So in the end, I gave up and filled a big bowl – one of *your* big bowls, the odd-shaped grey one with the wiggly orange stripe – full of milk, and pushed his nose in it. Like when you take a horse to water. Well, you'll never guess what he did next.'

Pauline had given up guessing some time ago, and simply shook her head.

'He walked straight into the bowl. Straight in! He was so small he almost vanished from sight. Below the level of the milk, his face was. Blind but absolutely fearless. And stupid. I was about to drag him out before he drowned when we heard this extraordinary noise. Like sucking. Like a … a great long slurping.' Her father provided a disgusting sound effect. 'And as your mother and I watched, the level of the milk started to drop, and it just kept on dropping – until his body came back into view, and he could start breathing again. Talk about a life force! I knew then that he was going to survive. Well, until today, I did! And he's been curled up by the Raeburn ever since, in a little dog basket. That is, when he's not round the house hunting and gathering and getting under Audrey's feet.'

The door was banged open by one of those feet.

'Tea!'

Tea was an understatement. Here was the overkill that often threatens to arrive when mothers say tea, and the three hefty mugs potted by Pauline came in on a tray with enough biscuits for a convention of vicars. It also came with a king-size hand-thrown teapot, plus the mail that had been overlooked in the morning's drama.

Audrey then joined them on the sofa, pleased that the focus of married life would, for a weekend at least, no longer be on the animal kingdom. These visits, four or five times a year, mattered more than she admitted. She sometimes worried about her daughter; although Pauline did not do drink or drugs, she did not do money either. The unworldliness gene, from which her mother suffered, had been handed down like some jokey rebuke about artiness. And as yet Pauline had not found the safe harbour of a partner.

The three sat snugly in a semi-silence, briefly content to eat and drink and say little. As a family, they were not programmed for idle and passive pleasures; the absence of a television was no showy refusenik credential but a blithe unawareness of the second-hand life. Even at the age of ten, Pauline was outdoors practising the pressing of flowers (and learning of Linnaeus just a little later). But for a moment, with Audrey sipping and Pauline dunking and crunching and Gwyn opening his letters, the world of domesticity descended.

'Fire's doing well,' said Audrey.

'Yes, soon be warm enough in here,' said Gwyn.

'I'm used to 1,200 degrees, you know,' said Pauline. 'That's the temperature *I* fire to.'

'I'm putting a new painting up over this fireplace soon. Cow parsley.'

'And that reminds me! I've got some pots in my bag for you.'

Ignoring entreaties to finish her tea, Pauline put down her plate and got up from the sofa. She had been gone from the room about three seconds when they heard her cry out.

She was stood staring at the kitchen table when Gwyn and Audrey entered. She pointed at Aristotle, who was still on his back, still dead to the world ... and once again at the far end of the table.

No one spoke for several seconds. Then mother and daughter looked to Gwyn the naturalist for enlightenment.

'Fairies,' he said. 'The fairies have been in.'

'Another scoop for the magazine,' said Audrey.

Again Gwyn went down the table and bent over the bloated body. Again he laid his finger on the cub's soft skin. Again no sign of life was to be seen.

'I just don't understand it,' he said. 'He couldn't move if he wanted to. And he's not capable of wanting to, not in his condition. Whatever his condition *is*.'

Gwyn gently prodded the cub, as if checking he were faking. But response came there none.

'Threaten to make fur gloves out of him!' said Pauline.

The family hovered around the cuddly little corpse-in-waiting, uncertain what to do, and without anything useful to say. Lost somewhere between life and death, Aristotle was beyond any human intervention. Audrey had – and hid – a disloyal wish that he might perhaps die, for a young house-fox soon graduates from cutely charming to demonically destructive, a persona to which it adds a vile stink.

'I wish I knew more about foxes,' said Gwyn. 'About their metabolism.'

He scooped Aristotle up in his hands once more, paused lest unbeknown to him the healing power of God was currently passing through his fingers, and then placed the cub back down next to the butter dish.

'I think we need to build a hide. And take turns watching him.'

'Well, you can take the first watch,' said Audrey. 'I'm going back to your fire.'

'Me too,' said Pauline. 'Sorry, Dad. There's only so much fox mystery I can take.'

She kissed him on the cheek, then picked up her bag, heavy with its cargo of unsolicited pots, and followed her mother out to the rising warmth that awaited next door.

Gwyn settled down into his geriatric armchair, with the subject of his vigil just a few feet away. Eight hours was his record for watching, and on that occasion he had been up a tree. His reward had been photos of a merlin and family, a rare coup whose memories still conveyed pleasure. But with bones that were beginning to creak, he now preferred his stake-outs more sedentary, and a kitchen was ideal habitat.

His eyeline was level with the corpulent cub, and he eyeballed him (in the lingo of the court) without a break for several minutes, in hope of a clue to his behaviour. But Aristotle remained serenely insensible, as if his body was grounded and his soul was in orbit. The coma drama continued. Gwyn came to fear a long wait.

He had rushed from the front room without putting down his mail, so urgent had seemed his daughter's call. And after several more minutes of staring at still life, he opted for keeping just the one eye on his patient while he flicked through the brown envelopes that remained. Dafydd, his former postman, had once told him that he held the record for the most letters ever received in a single day in the valley. It was a record Gwyn would gladly

210

have forgone, so tedious was much of his mail, so wearisome was the work of wildlife.

Last, and almost lost, among this day's post was a small, thin envelope, which had neither the weight to be an enquiry report nor the width to be committee minutes. He tugged at its tightly gummed flap and pulled out a single sheet of paper. He had reached paragraph three when his pointed jaw dropped.

'Good God!' he said.

And he read it again.

'Good God!' he said.

Gwyn stared in disbelief at the letter. And Aristotle let out the most enormous liver-powered fart. A fart of such force that it drove his unconscious little body toward the end of the table.

Chapter 34

The queue stretched for nearly thirty yards. It stretched all along the building. It stretched around the corner. Miss Stevens had never seen so long a queue before, not for any other of her exhibition openings. She was furious.

And now she was being asked to smile. Smiling did not come easily to her, even when she was happy (not that she often was). She was born tight-lipped, posing a problem for baby photos. Even aged six weeks, she had sensed that life was a serious business, and not a fit subject for mirth. Unusually, she had looked upon childhood as a time for arranging objects into collectible categories. Later, her doctoral thesis on cultural conflict in the Central Asian steppes had taught her that smiling was a social construct and unwise sign of weakness. A career in provincial museums had given her little cause to revise this view. And now the *Mid-Walian* wanted a smile.

As the victim of blackmail, Miss Stevens was ill-disposed to hoop-la.

She had, in the autumn, proposed an archaeological exhibition to depict the development of monastic influences on Abernant in the late Middle Ages. If yawns could clap, she would have had an ovation. The committee lacked a strong medievalist faction; their preference was for history that came with colour photos. The final decision was, of course, down to her, she being the artistic arbiter. But twenty-seven portraits of grass had not been a humdinger and council bottoms were said to be shifting in their grant-giving seats. As she made the case for long-dead monks and their fragmented artefacts, she had found herself squinting ever further down the barrel of a bureaucratic gun.

From then on, she had been working in a world of hints. Hints that *perhaps* her pewter and her primitive pottery parts might best be kept in storerooms; hints that *perhaps* the sixteenth (and seventeenth and eighteenth and nineteenth) century might be short on pulling power and best abandoned; and hints that, if she *were* more populist in approach, then *perhaps* some funds might be found to restore the museum exterior to its natural setting, viz. on the outside ... Followed by hints that, if not, her career could be over.

She stood in the heaving foyer full of former pediments and summoned up the smile.

The *Mid-Walian* had never, till today, shown any interest in her or her curating. No articles on the arts page, no profiles on the people page, no photographs on any page. Even the paid-for ads often appeared a week too late. But now her job was news, her gallery the hot ticket in town. Miss Stevens readied herself to give an interview, to eloquently express what were not her thoughts.

'The museum is very pleased,' she said, 'to give the public a chance to see –'

But before she could say more, before her silver-haired bun could be captured by the camera, the celebrity of the moment came beaming through the doors. And all attention shifted.

'Lovely to be here,' said Mrs Barbara Griffiths, widow.

She had clearly worked through her grieving and had moved on to grinning.

Death in a council car park lacked class as a method of bereavement, but had been the way she would have wanted him to go. And she did want him to go. Friends who had attended the funeral – an event with more uniforms than *HMS Pinafore* – spoke of her composure, and how she had winked when walking behind the coffin.

She had thanked the mourners who had paid tribute to his years of service, to his legacy of bandaged drunks. She had made show of admiring the wreaths, their flowers evocatively tied with first-aid knots. And she gave a little speech, movingly talking of how she had first met him as a lollipop man, so keen to help people to cross.

But after the body was buried, after the wake had dribbled to an end, there was a purging of his presence in their small terrace home. His boots were binned, his *Reader's Digests* sent to the dentist, and she took his outsize suits to the Sally Army, to help them bring Jesus to fat men. Her husband had also kept embroidered homilies, which hung hidden in recesses as if ashamed of their triteness. These his wife trashed with some vigour.

And then she brought the dogs in.

Her dogs were strangers to the house, banished by patriarchal diktat. Their yapping and their urine were felt not to be homely. But Barbara now made them welcome guests, puffing up the cushions and pointing out the sofas.

'Such a comfort,' she now explained to Clydog, the old-time journo, who had also done duty at the funeral. 'Do you have dogs?'

'My doctor advises against it.'

'I owe my dogs everything,' she said.

'How many do you have?'

'Six. They're my inspiration.'

'I can see that,' Clydog said.

' "Esmerelda and Friends",' said Barbara. 'A good title for the exhibition, don't you think, Miss Stevens?'

'Yes,' said Miss Stevens.

'Of course, I'm not a professional painter, but I do like a lot of colour.'

She had paused by no. 32, showing Esmerelda at dinner: seated, tongue lolling, at the head of the table, plate and knife and fork before her, red rosette upon the napkin neatly knotted round her neck. *Perfect Table Manners* read the caption.

'Twiggy of the doggy world,' she said proudly.

'Very good!' said Clydog, scribbling on his pad. Forty years in the fourth estate had, if nothing else, taught him to clock a good quote.

Miss Stevens said nothing.

'Before, with the shed, I was short of poses. But now I've got beds and baths and hearths and loads of props. So I can get my dogs to blossom, and show what cuties they are.'

She paused again, this time in front of three spaniels propped up on fluffy pink pillows. Like a centrefold for canines. Like a triptych with no altar. Like an advert for *Homes and Gardens*.

'*The Gossip Hour*. This is one of their favourites. I know that, because I show all my dogs their pictures, to see which makes them wag the most.'

She turned aside to sign an autograph, for a woman who claimed to be part of her fan base, and wrote at her request *Woof! Woof!*. The gallery had found a new demographic.

Clydog poised his reporter's pencil. 'And what are their three top poses, would you say?'

'Oh, any kind of costume drama – things like eyepatches and being pirates. You see, dogs love to be dressed up. They're show-offs at heart. Especially my Esmerelda, she positively flaunts herself. Come along, I'll show you the one I did where she has a bonnet and sits under a brolly. Very Jane Austen.'

Moving like a one-woman tidal wave across the gallery, Barbara was barely recognisable as the submissive stooge who stood in for the bruised and the burned and the sickly. Death had given her a second wind. She wished she had been widowed younger, found art earlier. Little did she know she owed it all to a dead cat. She used to watch her husband when he ate, when she fed him his multiple courses, and she used to listen to the sound of his breathing, as heavy as any late-night phone-pest's, as erratic as any post-op patient's. Sometimes she gave him extra, extra cream, in the secret hope of a food pile-up in his arteries, of his pink face going purple. But then she would ask herself if, faced with a flailing spouse, her instincts would not make her do the first-aid honours, her hating trumped by training? *In extremis*, would she have given him the kiss of life or not, when all other forms of their kissing had so long ago died out?

'And they stay still while you paint them, your dogs?' asked Clydog, as he and the curator followed her through the crowd of spanielistas.

'Oh, better than any human model, I imagine. Trained for Crufts, most of them. Sit, stand, heel, run, jump, lie on your back, it's all the same to them. So I just shout "Pose!" and they stay put!' She laughed uproariously at the idea and then came to a halt beside no. 51, in the far corner.

'There! *Miss Mansfield Park*,' said Barbara with a beam.

The choice of a sunbed in her garden showed an optimistic imagination. And her ideal of beauty challenged many a traditional norm. To be both coquettish and pug-faced is a big ask, even with a pink bonnet. Esmerelda lay pouting under her parasol like a canine Lolita, though critics might say the two bulging eyes undermined her attempt to be winsome. Also, the ice-cream sundae on the side-table was arguably an anthropomorphism too far.

Barbara radiated the pride of a mother as she looked upon her painting. 'I always think the secret to a work of art is for it to have an oval frame – don't you agree, Miss Stevens?'

'Yes,' said Miss Stevens, wishing for a bus to fall under.

Clydog had by now a full sheet of longhand notes for his readers, and was forced to turn the pad to a second page. 'How much time do these works of art take you?'

'I like to do one a day.'

'That's a lot of exhibitions!'

'Lot of people to please.'

Miss Stevens felt blood rush to her brain at the prospect. But then she did what she had done ever since the words 'doggy pictures' had first sullied her ears. She thought of the trade-off. And resolved, as an intellectual and a virgin, to lie back and think of swan-necked pediments and pulvinated frieze. *In situ.* As she too would be.

'And finally,' asked Clydog, 'how many have you sold so far?'

Barbara turned enquiringly to Miss Stevens.

Who said, through gritted teeth, 'Thirty-seven.'

Chapter 35

'So ... £210,000?'

'£210,000.'

Geraint J. Watkins did not hide the quiet enjoyment he got from uttering these words. He leaned back in his swivel black-leather chair, and smiled as he clasped both hands behind his balding head. This chair was the only concession to swishness in his ancient lath-and-plaster office in the eaves, where the copperplate certificates and battered box-files were proof pervasive of the firm's claim to be Est. 1873. Geraint's dress sense came from a similar era, involved a waistcoat in a mustard check, and suggested an Edwardian gentleman on the alert for chance royal visits.

He looked across at his old friend, on whose behalf he had fought some hard-won cases, and reflected that such palmy working days were all too rare.

Geraint knew the file backwards but he glanced down once more, like an actor with a prop that gives him pleasure, and said again what was already well noted.

'Plus the house.'

This was not a meeting on the clock, and seconds of silence ticked by.

Geraint added, 'And that's worth half as much again.'

The thought of the noughts lingered in the fusty attic air.

'I just hope she hasn't left me that bloody cat.'

'Cat ...?' Geraint purported to glance at his file to check. 'No mention of a cat, Gwyn.'

Gwyn relapsed again into silence, seemingly a silence of puzzlement, almost of sadness, at his unbounded good news.

'Though she does mention a friendship,' said Geraint.

Gwyn looked up at him, as if surprised by these words.

'… a friendship?' Gwyn gave out a sort of part-sigh, part-grunt, its source the pain of melancholy. 'A glass of lemonade … once, perhaps twice, a year?'

'Advice and kindness, she says.'

Gwyn did not reply, did not trust the distress mounting in his throat. His own recollections were of hurried departures, more pressing appointments, of other people still to see.

For a while he fiddled with a bandage on his hand, a very white and freshly tied bandage, though not quite up to St John's standards.

'Did you know her?' he asked Geraint.

'Only here, giving instructions.'

'Nice old stick. Good gardener, too.'

'Bit of a recluse, I gathered.'

'Yes, never strayed far from her garden. And there are no relatives at all?'

'None that she ever mentioned. Certainly no little side bequests.'

The quiet – and uncomplaining – horror of her lonely end left them both sitting in silence. The image of an old lady on a sunlit bench was the memory that lasted with Gwyn. And some long-forgotten Latin quotation on the subject of death kept banging loosely around inside his head.

'Even my own wife wouldn't leave me all her money!' he eventually said. 'And Audrey claims she loves me.'

'I see a lot of it,' said Geraint, like a comforting sage. 'Lonely pensioners, pretending to be dispassionate, casually enquiring about charities to will their life savings to. As though that had been the only purpose to their lifetime's work.'

'She was so correct … so reserved … so genteel … it's hard to conceive of such a gesture. Perhaps she was a wild child when she was young.'

'Miss Harpur did have one caveat,' said Geraint. 'A legal nicety.'

But Gwyn's troubled mind had gone wandering elsewhere. Led by a guilt too deep and private to share.

By some fluke of funerary mismanagement, by some Hardyesque turn of fate, the bodies that had died together had the following week been laid to rest at the same hour of the same day, but in different graveyards, at different ends of the valley.

It was rare for death to be double-booked and Gwyn had been caught in a quandary. No friend of the Sergeant, no lover of uniforms, he had felt no moving need to pay his respects. But, as Gwyn the JP, he was also a face and facet of the local legal system – whose members liked to be seen to stand together whenever one of their own had fallen (albeit in the face of kilos rather than killers). He had wavered, he had wondered whether not to play this petty game of politics. His heart said he should instead bid farewell to the nature-loving widow who lived beside the river. But, eventually, conscience came second. What decided him, what made him spend two hours suffering sentimental pomp and tosh, was fear of what might happen to his cardboard box. And what lot might befall any birds in need of a short-term respite home.

His hand was throbbing now, and he rubbed away at his bandage, knowing full well this was foolish. A faint pink stain had started to seep through.

Less than a dozen cars of neighbours, mainly old, mostly frail, had joined her last journey from Mill Cottage, winding up the valley to say their goodbyes at an almost empty Ebenezer Chapel. Now, too late, he wished he had gone there, wished he had known he had been her best friend. For he also knew how she would have hated the Revd Joshua Bennett-Jones. And his mane of messianic hair. She had never spoken to Gwyn of religion – perhaps she had lost her faith when she buried her husband so early in his life – but she was not a lady for oratorical flourishes, or for divine invocations. Mrs Harpur would not have taken kindly to being told her glorious, laboured-over garden was all part of God's great plan.

'*Expressing a wish …*' he heard Geraint say a second time.

'Sorry,' said Gwyn. 'Sorry, my mind went walkabout.'

'The caveat,' said Geraint. 'I was running through the caveat.' He began again. '*Expressing a wish, but imposing no binding obligation* – as we say in the trade – *that at least a portion of the money be used for the purposes of conservation.'*

'Oh, I'll use more than a portion all right!' exclaimed Gwyn, with uncharacteristic vehemence.

'I told her you would,' said Geraint.

'Oh yes,' Gwyn said. 'Oh yes!' But he did not elaborate. He had in mind to be a dark horse.

He reached out for the file, to see the full details of her farewell wishes.

'You're bleeding!' said Geraint.

'Oh damn!' said Gwyn.

'What's up with your hand? Stigmata?'

'Birds.'

'Birds?'

Gwyn felt himself look foolish. 'I've been taming a robin. First appeared in the winter, not looking very well. Going bald, like you. But I managed to get its confidence, got it to come into the kitchen for food and a bit of water. And now, if I stand outside the back door in the early morning, and hold out birdseed, it sometimes comes and lands on my hand.'

'Well, I've never heard of that before! That's remarkable.'

Geraint had, some years earlier, been press-ganged as lawyer to the Trust, and a little wildlife had rubbed off on him. But pressure of work and an allergic reaction to some of the Trust members had led him to discreetly stand down.

'Except this morning,' continued Gwyn. 'This morning he arrived, perched on my hand – and got dive-bombed by a sparrowhawk!' His arcing arm illustrated the high-speed descent of a sparrowhawk. 'Which missed the robin.' He re-enacted the missing of the robin. 'And hit me!' He depicted the impact of beak upon flesh. And then held up the bloodied, bandaged, hawk-damaged hand.

'Good heavens!' said Geraint, and he passed Mrs Harpur's last will and testament into Gwyn's good hand. 'How dreadful!'

'Well … yes and no.'

Something of the old Gwyn grinned, something of his true love resurfaced.

'I reckon it'll make a very interesting article for *The Abernantian Naturalists*.'

Chapter 36

Dafydd was fond of saying he knew everybody up and down the valley. He knew the remote and the solitary because he had delivered their mail; he knew the romantic and the tragic because he had delivered their flowers; he knew the hungry and the lazy because he had delivered their pizzas. And everybody up and down the valley knew him. They had seen him go from serious van to silly runabout to soppy pop-pop moped. And now he had gone one worse.

Misuse of a moped seemed a petty charge, and he said as much and loudly to Barri Bertolucci (aka Jones). But his visits to the Dragon's Head and his cruising past Marjorie's caravan had not gone unregistered by the rural commentariat. If walls have ears, hedges have eyes. And a man at large in pizza livery is more than a loose tongue can bear. Dafydd, fallen king of gossip, had become the gossipee.

Today, as he struggled up and down the valley in the May rain, he wished he knew nobody.

Yet again reduced to the ranks of the idle and the columns of the sits vac, Dafydd had found his post-pizza world offered only part-time prospects, few of them career-building. Mr Probert's firm, whose many mailshots used to add miles to his rural round, had posters to be put up. For every parish in the valley there was a notice-board, a place where the tom-tom drums could beat free of charge. And to each of these, with a sack on his back, Dafydd was now sweatily pedalling.

He saw himself as the victim of, well, he was not exactly sure what, but he was certain it involved unfairness, and possibly conspiracy, by whoever was in charge of life's rules. Chief among his causes for complaint were late-twentieth-century capitalism, management consultants, employment legislation, bureaucracy, feminism, and small print. His damaged image so exercised him that he had even begun working on an epitaph. *A man who worked too well but not wisely* was the latest self-pitying draft.

As he pushed the company bike up the hill and out of town, the rent-a-post farmer had given him a cheery wave, which Dafydd took to be mocking; as he paused for breath by the ruins of St Brynnach's, two passing cars had hooted, which Dafydd took to be derisive; and as he struggled off his bike outside the village hall, the WI yoga team had flexibly jogged past, which Dafydd took to be sarcastic.

He stood dripping in the concrete porch, with no helmet to hide his blushes, and thwarted by the few free pieces of pin-pricked felt. The social maelstrom of the valley fought for space with debilitating animal diseases, monthly fund-raising teas for Dial-A-Ride having to compete with vet talks on faecal irregularity. A genteel anarchy ruled the noticeboard, and left it like a mission-impossible jigsaw. Dafydd made a couple of feeble adjustments, decided the problem was above his part-time pay grade, and plonked the auction poster anti-socially in the centre.

'Never thought the day would come.'

Dafydd turned. Rhodri Richards was standing behind him, at the angle of old men in road signs.

'Never thought the day would come,' he said again.

'I'm very sorry,' said Dafydd.

'I'm eighty-something,' said Rhodri.

'I know,' said Dafydd.

'Land gets in your blood.'

'Bound to.'

'Land gets in your blood and you want it for your legacy.'

'Of course.'

'You wouldn't understand,' said Rhodri. He stared at the block capital letters that cluttered the poster. 'Wouldn't understand what it is to see your life's work all come to nothing.'

'Oh, I do understand,' said the ex-postman, 'I do.'

And the pair stood in silence, the old man's mind struggling with the news of the land sale now but days away. It was, apparently, *AN EXCELLENT OPPORTUNITY.*

The swirling wind tugged at their clothes and rattled the pane of glass that kept the notices dry and secure.

'Will you take a drink with an old farmer?'

'Well, I'm ...' Dafydd hesitated, the words 'busy' and 'working' on his lips.

But he was wired to be weak and he nodded agreement. He pushed his bike into the porch out of the driving rain, and laid his sack on top of the saddle.

And then he joined Rhodri in a slow wet walk across the road to the Dragon's Head.

Chapter 37

A notice had appeared on the police station door.

A photo of the notice had appeared in the *Mid-Walian*.

Letters about the notice, and the photo of the notice, had appeared on the *Mid-Walian* Readers' Page.

The notice referred to a consultation process and contained a lot of small print.

The letters denied there had been a consultation process and complained about the small print.

The notice announced plans for the closure of the reception area and its replacement by an outside intercom.

The letters criticised this as the abandonment of a public service.

The notice described this as an improvement of the service to the public.

Some letters asked how. The other letters were abusive.

The notice condemned the reception area as unfit for purpose.

The letters demanded to know what this was supposed to mean.

The notice of closure made no reference to the lately eulogised and long-serving hero of the reception, so sadly dead in action; or to his fact-filled posters.

Neither did the letters.

The notice was signed by the Chief Constable, who said access was his watchword. And that the decision was final.

No mention was made of cardboard boxes for birds.

Chapter 38

The three men sat silently in a row, their files and their papers laid out on the table before them. Subfusc and solemn, they stared into a vague middle distance. Each was of a different generation, yet each was in formal tweed with a tie, and each much attached to his dignity. The date of this scene, of these worthies with so detached a demeanour, could have been the 1880s. The event in hand could have been a tribunal, with a hanging as the outcome. Such is the importance of land.

The triumvirate had arrived long before the selling hour of six. The caretaker had set up the trestle-table as early as four, placing it facing the doors, at the far and focal end of the Jubilee village hall. For the three in charge, he had put out folding wooden chairs, kept for best in the cupboard. For the audience, for the buyers and the voyeurs, he had brought in plastic stacking-chairs, loaned by nuns in the hills. And left room for standing, side and back.

In the middle of the row sat middle-aged Mr Probert, all gravitas and gavel. This, though, was no occasion for the thigh-bone he banged upon the sheep pens, and today he had with him an antique of polished wood, pressing down on his document pile like a prize paperweight. On the right there sat the grand old man of conveyancing, Mr Geraint J. Watkins. Time had taught him to look on these events as theatre, his purpose not the pleasure of personal pomp but a performance as integrity personified, a bank vault on legs. On the left there sat the young bid-spotter (and pond-dipper), Mr Kevin Perkins. Time had taught him little, so he aped his elders' attitudes and posed with punctilio, as ponderous as a premature pensioner and giving no licence to so much as a smile. Their trestle-table stood beyond a tattered strip of green tape, believed to be for basketball.

The sound of 4 × 4s crunching on the gravel began more than thirty minutes prior to the off. Little knots of well-weathered men gathered in the doorway, hesitant to sit, reluctant to commit. They had come from a day on the land and many still wore the rough-and-ready clothes of early morning. Few were strangers to one another, and a jerky bonhomie began to echo through the hall. The occasion had a faint feel of harvest festival supper but without the food, a feeling given force by the numbers who had turned up without all their teeth.

The older farmers, a few with wives, were prone to the creaky, laboured gait that comes from a lifetime in the hills, and soon they chose to take a seat. But they filled from the rear, like children in a class. Some were canny buggers not keen to show their hand, others were unsocial creatures not certain of their setting. Sprinkled amongst them was the odd sartorial quirk, a nod to the occasion; for one, it was a white hanky moment in a battered breast pocket, for another, a rumpled woollen tie dragged from the back of a drawer. Steadily, as the car park wedged itself solid, the constant cries of greeting from friends and neighbours – neighbours not often seen so near at hand – edged the decibel level up close to a hubbub.

Yet this swelling audience paid no heed to the cause of their presence, the people with the paperwork up at the front. Familiar faces all three, from market days and livestock sales, now they were viewed as if across a ha-ha. No approaches were made, no words exchanged, no pleasantries passed. Born of old-fashioned formality, or perhaps from fear of impropriety, this odd divide said that tonight was a night for serious business. A night that nearly all the players in the Nant Valley had come to attend.

Gareth sat in the tractor for several minutes, letting its engine chug on and on. He had reached the end of the lane, the place where the tarmac turned into the track that ran up through his land to Pantglas. He had come here more and more in recent months. Nobody troubled him here. And with the stock now gone, no one had cause to walk these slopes, except the occasional rambler aiming for the moors.

He shut the engine off, and dropped softly down to the ground. The early evening sun was shimmering in a blur through the lightly trembling leaves. He neither paused nor looked around, but started toward the open field-gate.

All of a sudden, late in the wake of the tractor, Jessie came running along the lane. She ran to her master's side and nuzzled his hand.

'No!' said Gareth. 'No!'

He pointed the collie crossbreed back down the lane, back to the farmyard he had left her in. But commands that came without sheep were a puzzle to her, intelligent dog though she was, and she wandered a few yards off and then stopped. She looked quizzically back at him, an expression tailor-made for a collie. He walked over and gave her rump a little push, not out of nastiness but as encouragement. She moved a few yards further on; and stopped again.

Gareth turned around and went back up the lane and through the gate. Of late he left it open, pressed back against the hawthorn hedge, for it no longer had a function. But this time he took hold of its metal bolt and swung the gate closed with a clang. And then set off alone up the dingle.

'Ladies and gentlemen ...'

The pile of particulars had been distributed. If anyone had not fully known why he or she was here, then the four pages of facts and figures and photos, with terms and conditions and a coloured-in map supplement, had put an end to their ignorance. Almost all in the hall were now rustling their pages and murmuring, as if to prove they too were a contender.

'I should like to thank all those persons responsible for the very efficient paperwork,' announced Mr Probert, in the Victorian tones that were his trademark. And then slowly proceeded to thank, so it seemed, everyone short of the caretaker.

Gwyn glanced discreetly, nervously, around the hall. He had positioned himself near the front, where fewer people could detect the tic that would be his bid. He had come with his wife, who was to serve as cover, and thus put them in the category of nosy neighbours – the biggest category by far. Included were people here for the show, people here to see the state of the market, people here to calculate the latest cost of their acres. And some doubled as chancers, ready to pounce if they got whiff of a bargain.

Then there was the serious business.

Gwyn had taken some soundings, and tried to get the lie of the land-buyers. Most farmers saw land as more personal than sex and kept any bids close to their chest. But the Pritchard brothers had been heard – under the influence of too much free beer – to boast of their plans to get bigger. *They were clustered over to the side.* Young Rhys was fleecing a species more profitable than sheep and, so word had it, was ready to expand, to extend his land, and invest in the corporate capacity for intensive bullshit. *He was seated fifth row, centre.* The unfunny foreigner, whose name began with 'S', and who had bragged he could afford another valley as a spare, was thought to be keen on a vista, and daft enough to buy one out of vanity. *He was not yet to be seen.* And a possible long shot was Nico, said to have been machinating, known to have been miffed. *Always a man on the margins, he was hovering at the back, just inside the doors.*

'And, last but not least, the caretaker,' concluded Mr Probert. 'Now, before we start, are there any questions?'

Lu-lu-lu. Lu-lu-lu.

The melancholy notes washed unheard around his head. He no longer noticed birdsong.

Few were the sights or sounds of early summer that still reached Gareth's soul. He was dully aware that he now got no pleasure from a May morning. Or this June evening.

As he moved at a dossed pace up along the dingle, past the full-on flowers that so flavoured the day with scent, his mind was down in the valley.

He knew that his father had chosen not to leave the house, not indeed to leave his bed. On this sorrow at least, they were at one. Even as the son, he could not bear to be the public face. There would be no family witness to the losing of the land.

Like a lamb returning to the teat, his feet had brought him back to his favourite field. Where the only harvest was memories. Free now from farming, nature had run rampant, but all he could feel was regret.

He walked as if through a fog. He found no cause for pause, not by the babbling brook, not in the dappled shade.

He rarely raised his eyes from the grass on the ground, and then only to look up the hill at the half-ruined house on the ridge, where latterly he had so often come to escape the world. But had found himself unable to escape his thoughts.

'Well-hedged, well-ditched, easily worked, free of any restrictions, freehold, good shelter, good shade.'

There had been no questions. There had been no contact of any kind between those buying and those selling. Socialising would, so the room's mood seemed to say, destroy the magic and the mystery of property transactions.

'One hundred and ten acres. Land in the hands of the Richards family for over fifty years.'

A susurrus of sympathy rippled through the hall, a tribal courtesy that would not preclude the cut-throat bidding.

'Usual terms and conditions, contracts drawn up and ready, to be signed tonight.'

Mr Probert spoke at speed, almost a monotone: a man going through the motions, an audience who knew the rituals.

'And here to assist me, my two esteemed colleagues: Mr Watkins, Mr Perkins.'

Sober-faced; sober-sided; synchronised nods.

'Who'll start me off at £200,000?'

The village hall blanked him. Nobody moved, nobody waved, nobody winked. The conventions of battle had begun.

Gwyn had hoped the land might be in two lots, the higher land and the lower land, the rougher land and the softer land. The land with his bird and the land without. But instead he would have to bid for the whole caboodle, and sell off the better land later. Which made his margins tighter.

'£190,000?'

Hill pasture was perhaps a thousand an acre, the greener riverine grass something shy of double.

'£180,000?'

Both camps were old pros, neither prone to budge.

'£175,000?'

Like most of the serious players, Gwyn focused on infinity.

'£170,000?'

'You're having us on!' boomed the cry of a latecomer from the crowd at the back.

Stéfan had arrived – with Eryl his sidekick-cum-*claqueur* in tow – and had brought an outsider's approach to proceedings. He gave a long guffaw at the wit of his intervention, and seemed unaware that heckling was not the norm at an auction.

'£165,000?'

Gwyn wondered about the reserve price, and indeed if there was one.

'£160,000?'

In the wings, Ben Pritchard scratched his elbow. The bidding had begun.

'£160,000. I have £160,000. On my left.'

In quick succession, a series of other farmers scratched things.

'£161,000 … 162. 162. At the back. 163. 163. 164, in the corner. 164. 165. On my right. I have 165 … Help yourself, come in … 165, 165, 166 at the back. 166, 166. 166. High-class land. 166. We're obliged to sell land, not give it away.'

Bryn Pritchard tapped his nose.

'167. On my left again, 167. 168, at the back. 168. I have 168. Help yourself, come in. £168,000 I'm bid.'

The trick, the skill, was not to pause for breath, not to let the momentum lapse. Bidders must be made to believe they were aboard an escalator, rising, rising, always rising, with no way to get off it. And the audience must be sucked in by the drama, as they were tonight.

'169. With you again in the corner. Good to see you back, sir. 170 behind you. 170. Good-quality land, none of it known to flood. 170. 171. 172. 173. 174. 174. You coming in again? 174. £174,000.'

Brian Pritchard raised an eyebrow.

'£175,000. With you on my left. 175. Tonight's the night. 176, at the back. 177. Against you, sir. 178. And again …? 179. 179. 179. 179, in the corner. Must be worth £180,000, surely? This type of land doesn't come on the market often. 180, anyone?'

Brenig Pritchard rubbed his ear.

'£180,000. With you on my left. £180,000 … £180,000. Is there anyone else?'

Within less than three minutes, the bidding had gone to £180,000. And there it seemed to stick. All the likely farmers had dipped in and dropped out. The bidding was on hold. The Pritchards were in the lead and alone. Somehow poker-faced *and* smug.

The value of the land for the age-old purpose of agriculture had been reached. The expectations of the farming community had been fully confirmed.

… But now would-be bidders with other ambitions, more modern game plans, were watching and waiting, and keeping their bodily twitches in check.

Gareth never came here for the view. Unlike the townie owners, who had abandoned the remote long-house after a storm and a scandal, Gareth found no quasi-mystical pleasures in the panoramic sweep, no aesthetic uplift in the gorse or the broom or the hawthorn. He came here in hope of the solace that was thought to be brought by seclusion.

Old Pantglas and its barns were stood in a protective L-shape on the rocky spur, their muscle-bound walls of stone built as a bastion against the weather and the wind.

Gareth wandered leadenly through the dilapidated farmyard. The pond no longer had its quirky ducks, the water just a crust of hardened slime. Where once had rutted a Vietnamese pig, the weeds had returned to rule. And the wrecked remains of a wind turbine lay still embedded in the muddy ground.

This was the end of other people's dreams, but not until today had his mind made the leap to empathise. Not until today had he understood fully what their loss must have meant.

But *he* had no other world. He had no town to return to. He had no fall-back option. What would he do, what could he do, tomorrow?

He wondered yet again about his character. Was his failure always forecast, always so inevitable? When feeble as a child, was there no fork in the road? Had he known a life other than farming, might he have made himself a success? Or, at least, somewhat less of a failure? Had he met a local girl, who understood his nature, might she have loved him more?

He had reached the stone arches of the biggest barn. Here was the eyrie where he hid when he had hours to kill – as he so often did. Sunlight lay in slivers across the flagstoned floor, squeezed through the slits in the walls. Sacks of animal feed stood illicitly stored in the corners. His hedging bill-hooks rested beside the open doors, waiting to be sharpened.

Gareth looked around him, and then stepped into the gloom.

'180,000 and 1,' bawled Stéfan. As ever, anonymity was not a priority.

'Bids still in thousands, sir,' advised Mr Probert.

'OK, 181,000, then,' said Stéfan, with what he thought to be one-upmanship.

Rhys gave a subliminal nod.

'£182,000,' said Mr Probert.

Nico gave a subliminal nod.

'£183,000,' said Mr Probert.

Gwyn had a plan. (Courtesy of Geraint.) In military terms, it was to let his enemies fight and fight until financially depleted and mentally drained, and then, out of nowhere, plunge into the fray – and waylay their weary wallets with a killer bid. Or at least that was the theory.

'184,000,' called out Stéfan.

Mr Probert looked toward Rhys, who nodded again.

'£185,000.'

Gwyn knew this was a man with a business studies diploma on his hall wall, and so would have done his sums with care. Rhys would have profit and loss etched on his actions, with a red line not to be crossed.

Mr Probert looked towards Nico, who nodded again.

'£186,000.'

Gwyn knew less of Nico, and nothing that he liked. He was puzzled by his presence, and bemused by his motives.

'187,000,' called out Stéfan.

Rhys nodded.

'£188,000,' said Mr Probert.

Nico nodded.

'£189,000,' said Mr Probert.

The audience brightened up again. Now they had a game on.

Gareth dragged a feed sack across the uneven barn floor. Weighed down by its contents of chemical goodness – guaranteed to give better bone-structure to adolescent sheep – the plastic sack was awkward to manoeuvre, the concentrate pellets as unstable as ballast listing in a stormy sea. Gareth's own bones had been work-free for weeks, and with his body below its peak performance he struggled to stack the sacks.

He had chosen a position some six feet in from the arches, midway between the two side walls. The second sack he had slid up on to the first, plastic moving smoothly over plastic, but the third sack had proved wayward. He had had to heave it up, using his knees as a staging-post. The fourth sack took four goes, with a pause for a breather.

Gareth judged that the height was about right, that the beam above was spot-on, and he pulled his ball of baler twine out from his Barbour pocket. He did not wish to repeat Hefin's error, and risk his trouser belt, for Gareth too was a shy, sexually repressed man, and had no desire to be found dead in his underpants.

'Stay with me a little longer, sir,' said Mr Probert. 'At £190,000. 190,000 for this quality land.'

Rhys hesitated, not liking the sound of such a sum. His business was still by word of mouth, and the mouths all belonged to low-grade managers. No blue-chip company had so far signed up for his services, no captain of industry had yet been converted. To his chagrin, he usually had a clientele more keen to play at being Bond than bonding, men more eager to show off to those below them than work ensemble as co-ordinating cogs. And, for reasons he could not quite explain, almost half of every group was now secretarial, and thus exempt from paying full price.

'Still with you at 190,000,' repeated Mr Probert.

Rhys shook his head, as minimally as he had nodded, and withdrew from the fray. His brochure to utilise the rocky ridge, to entice queasy CEOs to try a fun bit of rope-work, would have, for now, to stay an aspirational concept.

'£190,000, then. At 190,000,' said Mr Probert, and turned his attention again to the back of the village hall.

Still going head to head, and standing side by side, were Nico and Stéfan. It was not about the land but the ego. Neither acknowledged the other, like duelling gunmen who had not been introduced.

Gwyn struggled to stay in no-nodding mode. He feared he would be done for by the crossfire as the target price moved ever upward, and threatened to go beyond his reach.

'I'll take 500s,' said Mr Probert.

Nico nodded.

'And 500.'

Stéfan raised a finger, buckling down to be conventional.

'191,000.'

Nico nodded.

'And 500.'

Stéfan raised a finger.

'192,000.'

Eryl smiled.

Nico nodded.

'And 500.'

Stéfan raised a finger.

'193,000.'

Eryl smiled again.

Nico nodded.

'And 500.'

Stéfan raised a finger.

'194,000.'

Yet again came Eryl's enigmatic smile.

Nico nodded.

'And 500.'

Stéfan raised a finger.

'195,000.'

Nico nodded, knowing the land was now far too overpriced to make a profit.

'And 500.'

Stéfan raised a finger.

'196,000.'

Nico nodded, knowing he had no interest in the land.

'And 500.'

Stéfan raised a finger.

'197,000.'

Nico nodded, trying not to catch Eryl's smile.

'And 500.'

Stéfan raised a finger.

'198,000.'

Eryl smiled again, for he knew the secret of the limit that Stéfan had decided on.

Nico nodded. He knew that limit too ... courtesy of Eryl.

'And 500.'

Stéfan raised a finger.

'199,000.'

Nico nodded, and got ready to savour the joy of defeat.

'And 500.'

Stéfan raised a finger, trying to keep a poker face as he approached his upper limit.

'£200,000.' Mr Probert paused. '... £200,000,' he repeated. 'You'll come in again ...? I'll take my time.'

But Nico did not nod, for he did not need to. He had won by losing. He had cost Stéfan an extra ten grand. For, if the land was not to be his, Nico's second greatest pleasure was to be a spoiler.

Stéfan punched the air in vulgar triumph, for he now was a man with a vista. And he had had revenge over Nico, who had trumped him in the past.

Eryl the surly handyman smiled one last time. This favour

done, he felt sure he would secure the money Nico still owed him. He was, of course, wrong.

'£200,000, being sold all the way ...' said Mr Probert.

Rhys chose this moment to quietly exit, feeling his plans to get the better of businessmen had been undone.

'... It's in the market,' said Mr Probert, 'at £200,000, it's being sold ...'

And he raised his gavel.

'Pssst!' said Mr Perkins.

Gwyn was having trouble with his tic. He had begun to panic as the price reached £200,000, close to the sum of his legacy, and so he had urgently felt the need to act. But the magistrate was not expected to be a bidder, nor accustomed to being one, and his tic was going unseen.

Gareth clambered with difficulty up on to the feed sacks, which moved like shifting sands beneath his feet. Above his head ran one of the great oak cross-beams, the wood carved and finessed by eighteenth-century axe-men. He held the end of the twine in one hand and tossed the ball up with the other. At his third attempt – and his failures did not tempt him to desist – Gareth looped his baler twine around the beam.

He picked up the bill-hook which he had rested on the sacks and cut the twine to a length that seemed appropriate for the task. Knots to him were second nature and with a countryman's unshowy skill he had soon tied on the twine and fashioned a hangman's noose. He tossed the bill-hook and the unwanted ball of twine back into the corner on top of his discarded Barbour. And took the noose in his hands. Even the fateful, melodramatic moment of slipping his head through a snare was not preceded by the slightest sign of doubt, by not a hint of existential stock-taking.

He tightened the scratchy noose and placed his feet together.

And then Jessie ran into the barn.

His instinctive response was not that of a man thinking of death. For he realised this was a dog that had come through a hedge – a hedge that he himself must have laid. And all he felt at first was a blow to his pride, and regret that his hedge-laying had left behind him a hole. A hole that any new owner would see.

But then Jessie sat down below him and gazed up with a winsome look. She whimpered, aware that something not normal was happening.

This was what Gareth had most wanted to avoid. He was Jessie's second owner; her first was Hefin. For a dog to have two owners kill themselves, in the same way, in the same barn, would do untold damage to her happiness of being. She would never trust again. He remembered Dafydd's sad description of how Jessie had behaved on the morning when, as postman, he had found her by the body. And he remembered her years of loyalty ever since, her role his only true companion. This was a harm he could not do her, a sight she must not see.

'Get back!' he cried, as he cried when she herded his sheep. 'Get back!'

But still she sat, devoted and waiting, her soft brown eyes telling of bewilderment.

'Get back!' he cried again. And he gestured commandingly with his arm. Unfortunately this sudden movement destabilised him, and he slipped from the feed sacks and snapped his neck. And left only his feet within reach of her desperate licking.

'£210,000, for the last time!' cried Mr Probert. And banged his polished gavel.

Gwyn leapt from his seat, untypically exultant, and raised both hands in the air.

An attractive middle-aged woman, with more bust than was normal in the valley, rushed over and gave him a big hug and a kiss.

'Do I know you?' asked Gwyn.

'I'm your new tenant,' said Marjorie Whitelaw. 'And I love you.' And without further explanation, she turned and bustled her way out through the crowd.

'Being a landowner seems to have perks,' said Audrey.

'But does she sing like a bird?' answered Gwyn.

The couple fought against the tide to reach the trestle-table and shook all the hands in sight. Gwyn felt euphoric, the moment felt historic, and he had to curb a minor urge to make a speech. There was a lot of pleasure round about him. The audience was pleased because the squire had been squashed and the bearded birdman left triumphant. Mr Probert was pleased because he had obtained a record price per acre. Mr Watkins was pleased because his old friend had realised a long-held dream. And Mr Perkins was pleased because for once he'd been useful.

They then gave Gwyn the climactic contract.

There followed several anti-climactic moments of reading through the slew of clauses and being complimentary about the 'very efficient paperwork' – though, in truth, Gwyn would have signed wherever and whatever he was told, and in triplicate.

And then they all shook hands again.

Gwyn turned to the honorary young herpetologist before departing. 'As soon as the fine print's sorted, the trustees must take a trip out to look at what we've got. I think there might be a surprise or two.'

The vital dullness of legalism dealt with, Gwyn took his wife by the arm and they joined the crowd on their slow shuffle out. Defeat of the favourite rarely fails to be a hot story. The village hall was now clogged with knots of gossipers and beaten bidders all dissecting the news of the night, each an expert, each bringing a personal spin. And writing it all down in laborious longhand was Clydog, whose years on the treadmill of copy had taught him the sexiness of land to his readers. The night's only absentee was Dafydd, never previously known to have lost his longing to be first with the valley latest, but now finally laid low by a soul that had a slow and patchless puncture.

Husband and wife edged forward through the throng in near-silence.

'You must be very happy,' said Audrey.

'Yes … and no,' said Gwyn, and gave her an unexpectedly sad smile.

'No?'

'It's the awful way that things work. Always down to whim and chance. If her cat hadn't hated blackbirds … if her husband hadn't been long gone ... if I hadn't been handy ... perhaps even if, as you say, I hadn't jailed poor Gareth. *And if she'd left £10,000 less ...!* That's not the way conservation should work. Picking up crumbs from unknown tables. Waiting for the fluke of a rich and kind – and dead – old lady. While nature disappears ever faster.' He sighed. 'I guess it's another article.'

The couple squeezed past a cluster of hulking men half-blocking the door.

'You played a blinder, Mr Hopkins!' said Brenig Pritchard. 'Congratulations!'

'Hear, hear,' said Brian, Bryn and Ben.

'That's very kind of you all,' said Gwyn. 'Thank you.'

'And we'd like to offer both of you drinks on the house.'

Gwyn hesitated, another plan on his mind.

'Free champagne?' suggested Brenig.

'Free sherry?' suggested Brian.

'Free wine?' suggested Bryn.

'Free gin?' suggested Ben.

'Perhaps another evening, thank you. I think I want to go and look at my land.'

The brothers laughed as one, each fully understanding such a primitive emotion. And with several slaps on the victor's back, the men disappeared off to the Dragon's Head. Off to their busiest night of the year, a night for more than just loners and losers.

Gwyn and Audrey turned away into the car park.

'*Your* land?' said Audrey.

'The Trust's land,' said Gwyn with a grin.

Then, ahead of them they saw Stéfan, who was clearly not going to any pub, not even his pub. Unlike Eryl, already gone. And of Nico there was no sign either, as was his Machiavellian practice.

Stéfan stood his ground and made a most unsquirely gesture.

'I'd have bought you a bloody bird, if I'd known that's what you wanted!' he shouted at Gwyn. 'I've got a friend who can get hold of those rare fucking parrots!'

And then he got into his big car and drove off with wheelspin and smoke.

'Perhaps,' said Audrey, 'you could jail that man and turn his estate into another reserve?'

'Come on. Let's drive up and look at this land. Before it gets dark. And see if my diva is singing.'

'All right, my love. Just don't get excited and drive too fast! One of these days you'll have an accident, and cause yourself no end of harm.'

ACKNOWLEDGEMENTS

This is a comic novel where some of the jokes needed research.

To Jeremy Langworthy I owe much gratitude, for I constantly pestered him on his two specialist subjects of ornithology and criminal justice and he gave uncomplainingly of his time and knowledge. Ed and Cathy Cooper were similar founts of wisdom on birds and botany, as they too had spent time at the chalk-face of conservation. Phil Morgan supplied help with mammals, on which he is a leading expert. Auctioneers Gareth Griffiths and Ryan Williams offered valuable guidance to the world of land, farm animals and agricultural auctions. Sue Jones gave me most useful insights into dog grooming for shows. The Bristol Branch of St John's Ambulance were very generous with their time, knowledge and access to blow-up dolls.

And, with unfailing kindness, Alistair Beaton not only provided world-class linguistic pedantry but continually gave me encouragement and moral support when I was flagging. Which was often.

To all of them many thanks.

The advice on penis replicas was anonymous.

A NOTE ON THE TYPE

The text of this book is set in Linotype Sabon, named after the type founder, Jacques Sabon. It was designed by Jan Tschichold and jointly developed by Linotype, Monotype and Stempel, in response to a need for a typeface to be available in identical form for mechanical hot metal composition and hand composition using foundry type.

Tschichold based his design for Sabon roman on a font engraved by Garamond, and Sabon italic on a font by Granjon. It was first used in 1966 and has proved an enduring modern classic.